Praise for Untold

"For lovers of Sophie Kinsella and Joanna Trollope, this novel combines romance and coming of age with a touch of mystery and some very smart writing"

- Cathy Utzschneider, Author of *Move!*

"Spitzfaden's command of dialogue and its tempo paint her characters likeable, unpredictable, quixotic, vulnerable, not to mention breezy and peppy as a preppy."

- Steve Sherman of *The Keene Sentinel*

"Quietly powerful, with an honest, yet romantic commentary on duty, expectations, and falling in love."

- Victoria Spencer, author of *Changing History*

"Seeing the plot unfold between her and Robin and watching as they both begin to realize what they may have been through in the past was fascinating and I felt my heart break a little as Katie made, what she thought was, the best possible decision for the two of them."

- *Ann Livi Andrews Reviews*

"A modern fairy tale with the perfect ending...Ms. Spitzfaden's voice is so clear and so compelling."

- Angela Breen

Other Titles by Amy Spitzfaden

Fingerprinted Hearts

*It's Funny You Mention Chloe**

Short Fiction

Storybook

"The Heartbreaks That Led Us Here" (*Surrender to Passion*)

**forthcoming*

Untold

a novel

Amy Spitzfaden

AMPHIBIAN PRESS

Amphibian Press
www.amphibianpressbooks.com
www.amyspitzfaden.com

First printing 2014

by Inkfingerz, a Division of 1st World Publishing

Cover design by Marissa Frosch

Cover model Kelsey

Chapter heading art by East Ashley Studio via Clipart Library

Printed in the United States of America

ISBN: 978-1-949693-91-1

To Grandmom,
if you'll excuse the language.

Chapter One

I can't believe you went. The words coming out of my pen surprise me. I was scratching doodles into the margin of my notebook while waiting for someone in the class to say something worth writing down, and then suddenly they were there. Presumably created by my pen, but definitely not by me. Who went where? I frown and run my sharpie over the sentence; three thick black lines and it's gone. With an effort, I drag my attention back to Dr. Owen Davies. He's a new professor at my college and he's explaining Yeats's view on… something. Davies is attractive for a teacher. He always looks slightly tousled as if he's just come out of the dryer, and he smiles more than most teachers do. Boring as hell to listen to, though. The man is obsessed with Yeats.

Stretching, I cast my glance around the room. A couple people are on their phones, but most are listening attentively, sparking a small feeling of shame in me. I glance down at the notebook in front of me and am startled by the bold lines inked across the page.

"I'd like to hear some personal takes on 'The Falling of the Leaves.' Anyone?"

I hear the girls around me shift, all trying to think of something to say. Personally, I've never had the professor fantasy. There's just something about tweed…

I miss you. I stare at the paper in front of me. When did I write that? Why did I write that? I don't miss anyone. There's no one to miss.

"What about you, Miss Winters?" I glance up at Davies, giving looking intelligent a half-hearted shot.

"I hate this poem." No point sugarcoating it. I'm too distracted to come up with a lie anyway.

"Why is that?" he asks in the excited way professors have when someone disagrees. So much for being too distracted.

"It's self-indulgent," I say, snapping my notebook shut. "People get so caught up nostalgia that they forget to look forward to what's coming."

"But it's the end of love!" cries Jemmy, a tiny tan-skinned girl who always has a romance novel in hand. "What's to look forward to at the end of love?"

"Your next love. If it's ending, then it wasn't that great now, was it?" I hear a general murmur of disagreement but press on. "Plus, it implies that there's a season for love, and that's stupid. Even if it's not meant literally—oh and by the way, using fall to signify sadness at an ending? It's been worn so thin."

"But what if Yeats was the first to use it?" Jemmy glares at me and I do my hardest not to roll my eyes.

"Yeats wasn't the first. Do you really think that the first time someone thought to use seasons changing in this way was in the late 1800s?"

Davies laughs and shakes his head and I see Caroline, sitting next to me, tap her friend excitedly on the wrist. I shrug and reopen my notebook to return to my doodling. I don't cross out "I miss you". Instead, I draw vines over the letters and shade it to make the words look ancient and forgotten. I'm not sure what started this, but I like the result.

There is something appealing about the concept of missing someone. The practice too, to some extent. I don't know what it is. Maybe it's the blend of that emptiness that compels us to draw blankets around ourselves and that unique sweetness that comes with any happy memory. Maybe missing someone reminds us that we love or loved that person, and that's what we find the most attractive.

"That's a very good point, Miss Winters. Can you elaborate on it?"

I blink. First, I hate it when teachers use last names to address their students and Davies just won't stop. Second, I didn't know I'd said anything out loud.

"Well," I hazard, "we don't miss things we hate. So if we miss something, even if it ended for a good reason, we're brought back to what we didn't hate about it. And that's a good feeling." I'm so much better at this in my head. Words have never been my form of communication.

"And how does that tie in with 'The Falling of the Leaves'?"

"It's why everyone considers it such a great poem." And why, I add silently to myself, I don't relate. I don't miss anyone.

Even my shorter classes seem too long lately. Davies's class is less than two hours, but by the end of it, I'm dying to go. When he finally finishes his lecture and wishes us a good afternoon, I'm already packed and ready to head out the door. It's a mild fall day, the kind where parents kick their kids off the TV and send them outside with stern words, creating a lifelong guilt that pops up with warm weather. I meander back to my room, taking the long way, which leads to a miniature bridge in a small thicket of trees right in the middle of campus. Today the river is decorated with brightly colored flower petals that someone must have thrown in earlier. I stand for a while and watch the remnants drift about. I wish I brought my camera.

My mood is so peaceful by the time I finally make it back to my room that I don't remember my door should be locked. The handle doesn't resist, and I open the door, expecting to find Pandora inside playing with our cat, which we keep here illegally. Instead, I'm shocked into stillness as my brain registers the scene in front of me piece by piece.

One of our end tables has been knocked sideways and the books that had been resting upon it are strewn across the floor. The couch cushions are askew and indented from recent contact and the green plastic lamp that Pandora and I picked out together at Target last week is lying on its side, the shade knocked to the floor.

Oh god, oh god, my camera. If it's broken or stolen I don't know what I'll… No, there it is, untouched on the shelf. I let out the breath I wasn't aware I was holding.

I move forward to investigate the scene, but stop when I hear a noise coming from my bedroom. I take a few deep breaths to steady myself, trying to figure out who would break into someone's dorm room in the middle of the afternoon and why. Before I come up with an answer, a tall, scruffy, and all-too-familiar form emerges from my room.

"Jude," I gasp, sinking to the floor. "You scared me half to death!" I look around at the debris, not as surprised as I should be. "What's with this mess?"

"Your cat attacked me," answers my brother, pulling a cigarette out of a carton and placing it in his mouth. As if on cue, my small gray tabby crawls out from underneath the couch and rubs against me, purring.

"Bad Santa," I say, picking her up and holding her to my chest. My heart is still racing, but the adrenaline is beginning to fade. Instead, seeping into my bones is the familiar exhaustion I feel only when Jude is around.

"Stupid thing to name your cat," Jude responds, retrieving his lighter out of his green coat and lighting his cigarette.

"It's short for Santa Maria, the name she came with. And don't smoke in here. I'm going to get in trouble."

Jude ignores my admonition and puffs quietly away on his cigarette for a while, not volunteering any information and not asking me for any in return. I watch him from my spot on the floor with a growing feeling of foreboding.

"So," he says finally, looking down at me dispassionately, "how are things?"

"Things are fine," I answer. I struggle to my feet, still holding Santa, and look Jude full in the face. He looks thinner than usual, and his coloring a bit peaky. He obviously hasn't shaved in a while, but doesn't yet have a full beard, just calico scruff. I want to ask him what he wants, or, better yet, push him out the door and lock it tightly behind him. Instead I stay where I am, and wait for him to speak.

"Taking any pictures lately?"

"Some." I offer a stiff shrug that gets Santa squirming.

"Still think you can make it?" There it is: the usual sneer. I glare at him and don't respond. Another half minute of silence, then Jude speaks again. "That guy still live here?"

I can only assume he means Michael. I shake my head and say, "Michael never lived here. He's just here a lot because of Pandora."

"Good."

Santa successfully wiggles her way out of my arms and falls to the floor, landing with a cat's trademarked grace.

"Is that all you want?" I try, I always try not to be sharp with him, but... he's Jude. I tug on the end of my hair in irritation, trying to ignore its remarkable similarity to my brother's.

"Yeah," he eventually says, looking at the floor and scuffing his shoe over what I hope isn't a spot of dropped ash. "That's all. Just seeing how you are."

"I'm fine." My answer is soft. Jude walks over to the window and opens it, allowing the outside air to rush in and diffuse the smoke from his cigarette. The sun catches his face and I realize: he doesn't look good. "Jude," I say, as he turns away from the window to pick up his bag, which he dropped on the floor, "how are you?"

He turns to look at me with a half-smile. "I'm fine, Katie. See ya." He straightens, throws his backpack over his shoulder, and leaves the room. I collapse onto the couch and Santa immediately jumps up and settles herself on my lap, her chest vibrations soothing me.

"It's okay, baby," I whisper. "He's gone now." Santa knocks her face against my hand and I oblige, rubbing the space between her ears with my palm. As soon as my shoulders begin to lower, the door opens again. I jump up and spill Santa onto the floor, readying myself for round two with Jude. But, instead of my brother, it's Pandora that pops into the room, beaming and brandishing a shopping bag.

"Look what I bought," she announces proudly, pulling out an outrageously pink scarf. She pauses and looks around. "Why does it smell like a bar in here? And what's with the mess?"

"Jude stopped by," I answer, trying to sound casual as I flop back onto the couch. Immediately, Pandora's demeanor changes. She drops her scarf back into her bag before joining me on the couch. Santa imitates her, jumping onto the cushions and settling herself between us. Pandy looks into my face, her blue eyes flicking back and forth, searching for some sign of how the encounter had gone. "It was fine," I say, waving my hand dismissively. Santa sits up and bats at it.

Pandora's expression doesn't change for a few moments, but then she snaps to awareness and begins searching through her bag. Her purse—affectionately known by us as Pandora's Box—although seemingly small holds just about everything that anyone could need. In the green cloth bag one can find breath mints, Band-Aids, lip balm, tissues, needle and thread, cough drops, makeup, a dictionary, you name it. I watch her, wondering what could possibly be the remedy for Jude.

"Lifesavers," she declares, dropping a wrapped roll of candy into my hand. I grin and tug the end open. Pandy always knows.

"What else did you buy?" I ask, popping a red ring into my mouth. I offer Pandora the next one, green, and she accepts. Seeing Pandy's purchases is always an interesting activity. Her wild blond curls, blue eyes, pale skin, and petite frame make her look as though she should be set on a shelf somewhere instead of out walking about, but she makes up for her delicate appearance by wearing exactly what she likes. She revels in the ridiculous.

I lean against her shoulder, letting the familiar scent of her hair calm me. I know the smell of Pandy's perfume better than any of my own—I can never stay on one scent—and although the fragrance is upbeat and mainly citrus it works to subdue me better than anything lavender or chamomile. Everything about her is always so clean and put together that I can almost forget the raggedy clothes and harsh smell of my brother.

Pandora reaches into her bag, then hands me an extra-large gray-blue men's hoodie that's remarkably soft. "Michael will like this," I say, unfolding it so I can see the whole thing. I imagine the soft fabric encasing the length of Michael's body and smile, before quickly dropping the sweater back into the bag.

"It's for me," Pandora answers matter-of-factly, bending down and rummaging through her bag. She reemerges from her purchases, holding a small box with both hands. "I got this for you."

She hands me a tiny glass perfume bottle and I take it, smiling with curiosity. I spray some onto my wrists and sniff. It smells like licorice.

"Thanks," I laugh, giving Pandora a nod of appreciation. "Where did you find this?"

"At this new store in the mall. I forget what it's called. It's kind of a janky place, but if you look through you can find some cool stuff."

I smile and give my wrist another sniff. Pandy and I became friends in eighth grade right after she moved to Hartford from California. I was miserable because my first-ever boyfriend had just dumped me for my newly-ex best friend, and Pandora was miserable because she missed San Francisco. We bonded over grief, but our friendship lasted well beyond that.

The door opens and Michael ducks through the doorway. His 6'3 frame doesn't make this task easy, but he's mastered it to the best of his abilities.

"Hey, sweetie," Pandy beams, lighting up the in the way that only Michael can elicit. I smile with her. I had a hard time adjusting to Michael when he and Pandora first began dating. I wasn't used to sharing Pandy's attention, and for too long I resented Michael's presence. Our world was suddenly full of violent computer games, rackety music (a phase that he thankfully outgrew), and snide comments during chick flicks. He somehow made it, though, that eventually things felt incomplete without him. When Michael moved to Maine for college, Pandy and I followed as quickly as we could.

I don't know if I would have chosen Travis University if it had been just me. A newly formed environmental group dug their claws Michael during his first visit. He came home from that weekend boasting about the sustainability program the school offered, and I quietly looked into their photography courses while Pandy researched the writing department. Now, here we are, cameras, pens, protest signs, and all.

"I brought food for the girls," Michael announces, dropping three plastic bags on our table. Pandy and I both shoot up from the couch to see what he's brought us. I grab a Styrofoam container of fries and Pandy takes a box of noodles. We settle ourselves back on the couch, content with our provisions and turn our attention to Michael.

Michael grew up in a family of five, the youngest child and the only son. He was, for lack of a better way to put it, spoiled. But instead of growing up vain and self-centered, he instead developed a love for spoiling others (not to mention a scary talent for getting his way). Of course, his generosity is almost entirely focused on Pandora, but I've been lucky enough to skim off his serendipity as well. *That's all it is with me*, I think as I bite into a fry. *Serendipity*.

"Hey guys? I have a question," I say, licking salt from my fingertips.

"Yeah?" asks Pandora. Michael makes eye contact and nods to show that he too is listening.

"What was my worst breakup?"

"Teddy," they both answer in unison. I wince. They're right.

Pandora slurps a mouthful of noodles, then wipes the corners of her mouth delicately with a paper napkin. "Why?"

I look out the window, trying to put the feeling that's been with me all day into words. "I feel like I miss someone and I don't know who it is."

"It's Teddy," responds Michael through a mass of chicken sandwich. "Teddy is a sexy man."

I grin. Teddy and Michael were best friends in high school, which was how I got to know Teddy in the first place. Their "bromance" was always a source of entertainment to Pandora and me.

"No," I say, shaking my head, "it's not Teddy. Sorry."

I do miss Teddy, but at this point it's only nostalgia. I don't miss him the way I used to. Teddy was the person who always made anyone he was talking to feel like his best friend. Dating him was an honor. It gave me a sense of specialness among my peers. I would see him talking to other people, smiling and listening to them as if they were saying was the most interesting thing he had heard all day, and all I would be able to think was, "That's mine." When he broke up with me for that tall German girl (although he never told me flat-out that that was the reason), I was devastated. That was almost four years ago now, and it seems more like a scene out of a TV show than something that happened to me.

"Maybe it's Johnny," Pandora offers, setting her takeout container down on the table in favor of a bottle of water.

I make a face. Johnny and I dated for two years and broke up six months ago, but I haven't missed him much. Our relationship ended with a fizzle, not a bang. We both lost interest but didn't want to hurt the other person so we ended up staying together about four months too long. Missing him would be ridiculous. Even though there is a part of me that wants to, I just don't.

"No, not Johnny," I say with a shrug, breaking a fry in half. "Maybe it's no one." But as I say this, I know it's not true. There's someone who I miss bitterly and desperately, and I have absolutely no idea who it is. "I should study." I get to my feet bringing the container of fries with me. "Thanks for the food," I say to Michael, then disappear into my room.

Once inside, I lie down on my faded cloud-patterned bedspread, kneading the question with my mind, trying to come up with someone to miss. It's not Teddy. It's not Johnny. I'm definitely not homesick, and both of my best friends are right here at school with me. So who's missing?

Chapter Two

By the next morning the tickle of curiosity has turned into a hollow ache. I feel terrible. It's one thing to miss someone and be able to fill the void with their face and the memories and impressions they left. But when there isn't anything at all that you can hold on to it causes an empty feeling so intense that I keep coughing to see if I can shake it. I blame Yeats. Him and his stupid "Falling of the Leaves". I need to distract myself.

Fortunately, today is the first day of my photography intensive. The scramble to get everything I need has me in a frenzy. In absence of a list, I'm darting around trying to remember everything I told myself I should bring: camera, case, lenses, notebook, pen, and textbook. I think that's everything. As I dress, I feel like my blood has turned into frogs. I still can't quite believe that I got this. Everyone in the photography program plus some general arts and communications students put in their names for one slot. Requesting to be considered was more of a whim than anything else but somehow I got the position. Now I'm off to meet my… mentor? Sponsor? Boss? Geri Martell.

For the first time ever, I'm starting to feel like I might actually become a photographer. I chose photography as my major simply because I like to take pictures. I liked the way photographs could catch a gesture or a moment and turn it into a whole story without moving an inch. Studying it was a natural choice only because I wanted to learn as much as I could. That I could make a living through this passion is only a recent idea.

Geri's office is toward the edge of campus in a tiny brick building that I've passed once or twice. I've never been inside. Being unfamiliar with her office makes me worry that I'll end up walking in on the wrong person, so I'm relieved when I get to the door and see that the office I was sent to— room 103—has the name "Geraldine Martell" pinned to the front. I dance from foot to foot, then raise my hand and knock.

"Come in."

Instead of the usual design that the inside of most professors' offices have—a picture of the family, maybe a mug from someone who appreciates the teaching profession—this one is decorated with brightly colored posters. Upon examination, I see they are advertisements for different kinds of liquor. There's one for Smirnoff, one for Jack Daniels, one with a picture of Kim Kardashian and something green in a martini glass, and, inexplicably, one advertising Gold Peaks Iced Tea.

The odd choice of decoration keeps me from noticing Professor Martell until she speaks. "Katie Winters!" I jump.

Geraldine Martell sitting behind her desk, typing rapidly on her keyboard. Instead of the middle-aged professional I expected, Geraldine is pretty, and only looks to be a couple years older than I am. She has curly dark hair that has been roped back into a ponytail, and the freckles across her give her a girlishly endearing look. I take to her instantly. She stands and gestures to the chair in front of her desk.

"Please, have a seat. I have something I need to finish up. I'll be done in a moment." Her eyes crinkle as she smiles. I relax down onto the plastic-y surface of an empty chair. Professor Martell's desk is covered with oddities, some of which I recognize, like a stuffed doll of the character "Gir", some of which I don't, such as a collection of novelty spoons with an intricate pattern that looks somewhat Celtic.

"There we go," she says. She hits send, then swivels around in her chair to face me. "Done. So, Katie Winters." She has a soft and high-pitched voice that adds to her childlike appearance, but her intonation has a maturity to it that radiates authority. I wonder if she's as young as I thought. "You must be pretty exceptional to have landed this spot."

Heat creeps to my neck and face, and I struggle to decide how to answer. "I'm glad I did. It's a great opportunity."

She smiles, seeming neither put off nor particularly interested by my response. A manila folder with my name across the front lies on her desk. "You're graduating this year, right? That's an exciting time. I graduated with my Masters two years ago." I make sure to look impressed as she continues. A stack of photos I submitted smiles up at me from her desk. "You obviously already know the mechanics of what makes a good picture, so I'm going to try and get you to go a bit deeper this year. We're going to start today with an exercise in observation."

"Okay." I bounce my head up and down with fervor. "I brought my camera."

"That's good," she answers encouragingly, eyeing the bag lying by my feet. "But we're not going to use it yet."

"Oh." I tuck my feet under my chair, feeling like an overeager kid.

"All you need today is your coat," squeaks Geri brightly, standing and leaning forward to turn off her monitor. "We're going to go outside and look around a bit."

"Sounds fun." I stand up and glance down at my feet. "Um, should I leave my bag here?"

"You can come back and get it when we're done." She gestures to the door. "Now, after you." I head out. Having no real idea where we're going, I wait by the door until she joins in the hallway.

"I was thinking we'd walk around the grounds today. We'll look for inspiration and you can tell me about yourself." She winks and leads us towards the front door.

I fight against making a face. I hate it, I absolutely hate it when someone asks me to tell them about myself. What am I supposed to say? She obviously already knows that I like photography and that I'm a student here. This is awful. But as I follow her out the door and onto the school's grassy common my resistance lifts a bit with the lovely scenery.

"About me," I hazard as we head away from the center of campus and down toward town. "Well, I'd love to be a travel photographer, because I'd like to see a lot of different places…"

"How about some stuff that wasn't on your application?" she prompts, swinging left as we approach the dorms and heading down a side street that I usually avoid. She isn't tall, but she walks quickly.

"Things not on my application…" I stammer, laughing nervously. Now that I've caught up with her, I let myself slow down. "What kind of things do you want to know?" She should take a little responsibility here.

"What's your favorite thing to photograph?"

I pause mid-step. The sidewalk catches my foot, almost sending me face-first onto the pavement. "Old things. I love history. Anything vintage, or dusty, or that looks like it comes from another era." *Or from a fairytale.* That seems a silly to say aloud.

"What about you is drawn to old things? Hi, Owen." She smiles and waves at Davies as he passes us. I wonder if we look like we're in a lesson or out power walking. I'm bright red and struggling for breath.

"I like thinking about where they came from, and what was going on in that time period."

Geri's ponytail bounces. "It sounds like you've got a lot of interest in the external. I want us to take a dive into the internal. What is it about you, right now, that's drawn to taking pictures?"

"I…" I'm drawing a complete and total blank.

"Tell me something that's bothering you today." We're coming into a part of campus where I haven't been before. There are more trees here than anywhere else I've been on campus, and I'm having a hard time keeping up the conversation and avoiding the branches that keep flying toward my face.

"I'm tired," I offer. It's the best I can do. I readjust my foot so it's firmly on the ground and haul myself over a knee-height tree that's blocking our path.

"Fatigue can lead to some interesting photographs," Geri says thoughtfully, "but let's dig deeper. What's in the back of your mind? What one little thing does your brain keeps coming back to?"

I scramble around in my head for those words, those stupid words that will help me tell her about what's been clinging to me since yesterday, but there's nothing. "I broke up with my boyfriend kind of recently."

Geri nods in sympathy. "That can be tough. How are you dealing with it?"

I duck beneath a branch, feeling a little guilty for using this example. "It's weird to not have him around anymore. I was pretty used to him for a while, there. But it doesn't actually bother me too much."

Geri pauses in her steps to give me a ponderous stare. "Tell you what," she says, running a hand over her hair as if to smooth it. "Why don't I tell you something that's bothering me, and then we can try you again."

"Okay," I say uncertainly. I've never had an interaction like this with a teacher before. Still, art is all about breaking boundaries, so I settle into the situation and wait for her reply.

"I'm worried about my little sister."

This next branch catches me, stinging me as a sharp edge puckers the skin on my cheek. "What has she been doing?" I know about sibling worries. I could definitely share that...

"She's in a new relationship, and she won't tell my family."

"Does she think that your parents won't like him?" I inquire, briefly wondering if he's like Jude. Good god, I wouldn't accept Jude into my family either if I could help it.

"Her."

"Ah." I step onto a rock and realize that the trees are getting thinner. Anticipation jumps up like a puppy. I've never been here before. I don't know where we're going. "How do you think your parents are going to react?"

Geri pauses to let me catch up, smiling as I crash forward. "That's the thing. We don't know. Alright, your turn," she says as I make it up to her side.

"But I don't have anything," I protest.

"Yes, you do. Now share."

Fair enough. "Fine," I sigh, stepping out of the thicket and onto some prickly grass. We're in a strange field. All of the roads, houses, and main pathways of campus have disappeared entirely behind what looks like a thin layer of trees but what I'm starting to suspect might be a legitimate forest. Geri doesn't seem content to stop here though. She's marching toward the other end of the field where the trees make what looks like a solid wall. "It's just," I say, running to catch up, "that the thing that's bothering me is kind of weird."

"All the better," she says, throwing me an encouraging smile as she walks. Maybe she's a little manic. I can't tell.

"What's bothering me is…" I try to collect my thoughts so I can explain my problem in a way that doesn't make me sound completely nuts. Before I can come up with something we've headed into the trees again and water seems to have erupted in front of me out of nowhere. "Oh wow, this is gorgeous!" I exclaim, looking around. The stream is surrounded almost entirely by trees. There's no sign of civilization to be seen, except for a small red house sitting almost directly across from us atop a steep incline.

"Not many people know this is here," Geri explains, taking a seat on a nearby tree stump. "It's one of my favorite spots on campus. The house used to belong to Alfred Travis, the man who started TU. I love this area. The road used to cross the river up that way," she points to her left. After a moment of gazing upstream, she turns back to me and says, "You were saying?"

She clearly isn't letting this go. "Alright," I say, sitting down on a pile of leaves. They're a little wet and I feel dampness seep through my jeans. I pick up a dried twig, and begin to snap off tiny pieces. Soon, my fingertips are brown. How am I supposed to phrase it? How am I supposed to explain that there's someone who should be next to me, but isn't? I could, of course, bail on that entire topic and tell her about Jude but… no. I don't want to go there. "Okay. What's bothering me today is that I miss someone and I have no bloody clue who it is." A piece of twig bark lodges itself under my thumbnail and I pick away at the fleck, ignoring the protests from my finger.

"And what do you think is causing this?" asks Geri. She leans forward and props her chin on one hand, examining me.

"I don't know." I squint down at my thumbnail and give up the fight. "It only started yesterday, so it's not a long-term thing. It might be insecurity that this is my last school year ever. Maybe it's a manifestation of the anxieties that go along with that." I like the way it sounds: clinical, thought-out, and reasonable. It's also completely false.

"Or...?" Geri prompts. She's looking at me as if there's an obvious answer.

"Or..." I flounder. Then I remember something that Pandora liked to talk about in high school. "Jung! He has a theory that every male part has a female part and vice versa. It's probably a spiritual disconnect." I try not to sound too much as if I'm reciting. Pandy loves the phrase "spiritual disconnect".

I expect her to look impressed at my mention of Jung, but she doesn't. Instead she raises her dark eyebrows and says, "Or maybe you really do miss someone."

"I don't," I say right away, shaking my head and tossing my twig pieces to the ground. "I went through everyone I ever knew and I don't miss any of them." An exaggeration, of course, but true enough.

"Well." Geri reaches down into her black netted bag. "Maybe you haven't met this person yet." She produces a magenta thermos, removes the cap and pours something steaming into the attached cup. "Tea?" she offers, holding it out to me.

"Thanks," I say. As I watch the steam spiral into the air (is it really that cold out?) I try to imagine that this could be true. Maybe he or she… Maybe it is out there right now doing something. Maybe this person is smiling at something that someone I don't know has just said. Or maybe they're getting some work done, sitting behind a desk. My shadow person is probably tired. It's the morning, but a morning that has followed a late night. "But how would that work? How would I miss this person if I haven't met him yet?"

Geri's eyebrows go up again. "So you already know a little about this person."

"No," I protest. "I don't know anything about them."

"Except that he's male."

"I…" I trail off, not exactly knowing what to say. Him.

Abruptly, I shake my head. "It doesn't make any sense. I'm probably making him up because I'm lonely." To punctuate this, I take a deliberate sip of tea, and burn my tongue.

"No!" cries Geri, dismayed. "Don't backtrack! I could tell that you were really there for a second! Look, in any sort of art, but especially photography, you're going to need to be able to see more than what's right in front of you. If you can't get past the walls you put up for yourself, how are you going to get in there with anything else?"

I take another, more cautious sip of tea. I can taste the flavor this time; it's both minty and earthy. I don't recognize it. "I don't mean to not open up. It just seems weird to make up a guy that I miss, and then convince myself that he's real."

I take the hazy figure that has just popped up in my mind and firmly show him the door. My gaze stays far away from Geri.

"Think of it like this: You've heard about people who when they meet claim to feel like they've known each other forever, right?"

"Yeah."

"What if you're one step ahead in this scenario? Could you be anticipating a meeting like this?"

The wind rustles up behind me, and I run my hands rapidly over my arms. Geri was right; I should have brought my coat. I shift on the log, made colder by my damp jeans, and squint at the stream. "I didn't know people anticipated those. I thought they just happened."

"Let me put it this way." Geri produces another mini cup and pours herself a cup of tea. "Why do you think meetings like that happen?" She tips forward slightly and takes a decisive sip.

I shrug. "Because they get along so well. They click. They have compatible personality types, so there's none of that awkwardness of meeting someone that you don't have anything in common with."

"But not everyone who is compatible feels this way upon meeting, correct?" She peers at me over her cup, looking more like we're having a cozy chat than a lesson for credits.

"I guess not." I'm taken with the strong desire to answer her questions correctly. I want to bring up some points that she hasn't thought of herself, impress her with my insight, but I feel like a stranger to this topic. I'm a photographer, not a philosopher.

"Do you think it's possible that there is something else behind it?" She's asking me.

"Maybe." My shoes are dirty. I scuff the toes a few times in the dirt, and imagine what it would be like to meet someone I felt I'd known forever. The closest thing I've had to that is Pandora.

"Could it be more than a coincidence? Perhaps they were meant to meet, or already knew each other in some way. Do you think something like that is the possible cause for that outstanding chemistry upon a first meeting?"

"I can't say for sure, but I guess I can't rule it out…" I've always felt unequipped to theorize on matters like these. How would I know if there's a destiny, or fate, or if everything is random?

"Do you think you could be in an earlier stage of that?"

"Hypothetically. But things like that don't really happen, do they?" I shift again on the leaves, but it's impossible to get comfortable. "And even if they did, how would I know?"

Instead of answering my question, Geri launches into end-of class behavior. She collects her things, tosses them into her bag, and then gives me my homework assignment. "I want you to consider this possibility. Explore the longing you feel and why you think it might be happening, and try to take some pictures that capture this feeling. Dive into the impossibility you're struggling with and show me what you're going through. We meet again on Thursday, right?" I nod. "I want you to have at least a dozen pictures to show me. Explore different locations, and get out of your comfort zone. You're not going to find anything looking where you always look. Choose the best ones to show me."

"Thanks," I say, rising to my feet. Geri smiles but stays where she is, perched on her stump with the little green plastic cup to her mouth. I hesitate for a moment, then give a little wave and traipse back to where I think campus is, not remembering that I left my coat and camera in Geri's classroom until too late.

Chapter Three

I've never bought into the whole "love at first sight" deal. I'd witness people meeting who switch straight into "we're the only two people in the room" mode, but I always assumed that it was because they wanted to jump into bed together and couldn't yet. Actually, the only first meeting between two love interests that I respected at all was when Michael and Pandora met.

Michael and I had been in school together for years, having both gone through the same offbeat private school system together, but we never spoke. All of his sisters had been adored, each in her own way, so Michael was the natural heir to their popularity.

By fourteen Michael was already six feet tall and handsome as anything. At least in the opinion of most of the girls at Riverside High. I chalked him up to be a shallow snob and never made the effort to get to know him. I was mostly put off by the way he treated his friends. He had a gang of guys who flocked him since babyhood that he didn't have any problem bossing around. Whenever I saw a group of them, it was clear who was giving the orders. No one dated a girl Michael looked at, took credit for a project Michael contributed to, or tried out for a team until Michael had a secure spot. I was so repulsed by this behavior that I never looked past the groveling and saw the mildness of the boy on the throne.

A couple years later when Pandy, new to the scene, began asking me about eligible guys, Michael never crossed my mind. Pandora was unimpressed with my suggestions, so for the first couple months of high school she kept to herself and didn't bother trying to get a date. Then, one afternoon at the beginning of November, Pandy and I went to the library to find books for a science project. We had no real idea what we were looking for and hadn't yet adjusted to the layout of the place, so we spent quite some time wandering through the shelves looking for our subjects, far too proud to ask the librarian for help. As we meandered through the stacks we heard some loud male voices coming from a back corner of the library.

"Who is that?" Pandy whispered. We peered through the shelf and saw Michael and a few of his friends sitting at a table, books pushed to the side and varsity jackets slung over the backs of their chairs. I rolled my eyes.

"Michael Lombardi and a couple of his friends."

"I've heard of him," said Pandy, leaning forward with interest. Her nose leveled with the top of the books and I let out a sympathy sneeze. She nodded approvingly. "He's pretty cute."

"But shallow," I informed her, prejudice pushing forward to sound like fact.

"I bet he's not," answered Pandy. She stepped out from behind the bookcase and strode over to where he and his friends were sitting. I stared after her in horrified amazement. Michael was a junior. No one just went up to him and started talking; he always had to make the first move.

"Excuse me," Pandy said confidently once she had reached his table. The boys looked up.

"Yeah?" asked Michael. He was a delightful cliche, sitting there in his varsity jacket. I bit my finger as I watched him take Pandy in. She was skinny and awkward, not yet having mastered her china doll looks. She looked like a joke with her round face, too-big eyes, mass of blond frizz, and painfully childish pink t-shirt reading "Angel". I slid further behind the books.

"I'm doing a research paper for my statistics class on attraction. Could I ask you guys a question?" She grinned brightly at them as she spoke. The guys at the table snickered.

"You can ask me anything babe," one of his friends leered.

"Great. What is the first physical feature you notice on a girl?"

The table rang with laughter but Pandy didn't flinch. She stood patiently as the guys around Michael called out their expected crude answers until they finished. After the boys had quieted down, she looked directly at Michael and said, "What about you?"

"Eyes," Michael said without even the slightest hint of irony.

"Thank you," Pandy said, offering a prim little smile. She then turned and sauntered away. Once back behind the shelves she grinned at me and said, "Eyes. Not shallow at all."

"He was probably just saying that to impress you!" I protested, turning as I spoke because Pandy kept walking.

"You don't really think that," Pandy said easily, and she was right. Pandy had won, and, much to my discomfort, I started to wonder if the two might be good together. There had been something going on as the two spoke that I hadn't witnessed before. Each had behaved in a way unfamiliar to me. I would spend the next six months fighting hard against Michael's presence in my life. But, underneath, there was always a feeling of inevitability that Pandora and Michael would be a couple. And they would work.

It's hard to do an assignment when you have no idea what you're doing it on. Existential angst has never been a favorite angst of mine. How does one visually portray the concept with any degree of subtlety? Subtlety can only come with a true and deep understanding. I, unfortunately, am in the dark.

I just… miss him.

I sigh as I get a patch of leaves into focus. After holding the button and hearing a satisfying click I look at my screen to see how the picture turned out. *Not too bad*, I think, squinting. The light coming through the leaves is more pronounced in the picture than it was from the viewfinder. The negative space has a nice effect, but not the one I'm looking for. I turn off my camera in frustration. I've been out snapping photos all day and so far have come up with nothing. There are a couple of pictures that I want to change to black-and-white, but who knows if that will do anything. I sigh again—exaggeratedly this time—and head back to my apartment to see if Pandora can help at all.

I know something is wrong before I even reach the door. The hallway smells like smoke and booze, indicating one thing and one thing only. My pace quickens and before I know it I break into a run. What is he doing back so soon? I push the door open and see Jude collapsed on the couch, his face freshly bleeding and his left eye swollen. I clench my teeth as I regard him.

"What are you doing here?"

"I need a place to crash." His voice is slow and slurred, his gaze is unfocused.

My stomach drops. "No," I say, shaking my head, "sorry. I have too much going on. You'll have to find something else. Why don't you go home? To Mom and Dad's?" My heart is pounding and exhilaration sweeps through me. I feel instinctively right in refusing my brother. Instead of answering, Jude leans backwards and closes his eyes. "Go away Jude," I plead. My moment of confidence falls away. All I want to do is climb into bed pull every pillow I own over my head. I can't deal with this. "How did you get in?"

"The door was left open. That pretty blond isn't here."

Pandora doesn't usually leave the door unlocked unless she's planning on coming back soon. This means I only have a couple of minutes before she returns to my festering lump of a brother.

I sit down on the couch next to him, hoping against hope that I'll be able to talk him out the door. "I'm sorry, but I have a lot going on. You can't stay here."

Jude turns and meets my gaze, his eyes bloodshot and serious. "I need to stay here Katie. I don't have anywhere else to go."

"Why don't you go home?" I repeat, desperate for someone, anyone else to take care of this mess.

He jerkily shrugs one shoulder and takes his gaze away from me. Up close he looks even worse. "Can't."

Pandy appears at the door, wearing purple sweats and chewing on a bagel. She stops when she sees Jude, tensing as most people who know him do. I mouth "sorry" to her. She briefly shakes her head. I love her so much.

"You have to go, Jude," I say, my resolve returning. Even if I can deal with Jude, I don't want Pandora to have to. Jude, however, continues shaking his head, his eyes back shut.

"I can't," he says again, this time with a snarl.

"You have to," Pandora says, her gaze lighting up in anger. Panic leaps up in my stomach. No, Pandy isn't supposed to get involved. This is my problem, my fight.

"What," Jude says evenly, opening his eyes to look at her, "do you have to say about it?"

"I live here too." With her fluffy blond ringlets and tensed posture, she looks like an angry kitten, ready to attack with her tiny claws.

"You shouldn't bother her," I hurriedly cut in. Jude has to know this is going too far. He's always been a pain in my ass but mostly he's stayed out of everyone else's way.

"No," Pandora says, gazed still locked fiercely on Jude, "you shouldn't bother *her*. Katie's your sister, not your sponsor. It's not up to her to clean up your messes."

"No it's really…" I trail off, suddenly wishing I hadn't always complained so much about Jude. Pandy has always been a fighter. Normally I like that, but today it's scaring me. The tension in the room is rising. I feel like a window could explode at any minute, and I almost want it to. Jude, now on his feet, is glaring back at Pandy, his teeth bared. I swallow hard and grab his sleeve. "Can you just leave?" I beg, trying to get him to look at me.

"You're a right bitch, aren't you?" he growls, jerking his sleeve away from me without taking his eyes off Pandy.

"Don't call me names," Pandora hisses, stepping closer to Jude. The two are almost face-to-face, standing only about a foot apart. It doesn't matter that Jude is nearly a full foot taller than Pandora; they somehow seem evenly matched. A slight wrinkle in the woven blue throw rug underneath their feet catches my attention. Bizarrely, I'm seized with the urge to run forward and straighten it. I force myself to stay put.

"You're a nasty troublemaker," Jude grumbles, finally turning away. He angrily snatches his worn brown bag up from the couch and heads for the door.

I'm just starting to breathe again when Pandora says, "And you're a no-good scum bag with nothing going for him except for his little sister, who only sticks around because she feels like she has to."

There's a noise, an onomatopoeia that has a name like "Thud" or "Bang", and for a second I don't register what happened. Then I see that Pandora is against the wall holding her head with both hands and Jude is in my face yelling, "Is that what you think? You think that too?"

Pandora is slumped almost to the floor now. Pain squeezes her blue eyes shut. "Get out of here!" I yell, planting both hands in the middle of Jude's sunken chest and shoving as hard as I can. My anger toward Jude has reached an all-time crescendo. Any will I had to help him has snapped. "Get out! I don't ever want to see you again!"

Jude stumbles backwards through the doorway, and I slam it shut. The room is abruptly quiet, except for Pandora's quiet sobs. I'm shaking. I rush over to Pandora and sink to my knees, trying to get a good look at her face but not wanting to see it.

"What happened?" I ask. Her hands are clamped tightly over the back of her head, but I'm beginning to see blood seeping through. "Jesus," I say, sitting back on my haunches. "Pandora... What happened?"

In answer, Pandy takes one hand from her head and points up. My eyes follow her hand I see that she's pointing to one of our wooden shelves hanging directly above her head. Sharp edges jut out dangerously. I suck in my breath as I realize what happened.

"Jesus." I say again. She's bleeding. Do I call an ambulance? How bad is it? What am I supposed to do, what do I ask? Fragments from things I've heard over the years zip chaotically through my mind. *Pupil dilation, constant pressure, first few hours are critical...* I have no idea what I'm dealing with. I need to get her to the hospital.

"What happened?" The new voice makes me start. Michael is crouching next to me, his expression serious but much calmer than I know mine is. When did he get here? I long to throw myself at him and start crying on his shoulder, darkening his shirt with tears. Instead I wrap my arms around myself and look down at the floor.

"Um," I breathe in deeply through my nose, "Jude." Shame carbonates my blood. I liked Jude at one point. I used to play with him. I wanted him to be happy. I am required by biology to love the person who did this.

"We need to take her to the hospital." Michael says, coaxing some bloody strands of hair away from Pandy's wound. I nod and stand, trying to figure out the next step. Do we pick her up? I bend over, and try to figure out the best way to pull her to her feet, forgetting all laws of physics and my physical limitations. Michael's hand comes to rest on my arm. "Ambulance?" I ask, straightening. My lips are so dry. If things were better, Pandy would give me some lip balm.

"No," Pandora moans. She's struggling to her feet, leaning against the wall for support. Michael and I ease forward, each grabbing one of her arms to steady her.

"We're taking you to the hospital," Michael says with gentle authority. He's slipped one arm around her waist and is using his free hand to carefully stroke the top of her head. Thank God that Michael showed up. I don't have a car, and I don't want to wait before getting her to the ER. An angry gash spans from just below her temple down to the middle of her ear. Blood leaks freely from the wound, staining Pandy's face red and brown.

She nods submissively. Michael and I help her through the door and out to his car, where we fasten her into the passenger seat. As Michael strides toward his driver's side door, I can't help but admire his calm. My shaking hands are hardly letting me open my door.

Instead of buckling my seatbelt I lean forward and use a t-shirt I found in the back seat to cover the gash. I'm not sure how sanitary it is but I don't care. I need to do something to fight the stream of blood. Michael is driving much more carefully than usual, taking extra time looking before switching lanes, and taking corners slowly and evenly. I want to appreciate this caution, but instead I feel angry. Why isn't he hurrying?

It's a fifteen-minute drive to the hospital. By the time we arrive, I've had to shift the t-shirt a few times to keep the blood flowing into fresh fabric. Pandora's moans have subsided a bit. I don't know if I should be relieved or worried. Michael pulls into the emergency parking lot, then reaches over to undo her seatbelt. Before opening the door, he leans forward and kisses her right next to the injury. Upon seeing this, everything in me jerks, but I don't have time to think about it. I open the car door and jump out, helping to escort Pandora across the pavement and into the building.

"I can walk," she protests, but we each keep a hand firmly on one of her arms. The emergency room is fairly empty; Wednesday afternoons must not be high time for accidents. Michael leads Pandora to the desk where they relay her information to the receptionist on duty. I take a seat on one of the sticky vinyl chairs. A child's toy sits in front of me, and I push a blue block back and forth across a red wire.

Michael and Pandora join me briefly after checking in, but are soon summoned away by a nurse.

"I'll wait here," I call after them as they move toward the door. I want to offer to go in with them but I seem be adhered to my seat. I sit for a while, kneading the bloody t-shirt in my hands. At one point Michael's phone, abandoned on the table, begins to buzz incessantly but after a while it quiets.

She'll definitely need stitches. What if she had a concussion? I remember hearing about people who experience pain weeks, or even months, after a head injury. The thought of Pandora in that kind of agony makes me want to bury my face in the bloody t-shirt. I can't sit here any longer. I need something to do. I get to my feet, and, unable to think of anything else to do, head to the bathroom, splash my face with cold water, and drop the t-shirt into the trash.

Ten minutes later I re-emerge from the clinical-smelling lavatory patting my face with a stiff paper towel. For the first time since I smelled Jude in the hallway I'm beginning to feel my panic ebb. Pandy doesn't have a life-threatening injury; all will be well again soon. As for Jude… I don't care about what happens to Jude. This time I'm done.

I round the corner back into the waiting room, trying to remember where I was sitting. I spot the seat and notice a brown and green striped hoodie lying on the char. How rude. Someone took my seat.

I glance around to see if the owner is anywhere nearby. The waiting room is empty. The only person I see is a man with white hair patiently reading a health and wellness magazine. Somehow I doubt that the hoodie belongs to him.

I pick the sweater up to move it, but, instead of shifting it to the next seat over, I slip it on over my head.

The inside is still warm, the body heat of the previous wearer pressed into the corners and creases. The fabric covers my torso, and, all at once, I'm catapulted into an overwhelming sense of familiarity.

The hood falls onto my head, brushing my face in the same spot where Michael kissed Pandora. Instead of lips on a wound, this is cloth touching unbroken skin. Again, my insides tangle. It's stronger this time, and soon the feeling overwhelms me. Michael, Pandora, this hospital, all of it falls away, leaving me alone. And empty.

I've pulled on sadness. Sadness, loss, and… joy. Joy, delight, comfort, and heartbreak wash over my skin and suddenly I can't breathe.

I miss him.

I've always hated déjà vu. Wanting to remember something that most definitely never happened drives me up the wall but this… this is different. This is worse. I can almost, almost remember. That callus right below his ring finger…

I pull the material tighter around my waist and curl up in the chair, closing my eyes and willing my emotions to sort themselves out. There's a rip in the seam of the left shoulder, and my skin chills against the outside air.

I think I stay awake but when Michael shakes my arm I feel like I'm coming back from a faraway place. "She's fine," he says, once I open my eyes. His blue eyes are alarmingly close. I sit up and pull back as he offers me a hand up. "The police want to talk to you."

Hello, reality. Unwrapping my limbs from my torso, I haul myself to my feet, and follow Michael into a small room. Pandora is sitting on the crinkly paper of the bed wearing a hospital gown. She's curiously fingering a bandage that's covering the side of her head. Her face is pale, and her eyes are tired, but I'm relieved to see she looks much better than before. Next to her stands a policewoman in uniform, taking notes on a pad in her hand.

"Hi," I say uncertainly. The police officer looks up at me.

"You're the friend who was there when the assault took place?"

I nod, my heart speeding up again. I glance at the officer and fix my gaze on a gray box of plastic gloves. I imagine pulling one out, then another, then another... "I'm also the assailant's sister."

I expect a reaction but the officer doesn't skip a beat. Maybe someone already told her. Out of the corner of my eye I see her writing something else down on her notepad. She asks, "And the assailant's name is?"

"Julian Winters."

I sneak a glance at Pandy to see how she's reacting to this, but she's distracted with leaning forward and trying to snatch her purse from Michael's hand. He doesn't notice.

"Can you describe the assault to me in your own words?" *As opposed to what?* I think dryly. *Quoting Sherlock Holmes?*

"I had just come back from a walk and Jude was there, looking for a place to crash. Pandora didn't want to let him stay..." I realize how this sounds and amend my statement.

"I mean, I didn't want to let him stay, I never do, and Pandora knows that, so she told him to get lost."

"This wasn't a unique incident?"

"No, not him showing up."

"Is this the first time he's gotten violent?"

"With Pandora," I give a minute shrug, not sure how much more I should say. "He's always had kind of a violent temper." Part of me wonders whether I should be trying to defend my brother but it feels good to be finally telling someone in authority the truth. "He got into fights in high school."

"Was he ever arrested?"

"No."

"What led to the assault?"

My breath catches as I remember. I don't want to relive it. "Like I said. Pandy asked him to leave and he wouldn't."

"Was any aggression shown on her part?"

"She was being forceful, but not threatening." Best to leave out the verbal abuse the two threw at each other. I'm here to get Jude in trouble, not Pandy. The room is quiet, with only the sounds of the police officer's pencil moving across the paper and the clock ticking at the wall. I glance over at Pandy. She's still struggling to reach the strap of her purse, only inches from her fingertips.

"That's all I need for now. We'll be in touch regarding further developments." The officer closes her book and heads to the door. Michael follows her out. I see him lean against the door, telling her something I can't hear. The officer nods, writes something down for him, then leaves. I watch curiously as he re-enters.

"What was that about?"

"Some procedural information."

I watch the officer walk away, pocketing the information that was given to her by Michael. I feel cold. "What's going to happen to Jude?" I feeling horrible for caring at all, but I can't help it.

"I'm not pressing charges," Pandora says firmly.

"What?" I stare at her, dumbfounded. This is too nice, even for Pandora. "But…"

"I'm not pressing charges. Now, Michael, will you *please* give me my purse?"

Due to the concussion caused by the impact, the doctors want to keep Pandora overnight for observation. After we say goodbye, Michael and I head back to campus together. We're both tired, shaken, and in need of some rest. The ride back is quiet and I squirm in my seat, trying to come up with a safe topic to break the silence.

"You missed a call by the way. In the waiting room. I didn't see who it was."

"I'll check it later." The car lurches out of the parking lot, causing my stomach to swoop unpleasantly. "Whose sweatshirt is that?" Michael asks eventually.

"Sweatshirt?" I ask, uncomprehending.

"The one you're wearing." Michael tips his head toward me. I look down and see that I still have the striped green sweater on.

I flush. Shoot, I stole it. "Oh. I don't know. I found it on a seat, and just... took it." I run my thumb over its tattered sleeve.

Michael lets out an abrupt laugh. "Thief."

I begin to giggle and it continues all the way back to the apartment. By the time we pull into the parking lot the giggles have turned into full-blown laughter, and Michael joins me. I don't know why either of us is laughing, but as we stumble out of the car I'm finding it hard to breathe. Luckily, I have Michael here to support my howling frame.

"Why are we laughing?" I gasp. We stagger forward and I fumble in my coat pocket for my keys.

"Because today sucked," he replies shaking his head. This starts another round of hysterics for me and Michael ends up almost having to carry me inside. Finally, we're back in my apartment and the laughter has subsided a bit. Exhaustion takes over. I flop down onto the couch which lets out a satisfying sigh as it accepts my weight.

"Today did suck," I say soberly, running my hand over my eyes. "Let's have this never happen again."

"Deal," answers Michael. He heads over to our fridge and pulls out a bottle of coke. "Just keep your lunatic brother out of here."

"He's..." I say, trying to muster up some defense for Jude, "oh I don't know." I grab one of our overstuffed red pillows and pull it over my face, enjoying the muffling effect it has on the world around me.

"Hey," Michael says, sitting down next to me. He pulls the pillow from my face and I wince. "It's not your fault, alright?"

He's leaning forward, trying to make eye contact. I look away. If I give in to his compassion I know I'll end up crying. "Yeah," I say gruffly. "I know."

"Come here," he says, pulling me into a hug. I snuggle against him, enjoying his familiar scent. I can't describe it, it's just... boy. But in a clean way; Michael always has impeccable grooming. When his friends were showering in Axe, Michael would smell of soap and peppermint. Except for his feet. His feet always stank. *He's much more of a brother to me than Jude ever was,* I think, trying to convince myself. Michael's hand moves to my hair and begins to stroke. I'm starting to submit to the relaxation pervading my body when I sit up and shove Michael away.

"You should bring Pandora some things for tonight. She'll want to see you again anyway."

Michael nods and gets to his feet, then turns to look at me. "Are you going to be okay?" His blue eyes—so close in color to Pandy's—are concerned. I wave a hand dismissively. I need him to stop looking at me like this.

"I'm always okay," I say wryly. Michael nods once and heads into Pandora's room. A minute later he comes out with an overnight bag, raises a hand in farewell, and exits. I nestle back into the nook on the couch and watch the door after he leaves. I expected for exhaustion to sink in now that I'm alone, but instead I feel restless. I get to my feet, grab my camera, and walk out the front door, picking up right where I left off.

Campus is too crowded. People are everywhere: lying on the grass, walking on the pavement, throwing Frisbees back and forth. Not one of them has any idea that Jude just hit Pandora. My footsteps echo my shame as I forge through the crowd. I need to find somewhere quiet to think. Or not think. *My brother. My brother. My brother.* My camera bangs against my chest, and I break into a jog, desperate to get away.

My first impulse is to head toward the highway, but instead my feet take me down the path where I had gone with Geri. I must not have been paying close attention last time because I don't recognize any of this. Soon, I'm caught in a thick mass of trees and there's no obvious way out. I pocket my anxiety and slip into the protection of the greenery, cradling my camera and pulling the solitude close. I don't try to find my way. Instead, I wander, following speckles of sunlight until I smell dampness and see a fairy-sized river jumping in front of me.

It's not the same part I went to before. Here the trees are thicker, the riverbed is wider, and the water gallops unbridled. Everything seems freer and wilder, dancing with life and secrets. I sprint toward the stream, and then, taking a giant leap, plunge my feet right into the water.

The river rises over my sneakers. There's a second's delay before I feel the liquid seeping in over my socks and down to my feet. It's bizarre and uncomfortable, but I keep my feet where they are, shifting around so I can hear the squelch of mud beneath my soles. I must have done this once as a child because the feeling is familiar. My feet are so very cold.

I stand for a while, listening to the distant highway. What would happen if the water rose and swept me away? The idea of frigid water overtaking my body makes me shudder, but I don't move. Instead I close my eyes and allow my teeth to chatter.

He'd find me here. He'd always find me, no matter how hard I'd try to hide. He'd come from the other side; probably find an easier way to get here too. He'd sit down next to me, put his arms around me, and whisper into my hair. The wind picks up and my hair blows back. *Why aren't you here? Where did you go? Who are you now?*

My eyes fly open as a sense of desperation grips me. I glance around, looking for something, anything to channel this chaos. A tall cement bridge about fifty feet away catches my eye. It looks like it used to be a road, but from its condition I'd guess it's been long since anyone's driven over it. It must be the one Geri was talking about. I make my way up the stream and stop when I'm directly under the heavy cement archway.

I'm fidgety. I'm restless. I search for an outlet for this energy and an old bucket of red paint comes into my sight. It's obscured almost entirely by tall grass. I'd be surprised if there's any paint left in there at all. But, even so, I struggle over to the can and look down into it. It's filled halfway with grassy maroon sludge. Good enough for me. Whoever left the can here didn't leave a brush, but that isn't a problem. I plunge my hand downwards into the chilly goo, then pull it out and begin attacking the wall. I slap and slash as hard as I can, feeling the bumps on the wall bite into my hand and tear away bits of my skin. My palm stings but I forge onwards, thrusting my hand back into the bucket each time my lines grow thin. Finally I step back and, pushing my hair out of my face with my muddy hand, I read what I have written.

I MISS YOU.

There it is. Right there for the world, or no one at all, to see. I drop to the earth, leaning backwards on my elbows and let my hair tumble down over my back. The paint on my hand is starting to dry, stinging my crackling skin. I feel exactly how I should.

Once I get my breath back I'll wash my hands and photograph my moment of raw insanity and present it to Geri with the nonchalance that always covers pride. After that, I'll have to see what else I can come up with because one good picture is never enough. I'll do all of that in just a minute but first I'm going to drop backwards onto the grass and finally close my eyes.

Chapter Four

"It's good," Geri says with an encouraging nod that is nowhere near the astonished admiration I'd been banking on. "Where did you find this?"

I scuff my shoe on one of the tiles that make up her office floor. "A bridge on the edge of campus. I think it's still campus. It's a pretty cool place. I found this there." Of its own free will my hand scoots into my pocket, even though the scratches on my palm have faded.

"This is all you did?" She holds up the single photo and I nod my head.

"I tried to come up with more, but it was really difficult, and my friend had to go to the hospital this week…"

"Is she okay?"

I nod quickly. After the bridge, real life made a rapid comeback. Pandy came home the next day all bandaged up, and I spent most of my energy trying hard to figure out how to act. I did try to find some inspiration but nothing, nothing caught my attention like the bridge. "She's fine, but it was a bit shocking."

Geri nods again, then tips her head and looks at me thoughtfully. Her brown eyes are calculating. I'm back in second grade with an unsigned homework sheet. I cough and pull down the hem of my denim skirt as Geri speaks. "I understand that this week was undoubtedly chaotic, but I can also see that you weren't giving this assignment your all."

I look down at my shoes, chunky vintage heels that I was pretty proud of when I got them for only eight dollars. God, I so don't deserve this. I'm a slacker of the worst variety. They could have chosen any of the top photography students and didn't, but I can't even come up with six pictures to show Geri. "It was hard for me," I say weakly.

"I can see that. So, I have another suggestion." Oh god, she's going to fire me. "Let's take a different approach. I'm starting to think that something like this might be too abstract to start off with. I'm going to give you another assignment instead: find an organization or group that you feel passionate about and tell me about it in a photo essay."

"Oh!" I say, instantly cheering up, "Okay!" That's something that I can totally do.

It's not until I'm back in my room that I realize that I don't care about any causes or businesses. "I don't know," I moan, sighing at the ceiling and watching the blades of the fan go around and around and around. Pandora, sitting on the arm of the couch, peers down at me curiously.

"What don't you know?"

I look at her upside down image. She's wearing a purple t-shirt that reads "Ha!" and what looks like wrapping paper clipped onto a scarf that covers her hair. If it weren't for the fact that she hasn't uncovered her head since she got back from the hospital, I'd almost think everything was normal. "I don't know what to do for my photojournalism assignment," I explain, reaching up and pushing one of her loose blond locks back behind her ear. "I totally bombed the last assignment Geri gave me, so she gave me an easier one and I have no idea what to do for it."

"What are the parameters?" Pandy asks. She pulls more wrapping paper from her purse and starts on my hair.

"It has to be a piece on an organization or business that I care about." I can't say this without rolling my eyes.

"I know!" Pandy straightens quickly and, in her excitement, almost topples backwards off the couch. "Michael's group!"

I snort, unable to summon up a proper appreciation for this joke. A bit of escaped wrapping paper rolls into a tube beneath my fingertips. "Right. But really, what do you think I should do?"

"Michael's group," Pandy says again. I frown at her, starting to wonder if she might be serious.

"What?" I roll onto my stomach and look up at her, trying to figure out the best way to explain this. "Pandy… We don't care about Michael's group. Why would I do an essay on them?"

"Look," Pandy says, holding up a bossy finger, "Michael has been bugging us for ages to go with him, right?"

"Yeah…"

"This way," she smirks, "we can shut him up *and* you can get your assignment done. And since it's an environmental protection group it can be all trendy and stuff. Your teacher will eat it up. Come on, it's not like you have anything better to do." She widens her eyes and blinks rapidly at me while puffing out her bottom lip.

"Fine," I sigh, and heave myself up off the couch. "At least Michael will be happy."

"Yay!" Pandy lets out a squeal and jumps up off the couch after me. "I can't wait to tell him."

"You guys want to what?" Michael looks from Pandy to me and back again, his back and shoulders stiff.

"We want to come to your EA meeting," Pandy repeats, stroking his arm while throwing me a wink.

Michael's tongue darts out of his mouth, then disappears again. My tongue follows suit. "Why?"

"Because we care about the earth!" Pandy flings her arms out dramatically. I clamp my lips between my teeth to keep from laughing. Michael looks at her suspiciously. His gaze moves to me next for confirmation. I try to look innocent.

"I have to do an assignment on a cause that I care about," I explain, hoping I sound sincere. Michael rolls his eyes.

"You don't care about my cause."

"We do!" I protest. "The earth is an important thing to protect!" This part is true; I've just never been able to see how

Michael's Earth Avenger's group has anything to do with it. Michael's always kept the specifics under wraps, but as far as I can tell, all the Earth Avengers do is complain about new highways and yell at each other. And dear god, what a stupid name they have.

"If you guys are coming along just to make fun of it…" Michael's sternness almost gets me going but, thanks to Pandy's foot on my toes, I stay serious.

"We're not," Pandy coos, stepping close to him and taking his hands. "You care so much about it, so I should at least give it a try. Now that I've convinced Katie to go too, I won't feel as uncomfortable being a visitor."

Perfect. Michael de-solidifies and gently wraps his arms around Pandy, who snuggles in closely in return. A slight twinge goes off in my chest and I cough, trying to loosen the tightness, but it stays right where it is.

Two days later Michael and Pandora head out to the car, hand-in-hand, Pandy skipping a little. I trail a ways behind them, just outside their bubble of awareness. We reach the car and all climb in, Michael driving, Pandy in the front seat, and me in the back. Michael turns on the car.

"Everyone buckled?" he asks, looking at me in the rearview mirror.

"Yes," Pandora and I answer obediently. Michael shifts the car into gear and we trundle forward toward the meeting's mysterious location.

"How long are these things usually?" I ask, trying to sound casual. The trees flicking by outside the window show me that we're heading west of campus—a direction I don't usually go.

Michael catches my eye in the rearview mirror and grins. "Don't worry; you can leave when you want."

I tug my hair down over my shoulders but Pandora says, "Katie needs to complete her assignment, so we'll probably have to stay for the whole thing."

Michael laughs and I flop back in my seat, spacing out until we arrive at the meeting place. I don't know what I was expecting, a lecture hall, or an abandoned warehouse maybe. When we pull up to the curb, though, I see that we're in front of a house. It's fairly nice for the neighborhood—two stories and an even paint job. Curiosity begins to stir as we approach the front door. Michael knocks his gloved hand against the front door. A guy, probably a few years older than Pandy and me, answers. He's clean looking for an environmental activist—at least how I've always pictured them—and almost a little bit handsome. His skin and eyes are dark, and beneath the sleeves of his blue button-down it looks like he has pretty nice arms.

"Michael, hello. Come in. And who are these lovely ladies?"

"My girlfriend Pandora, and this is Katie."

"Pleasure," he says smiling. His manner of speaking is so formal that there's no hint of flirtation in his voice. Shame. He introduces himself as Shane, and then leads us through a small hallway to a room that looks like it was originally intended to be some sort of bedroom. Instead of a bed and dresser though, the room is crammed with chairs and a couple of couches. A giant screen boasting the name of a brand unfamiliar to me covers one wall. I glance backwards and see a huge, and undoubtedly expensive, projector. How environmental.

Michael stops in the doorway, and begins pointing in turn at each person in the room. "Jessica, she's Shane's sister, Gil, Amanda, Mark, Russ, Francis, and Ducky."

"Ducky?" Pandora repeats. A short guy by the window looks up and waves.

Jessica, having all of Shane's features but softer, is devastatingly beautiful. She's the kind of woman that would make me feel underdressed even if I was wearing a ball gown and she was in a t-shirt. She's talking to one of the guys—Gil I think?—who has his gaze fixed on an iPad. Huh. If I was a guy, I don't think I'd ever look away from Jessica.

Amanda and Mark are clearly another set of siblings. They both have strawberry blond hair, and pointed noses that end in a strange little crevice. They're sitting next to each other but not talking. Mark has a book out, and Amanda is trying to get Russ's attention. I can't say I blame her. Russ is a bald, bearded hunk of chiseled muscle. I nudge Pandy and she gives me a knowing wink before giving Michael a kiss on the cheek. Francis is older than the rest, looking to be in his mid-thirties, or even forties. He's stocky and scowling, with a mass of damaged hair roped into a bun.

"Watch out for him," Michael murmurs, as if hearing my thoughts.

After figuring everyone out, I plop down on the end of the couch nearest the door and snuggle back into my hoodie.

It's time for some lazy strategizing. Since I don't have to turn anything in for this assignment until right before Thanksgiving break, I think I'll spend the first meeting getting to know the group and take some preliminary notes (yuck). As tempted as I am to jump right in, I think I'll save picture-taking for the next meeting. I do have my camera with me, just in case I see anything I can't miss. The poor lighting isn't giving me much hope, though. The camera's ISO is already set high, but my test shots are still dark and blurry. Something tells me that this isn't going to be very fruitful.

"Almost ready to start. We're just waiting on Robin," Shane says, looking around at the group assembled.

"He's not coming. He's taking Vin to get her cast off," Amanda replies. Russ finally spares her a glance. She throws an entire birthday's worth of delight into the one smile that he sees, before he looks back down at his iPad. Poor Amanda.

Shane frowns and tips his head to one side. "Is Vin doing okay?"

Amanda nods. "Better."

"We'll start, then. First, I'd like to welcome two new guests today." I flush as everyone looks in our direction. Pandora, who has squished herself in next to me, grins and waves at the room. Her confident posture and bright expression make her seem like some sort of VIP. I guess that makes sense since she's Michael's girlfriend, but I'm not sure what to do. Smiling uncomfortably, I pick out a few faces to nod at so I don't look unfriendly. There are a lot more faces than Michael pointed out. I'd guess there are at least fifteen, twenty people at this meeting. I'm never going to know them all. After I finish looking around I relax, welcoming the shift in attention.

"Good to see you all again. We'll be looking at some updates from our last project, but first I have some news. Velke Corp is starting a training program for anyone interested. Talk to me if you want to travel. We're still working out details, but the program should be ready by the summer." A murmur of interest goes around the room. "I'm gonna tell Rob," I hear someone mutter. A cell phone lights up as the projector kicks to life.

I raise my eyebrows and look at the screen. No need to advertise how boring I expect this to be. Shane turns off the lights and the room grows quiet. I squint at the slightly out-of-focus pictures, forcing myself to pay attention. I'm going to need an angle; I'm going to need to give the impression of passion. If I can find one thing, anything, about this group that catches my interest…

"I got a letter back from the Allensdale Board of Trustees. They've heard us, but they're not listening. We might want to reconsider our approach."

"Screw them!" yells Jessica. Shane looks at his sister and she quiets down. I hear murmuring around me, but I can't make out if it's in favor of Jessica or Shane.

"The samples we took from the Nature Reserve are being processed. I'll send out an email as soon as we get the results. In the meantime, stop collecting more. I'm serious." He casts a critical gaze around the room. This time I can tell the grumbling isn't of a happy nature. Shane gestures to the girl at the projector. The EA logo—two letters surrounded by enough swirls to make me wonder if they didn't want to think of a logo—disappears, and the first slide pops up.

I hurriedly write down "Reserve samples" and turn my attention to the images before me. The pictures are atrocious. Most of the faces are washed out by flash, there is nothing dynamic about the angles and framing, someone's finger is partially obscuring the lens in about half of them and everything looks painfully staged. For each picture that flicks by, I occupy myself by making a mental list of improvements. It's not until Shane pauses for a question that I realize I haven't heard a word since the slideshow started. When Mark pipes up with a question about tar sands (there was a confused moment there when I thought he said "Tarzans), I try and focus back in, but I'm too far gone. It's biology class all over again.

"… The budget has gotten tight, so we might have to postpone the whole thing until March."

A collective groan goes around the room. I pull on my sympathetic face a second too late. Thankfully no one is paying any attention to me. I squiggle down deeper in my chair and begin counting the white flecks on my fingernails. There's still a bit of maroon around the nail beds of my left hand. I wonder if anyone noticed.

Eventually Shane's words sink down through my mire of boredom. Whatever project they're talking about may have to wait until March. Does this mean that I have to stick around until then? That's six months away! A grim image of me doomed every week to sit in this room with these people flashes before my eyes. I need to get out. Planting my hands firmly on either side of me, I rise slightly to see how crowded my path to the door would be. Dear lord, I'm trapped.

I don't have to leave right now, I reason, letting out a breath and lowering myself back into the indentation I left on the sofa. *I can at least wait until this session is over.* But if it's going to take six months for me to see any real work in action, then I am leaving, and never ever coming back.

The presentation is not ending. Picture after picture meanders by, each one feeling like that chatty person you dread running into at the grocery store. Shane's stamina doesn't falter for a second. He seems just as excited about each new slide as the one before, taking at least five good minutes to explain each one. I wait for the pace of the slides to pick up or for Shane's voice to flag, but he keeps going on and on and on.

I start counting the pictures as they go by. One… two… three… Maybe this will put me to sleep. I hit fourteen, and see it.

A young man with light brown hair kneels by the edge of a river in an outfit that seems to be constructed of colorful plastic sheets. He has a yellow rain cap on his head, and dark green rubber boots on his feet. He's smiling widely as he holds up a vile of murky water.

"… As you can tell, Robin was pretty excited about our findings." Click, and the picture is gone. I blink with disorientation, staring at the place where he had just been. It's occupied now by Amanda and Ducky, who are talking to a man with white hair.

That was him. That was *him*. I look around to see where Pandora is, but she's looking at the screen, laughing on cue with everyone else. I stare at her for a few seconds, willing her to look at me, but quickly realize that if she looked I'd have no way to communicate what I just discovered.

That was him. Robin. His name is Robin. His name is Robin and I haven't met him but I miss him more than I even knew. His is the face that was missing from my mind. He's the one that should be kissing me right on the forehead, in that spot reserved for tenderness.

He's the one that should have found me under the bridge.

The lights finally flick on and people around me rustle. Conversation leaps puppy-style around me even though Shane is still speaking. I stay where I am, transfixed by the blank screen.

"No need to protect anyone's image. Let's go and get the word out there."

"We have our own image to consider."

"And we want the image of people who get things done. What's the next step?"

Can't they all be quiet? This isn't what I expected to happen when I came here. This isn't it at all.

I'm the only one still sitting. People are on their feet, chattering away while they work toward the table that now magically bears sandwiches. I look through the crowd for Michael and Pandy. They pop up right in front of me, Pandy wearing a smirk and Michael an expression of understated pride.

"What did you think?" she asks, irony sparkling in her blue eyes.

At the exact same time Michael says, "Well?"

Both of them are staring at me expectantly. Both of them know that I hate to lie.

"I think," I feel suddenly giddy, like I could start laughing and never stop, "that you need a new photographer." I lean my head on Michael's shoulder, smiling as he shouts triumphantly.

We all head back to the car, Pandy's drifting off to the side. The look she's giving me borders on doubt, even suspicion. I will her quietly to stay silent until we get home and I can tell her everything.

"I still can't believe you want to join," Michael says, shaking his head.

"Well," I say, leaning forward from the back seat. I rest my cheek on Pandy's chair, letting the fabric brush my face. "I have to pick something, and your photos suck. The whole thing seems pretty accessible. I like it."

Michael puffs up further, taking my lukewarm praise to heart. Pandy doesn't move. Her blonde hair is covering her face from this angle so I can't see her expression. I poke her arm playfully but she stays still.

"There were some interesting concepts raised," Pandy agrees finally. She shoves her hair back and tosses me a superior look in the rearview mirror. "But I don't think you guys are going about everything in the most effective way."

Maybe not, I think, *but this is the only way that I get to meet him.* It takes me a second before I realize that she's talking to Michael.

"What would you do differently?" Michael inquires. He cranes his neck to see into the oncoming traffic and swings us onto the highway.

Pandy wiggles her lime green Converse sneakers on the glove compartment. "Your group seems to have quite an aggressive approach to things," she says carefully. "While I think it's good to take action, it seems like some of the stuff could get you into trouble."

Michael accelerates and swoops into the left lane, cutting off a blue convertible. "An aggressive approach is what you need. No one is going to change anything if they're not forced to. We need to show them that we're not going to take this lying down. Corporations like them feel invincible. We need to show them they're not." The convertible blares its horn and Michael gestures rudely in the rearview mirror.

"That makes sense," I offer from the backseat. I don't actually have an opinion, but I feel closed off from the front, so I vie for inclusion.

"I get that," Pandora says, giving an apologetic wave to the blue car, which has now almost passed us again. Her curls bounce around her head. I'm abruptly struck with worry for what this motion will do to her injury. Is it all healed or is there still cause for concern? "I just don't think the plans are the best thought-out. I mean, are you even sure you've got the story right? APM is a pretty big company. It doesn't seem like the best idea to start a smear campaign."

"Shane knows what he's doing," Michael says, and the discussion is closed.

"If you'd listen to Shane," Pandy replies, too quietly for Michael to hear.

We drive back to the apartment in silence. By the time we get to campus, discomfort is creeping up on me like an unwanted shoulder rub. I was so focused on how this is going to get me to Robin (Robin!) that I hadn't even thought about what the group is representing. I assumed it must be good, since it's a fight for the environment that Michael's a part of. I've heard, however, of things like these going too far.

As we walk inside, I can't help noticing the tension in Pandy's shoulders. She isn't talking much to either one of us. Is that why she's angry? Because I've agreed to be part of something immoral? Michael, claiming a busy evening ahead, stays in the car and takes off. Pandora waves affectionately as he pulls out of the parking lot, then turns to frown at me.

"What's with that?" she asks sternly, breaking her silence.

"What's with what?" I ask. It's always better not to guess.

"What's with your sudden interest in all things eco?"

I push past Pandora, shove my key into the outdoor lock, and twist. The thunk of the turning lock competes in volume with my voice. "You know I have to do a project on something and we chose this together. What's the problem?"

"The problem," Pandora says impatiently, taking the thick metal door handle from my hand and letting herself in first, "is that you're totally sucking up to Michael."

Her tone is casual, but I'm rendered motionless.

"What?" I look at Pandy. She's leaning against the door, holding it open with her small frame. I can't step forward. "Pandy, that's crazy. Why would you think that?" My heart kicks into fifth gear and my hands begin to tremble. I hope she doesn't notice. I hope she thinks that I'm cold.

"We never had any interest in this group, ever. We got to a meeting and not only is it boring, but it also seems pretty sketchy."

"Not all of it!" I protest, thinking of Robin's earnest grin.

"No, not all of it. But, Katie, you didn't listen to a word they said. Now you're diving headfirst into being their photographer?" She isn't angry. She's looking at me expectantly, waiting for me to explain myself. I want to. I will. I don't know how.

"I didn't notice that it seemed sketchy…"

"Because you weren't listening. Because it was boring." Pandy speaks slowly, punctuating each word with a nod of her head. "But at the end of it suddenly you're 'Miss Environment' and acting like it's the most important thing in the world to you. Come on, Katie!" She stamps her foot in frustration. "Why do you always have to get like this when it's something Michael likes?"

"I don't!"

"He's not your boss, you know. You don't have to be like everyone else."

Her words slap me, hard. Images of those boys in high school come flooding back to me in a nauseating wave. Raking my hands over my head, I yank my hair back from my teddy bear earrings. "Look, Pandy, if you would just chill for one second and let me explain…"

Pandy sighs and I see her slump. "I'm sorry. You don't need to explain." She pushes the door wider, inviting me inside. "You need a project; they're a good group. I was being dumb. It's just that," she releases the door once we're both inside the building and it begins its slow whine closed, "I wanted us to both hate this together. And now you're all into it and so is Michael and I guess it made me feel left out."

"Pandy." I stop walking. "The reason why I'm excited about this has nothing to do with Michael or even what the group is doing."

She looks at me sideways and doesn't say anything.

"The reason why I'm excited to join is... One of the guys in the pictures... The guy by the water looked so, so familiar. And I don't know who he is, but there was something about him I recognized."

Pandora's expression freezes and her lips tighten. A second later, she's laughing. "Katie," she chuckles, shoving her hands into her coat pockets, "That is so like you."

"It is not!" I protest. "I've never done anything like this in my life! There's something about this guy. I think his name is Robin. And he felt... he felt so familiar. I can't explain why."

"I can," Pandy answers, cocking an eyebrow and pointing at my chest. "You're wearing his sweater. He had it next to him in the picture."

Michael comes by a couple hours later only to find that Pandora has gone out for a run.

"She'll be back soon," I say, tossing him an apology soda.

"It's cool." Michael cracks the can open with two fingers. The motion takes me back to high school, when the way Michael so confidently opened beer was a constant fascination of mine. I drag my mind back to the present, dismissing any recollection of high school.

"So," I say, leaning back against the counter. The tile is cold beneath my hands and the grouting between them scratches my palms. I pick my hands back up and rub them together. "Pandy seemed freaked by me offering to be your photographer."

The left half of Michael's mouth rises into a smile. "It's a weird request. Especially since you started off only wanting to do an essay."

"But it's okay, right?" I press, glancing at Michael's face. He catches my eye, and I quickly look over at the cow clock that hangs over the sink. The second hand moves over the cow's udders, and suddenly I feel embarrassed.

"Sure, it's fine. Why wouldn't it be?" He knows. He knows exactly why it wouldn't be. I level my gaze with him and hold his blue eyes with my slate ones.

"Pandy said it made her feel left out. At first she thought that I was joining..." I force myself not to stammer over this part, "because of you."

Michael doesn't look embarrassed. He doesn't look ashamed. Instead his eyes stay still and he grins. "Are you?"

"No!" I want to hit him. I look around for something acceptable to throw but only find a potholder. That just wouldn't have the heft. "Michael, don't. Just don't. Okay? I want to join for my own reasons."

"Just seems weird," Michael says with a shrug. He looks down at the soda can in his hand and takes another swig.

"It is weird," I agree. "But it's a weird that has nothing to do with you. I'll tell you the real reason later."

"Fine." Michael shrugs and sets his empty can on the counter. He's always been able to drink remarkably quickly. "I gotta get going. Tell Panda I stopped by?"

"Sure." He turns to go. "Michael…"

"Yeah?"

"I think this is Robin's sweater." I pick the hoodie up off the chair next to me and, with a pinch, toss it to Michael. He catches it. "Give it back for me?"

Michael glances down at the hoodie and drops it into his bag and out of sight. "Sure. When I see him."

"Yeah. When you see him."

Chapter Five

THREE YEARS AGO

It was at a party, and neither of us should have been drinking. Michael—back already from his second year at college—had promised Pandora he wouldn't, and alcohol was something I didn't have a taste for. That night, though, I'd found something pink and fruity and enjoyed the lightness that sipping it brought. Michael was on his third beer.

"Pandy's gonna kill you," I sang, flopping down next to him. He grinned and raised the dark bottle to his lips. They were nice lips. Michael's always had nice lips.

"Do you really think she's not doing the same thing?" he asked, after he had taken a righteous swig. Pandora was spending that weekend at her cousin's wedding. Michael and I both knew that she had a tendency to indulge too much at family events.

"But you two are supposed to be cutting back together," I said, primly taking a sip of my pink drink. "I don't have to, because I'm not sleeping with either one of you."

Michael snorted. "No, you don't have to because you don't drink."

"I do so!" I protested, brandishing my plastic cup. Bubblegum liquid danced up to the brim before settling back into place. "It's pink, and delicious, and I like alcohol now."

"And you've had less than one cup and you're wasted."

"You're just jealous cuz I can get there faster," I said smugly. I was feeling comfortably warm. The party atmosphere mixed with my drink pulled me towards wanting to sleep. Taking a sip from my cup, I snuggled back on the couch and let my head drop to Michael's shoulder.

"I can see your bra from here," he commented.

"Then stop looking," I answered with a yawn. "This party's too noisy. Want to go outside?"

We headed out to the patio, overlooking the host family's enormous fountain. It was lit up and a beautiful sight to see, despite Pandora's many complaints that it was tacky.

"Can you believe me and Pandy are graduating in a month?" I said, leaning sideways and tipping my head to see what the fountain would look like from a different angle.

"Not with the way you're acting," Michael teased, catching my arm and straightening me up.

"Boo," I pouted, "I'm eighteen and drunk. Isn't this how I should be acting?"

"I guess," Michael shrugged, taking a sip from his bottle. I noticed it was full again.

"The magically refilling bottle," I intoned, snatching it from him and taking a giant swig. As soon as the liquid hit my mouth I pulled the bottle from my lips and spat the beer out onto the ground. "Gross. I might like liquor now, but I do not like beer."

"You and Pandy both," commented Michael, reclaiming his drink.

"Pandy," I said dreamily, "I miss her. I wonder where she is now."

"Probably dancing her ass off."

"I bet she looks ridiculous," I giggle, imagining Pandy in her puffy pink bridesmaid dress.

"I bet she looks hot."

"You always think Pandy's hot. Pandy and no one else. Lover boy." I uttered the last three syllables slowly, aware that I was acting a lot more drunk than I felt. But isn't that what alcohol did—make you do silly things but not care?

"I think you're hot," Michael said, turning to face me fully. He was so much taller than me that I had to tilt my head pretty far back to look into his face. His blond hair was slightly matted, probably from being in the warm room for so long. His gray t-shirt clung nicely to his shoulders and chest. Without Pandora around I was starting to see Michael by himself, and I liked it.

"Lover boy," I said again, at a loss for what else to do.

"Lover girl," he answered, a silly and nonsensical response that pushed me into a fit of giggles.

"Lover man."

"Lover woman."

And then we were kissing. I remember thinking how strange it was to be having this new experience with someone so familiar. I had watched him kiss Pandora so many times, but this time it was me.

I broke away.

"Shit," I gasped, wiping my mouth as if that would somehow erase the sin. "Michael. Shit." I looked up at him timidly, afraid that more eye contact might lead to a repeat offense. Michael was positioned so that shadows covered his face. I couldn't see his expression.

"We're drunk," he said calmly. "This means nothing." And with that, he turned and walked back into the party. Hot with despair, I took my cup and threw the contents over the railing.

"Hey," I heard someone say as they stumbled out of the main room and onto the patio. "Why would you do that? That's bad for the plants."

I turned and saw the host, Tina Beddingfield fumbling in her pocket for a cigarette. Although I didn't know her well, I was taken with urge to confess everything. I wanted nothing more than to fall upon her shoulder and start sobbing.

But when I opened my mouth the only thing that came out was, "I'm drunk."

"No you're not," Tina said, clearly amused, "You've been drinking sparkling grapefruit juice all night."

I'm woken by a phone call from my mother. She's calling about Jude, of course, and the awake part of my brain wonders why it took her so long to contact me about this. Talking about Jude is hard when I'm fully conscious, so having to do it while I'm half-asleep is practically impossible. I hardly hear anything she's saying except for a couple choruses of, "I don't know what to do with him!" I nod along sympathetically, keeping my eyes closed for as long as I can keep awake.

"It's tricky, Mom," I mutter.

"I just don't know what to do," my mom says again.

"You know that Pandy isn't pressing charges, right?" It feels strange to use Pandora's nickname right now but I can't get my mouth to form her whole name. I open my eyes and force myself up, realizing that this conversation isn't going to be over soon enough for me to get back to sleep. My mom is quiet for a bit.

"I almost wonder if she should," she says finally.

"Maybe." I pull my feet up to my chest and look down at my toes. There's a band of white around one of my toes from the toe ring that Pandy gave me at the beginning of the summer. It was a cheap little thing. The whole band is rusted now. But I felt fancy all summer, running around with bejeweled feet. Pandy's matching one is still, no doubt, intact.

"I'm so sorry, baby. I know this has to be hard for you," my mom says softly. "I just don't know what to do."

"We'll figure it out," I promise. Helplessness renders me limp.

"Thank you, sweetie. I'll let you go now."

"Bye mom."

I hang up and stare blankly at my bedspread for a few minutes. It's light blue with clouds covering it and so old that

I don't even remember when I got it. Still, I insisted I take it to college even though my mom offered to buy me a new one. I wanted that connection to home. I don't know why. I rub my thumb over the worn material, then get to my feet. I need to go. I need to get out and move and not think about Jude or Pandora or Michael. I need to go.

I look around for the moss-colored hoodie, which I've gotten so used to wearing, before I remember I gave it back to Michael. My shoulders slump. As a replacement, I pull on my high school drama club sweater. It lacks the softness Robin's had, as well as that heaviness that only comes with sweaters worn by guys, but it covers me. At least I'm warmer than I was.

The sunlight outdoors feels inappropriate. The people around me seem like a cheerful movie left on in the background while you're in a fight. Why are so many people up so early? I need to be alone. It's time to make a dash for solitude.

The wind is active, slapping dust into my eyes like a bully. I don't go back and retrieve my sunglasses, instead I forge forward. A climb up a grassy hill, a stumble down a muddy incline, and I'm at my defiled bridge. I wade through a puddle and make my way over to the offending lettering, unsure if I'm proud or mortified. I've never done graffiti, or any other kind of vandalism, before. I wonder if there's some way to undo it. I know it's unlikely, as the paint was permanent, but I want to try.

There's more graffiti on the bridge than I remember and it takes me a moment to find my own. My gaze skims over the other proclamations: GM+OD, Andy waz here...

There it is. Wait. I thought I wrote mine in red. The letters before me are shining brightly in standard blue. As I look at more closely at the words, I see there's one more than before:

I MISS YOU TOO.

My breath catches and I step forward, pressing my hand against the cold concrete. The paint is dry.

I CAN'T BELIEVE YOU WENT. The letters are splashed up on the wall before I even know what I'm doing. I'm crying, my tears keeping me from seeing my words. *Shut up*, I think viciously at the four blue words. Kicking the wall until my foot smarts, I fight back the urge to scream. *Liar!*

It's probably just the work of an art student. Someone who knew about this spot and wanted to add their own story to the new graffiti. But, as I stand here by myself, it doesn't matter. I'm wrapped up in the words, and to me, he wrote them. *I want you*, I mouth, running my fingers again over the blue paint. *I miss you so badly.*

Chapter Six

Fall has come along and swept me up into a frenzy of optimism, quite unlike how our friend Yeats described it. The leaves on the trees have finally burst into their gaudy displays of yellows and reds. Every chance I get, I'm outside with my camera, trying to romance the scenery into giving me the best shots. Geri likes my these photos, saying that I'm doing a great job with capturing emotion. They've also done the delightful task of keeping her attention off my EA essay. My selection of a group seems to be enough thus far. My lack of passion has been neatly tucked out of Geri's view, but it's not making the assignment any easier.

He must have looked like someone. I can't remember who, but I'm sure that that's all the recognition was. Maybe he had the same expression as an actor I like, maybe I saw pictures of him on Facebook with Michael, or maybe I did just recognize him because of his sweatshirt. I'd been rocking the green and brown stripes for almost two weeks before I saw that picture. That must have been what was so familiar. My project has been tugging at me for the past three weeks, whispering for me to go to another meeting. But for now I'm keeping my distance, spending all of my time creating my Halloween costume.

Originally I wanted to be a character from Jane Austen, Emma maybe. But first, no one would recognize the outfit and second, I'd have to be sure to wear clothes consistent with the time period. With everything else I have going on, I didn't have the energy to research that. I'm opting instead for a non-character-specific old-fashioned dress with a big skirt, lots of curls, and sleeves that start below my shoulders.

I think Pandora might be getting annoyed with my craft supplies covering our floor because she's been spending less and less time at home. She and Michael have some surprise costumes that they're crafting. She's over at his place "working on them" constantly. I don't mind her absence. I'm happy to spend my afternoons alone, cutting, pinning, and sewing away with 90s rock blasting from the radio.

Halloween is on a Saturday this year. The school is throwing a big party complete with decorations, a magic show, and a costume contest. I have a theory that the effort put into the party is largely to keep the students out of trouble, but I'm glad for a school-sanctioned way to celebrate. I decided a long time ago to permanently and steadfastly avoid all things alcohol related.

Friday night I'm on my knees, trying to get the bustle right on the skirt, when Pandora emerges from her room. She's wearing a short gray cotton robe over a black pair of underwear that reads "Bride" on the front and "Mrs. Lewis" on the back.

"'Lombardi' wouldn't fit?" I ask, nodding to her underwear.

"What?" she glances down at herself as she saunters past me on the way to the refrigerator. "Oh. They were on sale. Almost done with that?"

"Amoft," I answer around a mouthful of pins. I pull a blue end from between my lips and hitch up another section of material.

"Better get it done by tomorrow," warns Pandora, grabbing a soda from the fridge. She plops down on the couch and watches me work.

"Yours done yet?" I set my pins down on the wooden part of the floor to ensure that they don't get lost in the plush carpet. That would not end well.

"Yup, Michael and I finished last night. They're awesome." She takes a satisfied sip of her soda. Leaning forward, she picks up the back of my skirt with one hand and examines it. "This is really good."

"Can't get the bustle to work," I sigh, shoving a handful of hair out of my face. I again find myself regretting the bangs I got in the spring. It seems like I always have hair in my face now.

"Hm. Anyway, I have some gossip about the dance." Pandy, the master of the non-sequitur.

"Let's hear it."

"There's a rumor going around that there's going to be some kind of mischief."

I roll my eyes. "Can't people behave?"

"I think it'll be fun. It's supposed to happen at midnight." She squiggles into the sofa as if readying herself for a good show.

"So, when it's not Halloween anymore."

"You're no fun." Pandy crosses her arms over her chest and pouts. "I'm only telling you because it might make a good story. You know, one you could write for the school's blog or something."

Comprehension dawns. "I could bring my camera…" I say, slowly nodding. I live with the paradox of hating any sort of trouble but working toward a profession that revolves around finding it. A good journalist looks for trouble wherever she goes. "Midnight?"

"Yeah. And if you get famous from this story, you owe me."

"A good journalist never reveals her sources," I say primly, stabbing a green-threaded needle through three layers of fabric. Pandy rolls her eyes and gets off the couch.

"I'm going to go put some pants on. It's freezing."

Halloween dawns cold and appropriately gray, making the leaves seem extra bright against the whitewashed sky. I can feel the air prickle with anticipation for the night ahead. I pull on a thick sweater and make myself a cup of tea, ready to sit on the couch and watch anxiously as the clock ticks forward, bringing me closer and closer to the party.

I finished my costume last night, but once I'm back in front of it, I begin my busied search, looking for anything and everything that I can add or fix. Since it was meant to be a quick look-over, problem after problem materializes under my fingertips. Soon I'm saddled with more than I can do and a panicked heart rate. By the time Pandora stumbles out of her room, sleepily asking me if I'm ready to go to lunch, I'm near to tears with frustration.

"It's awful!" I say, throwing my handful of ribbons to the floor. Pandora nods, eyes half closed, then grabs my hand and pulls me to my feet.

"Lunch," she instructs. The two of us head out toward the campus dining hall, Pandora still only in her panda bear pajama pants and one of Michael's t-shirts. Inside the dining hall, we're greeted by the smell of fall spices and the sight of slice after slice of pumpkin pies, there for the taking. Pandy and I skip the entrees, and go straight to the pie, taking two slices apiece and grab one of the smaller tables by the windows. Pandora, not wasting any time, immediately digs into her first slice. I lazily take a forkful and lick at it, gazing around the room.

I spot a few people with cat ears or clown noses, but for the most part the costumes are waiting until tonight. A nearby table passes around a giant bag of candy corn. I briefly consider asking for some but as soon as my pie hits my mouth I decide not to. I'm about to start on my second slice when a flash of earth tones flits through the corner of my eye. I frown and swivel my head toward where I saw it. The dining hall is functioning in its routine manner, and nothing clicks into place for me. There's something pulling at the corner of my mind but I can't identify what, so I return to my pie.

The evening can't come fast enough. At about ten minutes to seven I've fidgeted with my costume until even I can't find anything else to change and there's still over an hour until the dance officially begins. Of course, it's more like two until anyone actually shows up. I'm usually fine with hitting a party early and leaving before it gets too late. But tonight my obligations ensure that I have to stay at least until midnight. I'll head over around nine so the early attendees can have plenty of time to see my fabulous costume. I can catch the show after and then only have an hour and a half to kill afterwards before the evening's promised finale.

Pandora had better be right, I think, sitting on my bed and breaking off the end of a granola bar. Crumbs scatter onto the bedspread. I wipe them off impatiently, hearing the little rainstorm hit the floor. I'm going to regret that tomorrow. Sparkling up at me from my lap is a book of fairytales that I brought from home, seducing me with ideas for next year's outfit. I've always been enamored by the translucent skirts and tight bodices of fairy outfits. When my eyes are closed, I sometimes imagine a world where I could garb myself in such outfits daily. But would magic still seem magical if we experienced it regularly?

I've just gotten to my favorite picture—one of a woman with long black hair and dark eyes wearing a torn purple dress—when Michael and Pandora burst into my room, wearing long white capes and cushioned crowns. Michael has on a red shirt with black pants and Pandora looks stunning in a long crimson velvet dress.

"Ladies and gentlemen: The king and queen of hearts!" Pandora announces, brandishing a golden scepter in the air.

"Fabulous!" I exclaim, walking over to inspect them. Their capes have red hearts sewn in strategic spots all over the snowy material. Pandy's imitated the look with a matching heart drawn on each cheek. Their synergetic creativity draws up a moment of insecurity about my own simple dress. The work I put into the outfit doesn't like this feeling, and stomps out the doubt.

"How's yours coming?" Michael asks. His arm is locked around Pandora's waist. His large-knuckled hand makes her waist seem extra tiny. I smile at the pairing.

"It's done." I shrug. "Should I change into it?"

"Yes," Pandy decides. "Then we can do pictures and make it over to the dance in time for the show."

The next hour is spent zipping me into my dress, teasing my hair (thank god I have Pandy for that), fixing all of the last minute problems that somehow escaped me (how was I to know my zipper would get caught?), and finally taking pictures: Michael and Pandora both together and separately, beaming, blowing kisses, and looking every inch the whimsical royalty that they're enacting. When it's my turn to be documented, Michael takes over since Pandy and cameras don't mix.

Finally it's time to traipse over to the art center where the party is being held. This is the first Halloween in I-don't-remember-how-long that I haven't worn heels. I delight in the warmth and comfort of the solid brown combat boots I opted for. They're not exactly period appropriate but there are big gold buckles on the side, which makes me feel pirate-y. I reach the arts building a bit before Michael and Pandora do, since Michael has to help Pandy teeter over the rocks in her high white heels, and I excitedly dip into the party.

Smells of popcorn and caramel greet me. Everyone in the room looks fantastic. There are characters I recognize, (Winnie-the-Pooh, Iron Man, and of course at least one Jesus), and the inevitable tropes that make their appearances at every costume party: vampires, priests, pimps, etc. Then there are colorful costumes full of so much detail that I'm sure there must be a story behind each one of them but I don't recognize any. The music, of course, is atrocious, but the beat is strong enough that I'm able to skip out onto the dance floor and start shaking my hips without too much trouble.

A couple minutes later, Michael and Pandora make their entrance. Soon we're all twirling, jumping, and laughing so loudly that we can almost hear ourselves over the music. As we dance, I remember in high school how I couldn't be near Michael and Pandora at dances. They were so embarrassingly physical with each other that I liked to pretend that I didn't know them. I smile indulgently at the memory. Their current style is sort of modern ballroom, and a lot more fun to join in on.

After greeting the familiar faces at the party and the giving and receiving of compliments, it's time for the show to start. Pandy, Michael, and I all manage to push our way up to the front. Pandy and I settle ourselves onto the floor, scooting around so our costumes minimize our contact with the floor. The wood usually leaves me with an aching rear, but sitting on an uncomfortable surface is far preferable to standing for forty-five minutes and ending the show with throbbing feet.

The performers are the same group who did the show last year, a talented bunch whose acts are mostly dancing with glow sticks with some sort of big pyrotechnic finale. Pandora and I watch in festive delight at their standard routine. Michael stands behind us, occasionally crouching down to whisper something to Pandora. Each time, she giggles.

As my interest in the show begins to wane—the performers always go on about seven minutes too long—I look around the room at the crowd to see if there's anyone I've missed. I see Jemmy, dressed as Princess Jasmine, next to a boy dressed as Aladdin. I smile. That's a cute costume. There's Georgia, a girl from my photography class who always seems to have a cold. She's dressed as something with tall ears, a leotard body, and a fluffy tail.

And there's the hoodie.

I can see its striped sleeve sticking out, all the way up to the start of the rip. The rest of the hoodie and wearer are blocked by a clingy couple dressed as a cave man and woman. I twist around, intent on getting a better look. Unfortunately, no matter what angle I take I still only see the sleeve. Dammit!

"Getting uncomfortable?" Pandy whispers sympathetically. "The show should be over soon."

I nod, and take a few deep breaths. I force myself to still, only trying to move my eyes as far sideways as they'll go, just in case I can catch a glimpse of his face. After the show. I'll see him after the show. As soon as the finale is finished and people start clapping I'll stand up and go over to that sweater… I allow myself one last turn of the head and it's gone. It's gone. I kneel as high as I can go and look frantically around, but all I see is the dull normality of the people I know. He left. The show was too stupid for him and he left.

"You okay?" Michael whispers, sensing my distress. I feel his hand on my shoulder and I relax back down onto the floor. I nod. Pandy looks between the two of us, then scoots backwards to lean against Michael's legs. He moves his hand from my shoulder to her hair and she relaxes, nestling her head backwards into his palm. I watch them dully. I hate that I missed the sweatshirt. I should've been paying more attention. I should have gotten up right then and gone over and… Then what?

Not even the fireworks can cheer me up. The bangs and flashes jar instead of thrill me. My back is sore, my brain is tired, and I ache for the whole thing to be finished. Finally, the audience breaks into applause. Pandy and I haul ourselves to our feet.

"How did you like it?" Pandy asks, weaving her way through sweaty bodies to escape the densest part of the crowd. I shrug.

"It was alright. Kind of boring the fourth year in a row, though." I'm tired. I want to go home. I feel like a deflated beach ball: colorful and shiny on the outside but unable to rise to the festivities. But I know Pandora and Pandora knows me. If I tell her I want to go home she won't let me. I'll stay, but only to avoid the argument.

The music starts up again. We three resume dancing, Pandy and Michael with as much gusto as before, me with a little less. But after a few minutes the spirit of the thing catches me, and soon I'm almost back in full swing. I spend the next hour alternately dancing with Michael and Pandora and making trips over to the refreshment table for water, popcorn, and people watching. I'm so distracted by the revelry that I hardly notice midnight approaching. It's not until Pandora sidles up to me with an important look on her face that I remember the promised Halloween event.

"It's pretty much confirmed that something's going to happen," Pandora whispers conspiratorially. She's taken her cape and crown off and her hair is a pile of buttered spaghetti. The sweat on her cheeks has set the red hearts bleeding. My informant, ladies and gentlemen. I look at the giant grandfather clock that someone hauled in for decoration. 11:40. Twenty minutes to go.

"Any idea where it will be?" I look around the crowded dance floor, hoping the kids behind these shenanigans aren't going to do anything dangerous.

"Hard to tell. I heard outside, but that could be a red herring if they don't want the info leaked."

I nod, and debate leaving. Twenty minutes of my life is quite a commitment. I dislike the vagueness of the hints, and will be furious if it turns out to be nothing. Pandora's pretty good with unearthing secret info though, so if she's saying this, then it's probably a go. My mind flashes to the EA assignment I've been avoiding and my resolve tightens. I'm going to get these pictures and they will be amazing. I'll make Geri proud.

I walk back to coat check and extract pull my camera from the ostentatiously boring row of coats. Everything, thank god, is as it was, untouched and ready for action. I busy myself with the photography prep that always makes me feel delightfully legitimate. After settings are adjusted and test shots are taken, I look at what I have to work with. There are a few electric torches outside, plus the light coming from indoors. It's not ideal, but it's all I have.

As I'm at the door a flash of earth tone stripes catches the corner of my eye. I whirl around. The back of the hoodie is vanishing into the crowd.

"Wait!" I bellow, but the pounding bass and excited jabber drown out my cry. I rush forward, shoving aside a couple of girls dressed as nurses. My ankles waver precariously as I lunge forward, trying to keep the sweater in sigh. But before I can catch it, Pandora appears in front of me and shoves me toward the front door.

"It's starting!" she squeals. "Turn on your camera! Let's go!"

I spend a second resisting. Outside, I hear a loud crack and human shrieks, and my mind begins to race. The sweater, the *sweater*, but then… The EA is my pathway to meeting him. This Halloween event is one time only. This is for me. I want this. I need this. I deserve this. *I'm sorry.* I turn around and sprint out the door.

Relief and fresh air hit my lungs. It looks like someone got hold of the performer's backup fireworks and is setting them all off at once. It's pandemonium. People are screaming and shrieking, some with laughter, others in fear. I pull out my camera and start grabbing every shot I see. For once I'm doubtful if photographs accurately capture the scene: the fireworks as they graffiti the air, and the panic of the people on the green. I shoot and shoot until my finger hurts, praying to God that some of these will be salvageable. It almost might not matter that I let that figure slip away.

The fireworks end just as security comes on the scene, talking through megaphones and calming the frightened people down. The question of "who did it?" spirals around and up into the sky. No one seems to have the answer. The whole party is outside now, and I take this opportunity to capture the crowd. The people's expressions are priceless, ranging from delighted to disgusted, made better by the fact that they're all in costume. I whisper a little prayer down into my camera, asking it to help me portray even a fraction of this farce.

Security gets things under control within a few minutes. Soon everyone is packing up to leave. I don't lower my camera until the scene feels like a ghost town. Then Pandora is at my sleeve, telling me that she and Michael want to go home. I look around. There's only about half a dozen people left in the building and "he" isn't one of them. It's just the students who put on the dance, taking fake cobwebs down from the ceiling. I quietly put the lens cap back on my camera. I wrap my coat around me and trudge after Michael and Pandy back toward the apartment, wondering what this melancholy is that's firmly settled into my stomach.

Once we're back, we all say goodnight. My friends retire to Pandy's room, to sleep or to live out their costumes, I don't know. I head into my own room, my door becoming a pillow on the barrel of a gun. I set my camera down on my desk without turning it back on. I'll look through the pictures tomorrow. *I'll tell you tomorrow if it was worth it.*

"Great emotions here," Geri says with a nod as she flips through the stack of pictures. We didn't have a meeting set up for today, but as soon as I looked through my shots from last night I found myself running to her office. Thankfully, her workaholic tendency ensured she was there, despite the fact that it's Sunday. Most of my pictures were blurry and unusable, but a couple turned out remarkably. My favorite is a silhouette of a girl holding two fireworks above her head, watching the colors above her explode. You can see the bottom of her face but the rest of her appearance is hidden by darkness or too-bright light. I wait for Geri to stop at it and comment on its beauty. To my disappointment, she flips past it to the next picture.

"This is something to be proud of." It was previously my second favorite but seeing it in Geri's hand with my favorite left forgotten on the table, it's slid down in ranks to last. The profiles of three Halloween attendees in a row are staring in horror at the scene before them. The guy closest to the camera is masquerading as some kind of gray-green devil with short stubs of horns attached to his bald head. The girl next to him has wings and glittery blue face paint. Behind them you can see a clown's wig and a hand raised to the person's face in surprise. The picture is so preternatural that it looks like something straight out of a Tim Burton film. "It captures a great balance between the playful nature of the event and the serious side of civil disturbance. Do you think you could write up a piece about this for me and have it by next Monday?"

I wince. That gives me over a week, but still. Pictures are how I express things; words just get in the way. "Sure, I guess so. Does it have to be on this one?"

"If there's another one you like better you could do it on that, but I feel like this one has some great symbolism going on."

I glance down at the discarded picture that I liked so much. Now it seems trite and superficial. "I'll do the one you picked," I say, trying not to sound like I'm sulking. Geri smiles.

"I hate writing," I moan, dropping my head down on my keyboard and adding some gibberish to my essay. At least that'll help get the word count up. Pandora hums in sympathy from her spot next to me and gives me a pat on the back.

"Mike'll be back with the food soon," she says for encouragement.

"I'm starving." I straighten up and tug my sweater around me, thinking longingly of french fries. I really hope he brings french fries.

"Here," Pandy offers, pulling my computer toward her, "take a break and show me your pictures from the dance."

"You already saw the best ones," I say, running my hands over my dry eyes. I watching as she clicks on "My Pictures" and scrolls through the mess of folders, trying to find the right one.

"I want to see them all! The bad ones are always the best."

"Alright," I say, giving her a warning look, "you asked for it." I take my computer back, click on my "Events" folder, click on "Halloween", and select "Year 4". A whole display of dark pictures pops up. I click on the first one. Pandy leans in, her hair brushing my shoulder as she looks eagerly on.

She laughs at all the right pictures and keeps politely silent at the blurry or underexposed ones. We skim the few that I took indoors before getting to one of the whole party outside on the lawn. Pandy and I point at the screen, identifying all of the people we recognize.

"There's Felix! Who knew he looked so good without a shirt?"

"Is that Professor Davies? I never thought I'd see him dressed as a cat!"

We go on until we're out of people we recognize. I'm about to switch pictures, but a question is rubbing at my lips and I have to ask it. "Hey Pandy?"

"Yeah?"

"You know that hoodie I found at the hospital? The one that belongs to the guy in the picture?"

"You mean the one you wore all the time and it was totally gross because you found it at the hospital and you didn't know what kind of germs were on it?"

"Yes. I think its owner was at the dance."

Pandy's eyes light up with excitement. "You mean Robin was there?"

I blush. "Maybe. I don't know though. I just saw the hoodie, but I'm pretty sure it was the same one…"

Pandy pulls a face. "That means he was at the dance without a costume. Lame!"

I force a laugh. "Yeah. Lame. Anyway, did you see him there?"

"No, but Michael's almost home, we can ask him. He knows the guy anyway, right? So maybe they saw each other and said hi or something."

As if on cue, the door handle turns. Michaels enters, a vision in blue, holding a large pizza box and a greasy paper bag.

"Fries?" I ask hopefully.

"Since you two have been working so hard," Michael answers, bequeathing the bag to us. We take it and get to work pulling out as many fries as we can before we're faced with the distraction of pizza.

"Katie has something she wants to ask you," Pandy waves a one of the golden sticks in front of her face to cool it down.

"Yeah?" Michael asks. He looks over at me as he puts the pizza box down on the table.

I cough, unprepared for this intro. "Um, yeah. Actually, I was wondering about your friend Robin."

Michael walks to our kitchen, pulls out an unopened pack of paper plates and tears the plastic away. "What about him?" He pulls three plates away from the top of the stack, then sets in on a pack of napkins.

"It was his hoodie that I stole, right?"

"Probably."

"Was he at the Halloween party? I thought I saw him there." I'm trying to keep my voice calm but inside I'm trying to decide if I want to hear the answer or run and hide in my room. Tension builds until I want to scream. I don't know why, but asking about Robin feels monumental.

"Huh." Michael returns to the table, opens up the pizza box and starts separating slices. He hands one to Pandora, puts one in front of himself, and hands the last to me. The plate is a little too thin and I feel heat and grease seep down into my palm. "Didn't see him."

A puff of air escapes my lips. I don't want this pizza anymore. I want to sleep.

"Your EA guys didn't have anything to do with that prank, did they?" Pandy asks, pulling all the cheese off the top of her pizza.

"Course not." Michael sounds annoyed. I bite my lip, hoping that this question didn't give Michael the wrong idea.

"I didn't think so," I quickly explain. I realize that I need to offer a new reason instead. What do I say? "I think Robin sounds nice. That was the only reason why I was asking."

"You don't know him," responds Michael brusquely.

I recoil as scalding cheese drips onto my fingertips. "Why?" I shove my fingertips into my mouth in an attempt to cool them down.

"He's not your type. The EA's his whole life."

A mixture of indignation and amusement bubbles up in me. "I just said he seemed nice, Michael. I'm not looking to marry him."

Michael jerks his shoulder. "He's fine. I don't know how you guys will get along though." Pandy, rising from the couch, and whispers something in Michael's ear. After she straightens she moves into the kitchen to get herself a soda from our fridge.

"That's not up to you to worry about," I say primly, tossing my hair back over my shoulders, feeling lighter again. "It's up to me to worry about. At your next EA meeting, which, you probably remember, I will be attending as your new photographer."

Chapter Seven

The good thing about Michael is that he doesn't lie. He's been acting weird about my EA decision, making me suspect he might be withholding information about the next meeting. I had to ask him flat out for him to tell me. Now we're on our way over together, Michael broodingly quiet. Pandy opted to stay home, claiming that she had better things to do than care about the earth (I'm pretty sure she said this just to set Michael off). I'm too busy fiddling with the settings of my camera and clearing old pictures off my memory card to care about Michael's mood. I'm a pack rat when it comes to digital space. It's hard for me to delete even if I have backup. I need space for today, though, so each blurred image from Halloween is getting dutifully clicked away.

As I start my hundredth round of clearance I've still got a spark of hope that I captured a picture of Robin. I don't know why. I probably wouldn't save it. I'm going to see him in person in a few minutes and have the whole fantasy destroyed, but I like the idea that I've been carrying a bit of him on my camera this whole time.

"This is the last meeting before holiday break," Michael says abruptly.

"What?"

"We're not meeting again until January."

"Noted." I wonder why he's telling me this. They'll probably go over it at the meeting. If anything, it's more incentive for me to attend. Michael can be weird sometimes. We pull up in front of the house, and my stomach leaps. I might as well be a teenager assigned to the same work group as my crush. I unbuckle and spill out of the car, tumbling toward the front door. I get there before Michael and reach forward and ring the doorbell.

Shane answers. It occurs to me that this is probably his house. I smile brightly at him and he stares back uncomprehendingly for a second until he sees Michael and places me. "Hi Pandora, good to see you again," he says, stepping aside to allow me to come in.

"It's Katie," Michael corrects, coming up behind me and shaking Shane's hand. "Pandora's not coming today."

"That's too bad. Well, Katie, it's good to have you. Go ahead inside; everyone's in the meeting room." I remember the way much more easily than I expected and step through the door, feeling like a celebrity entering a party. Not to toot my own horn, but I look *good*. I'm wearing a charcoal blue sweater, black skinny jeans, and the most gorgeous pair of brown leather boots anyone has ever seen. My hair has been coaxed into demure waves that lie obediently around my shoulders. I feel ready for anything.

Except for what happens.

There he is, flopped sideways on one of the chairs, chatting with the people on the couch. Robin. He looks different than I expected, taller maybe, and his hair is cut shorter. Still, I recognize him right away. And I feel angry.

I stand and collect myself. I'm trying to work through the urge to turn around and walk straight out of the room when Robin turns and looks at me. His eyes catch mine before I can look away, and in the second where I'm struggling to decide on my expression when I notice it. Robin looks shocked. It only lasts for a moment, but in that half second his entire expression widens and I almost see… hurt. Then his face relaxes into cheerful curiosity and all recognition is gone.

"Hey," he says, rising from his chair. I shift my weight from foot to foot, trying to remember my natural stance, but it's gone. In a second he's right in front of me. He is definitely taller than I expected. Thinner too. I remember him being closer to my height, broader. The top of my head was at his eye level then and now I barely reach his nose… I step back and give my head a tiny shake. I'm thinking of someone else.

"Hi," I say politely. It's nice of him to greet the new girl. This group seems to have pretty good manners. I'm about to open my mouth to say something generic and formal when Robin surprises me by asking, "Are you Katie?"

I stop. "Yeah," I eventually manage with a stiff headshake. "How did you…?"

"That's great!" Robin says with enthusiasm, grabbing my hand and giving it a firm shake. "Hey guys," he calls over his shoulder, "Katie's here!" His friends out the couch—a new group than last time—whoop and laugh. I grin along with them. "I've been telling Mike to bring you," Robin says, nodding as if this is the only obvious conclusion.

"Naturally," I say, raising an eyebrow.

"I have, it's true! Ask Mike, he'll tell you. Every meeting I've been saying, 'When are you going to bring Katie?'"

I laugh again and think for a minute that this might be true. Warmth and happiness inflate me. The swelling in my chest feels like it might pull me up to the ceiling. "Sorry it took me so long."

"That's alright." This time, Robin's answer is quiet, and a little soberer. He's looking me right in the eyes again, and the room suddenly seems quieter.

"I really am sorry…"

"Time to start!" Shane says, clapping his hands. The moment snaps. I run my hand over my cheek, smile tentatively at Robin, then drift over to an empty seat, not entirely sure what just happened.

"Hey Katie?" Robin says, leaning forward so I can hear him as the lights go off and Shane begins to speak.

My heart leaps. "Yeah?"

"Thanks for returning my sweatshirt."

I don't look at Robin for the duration of the meeting. I also don't hear a word that Shane says. There's something hovering around me that I can't seem to catch but I want to examine. Once I recognized Robin in that picture, I think I assumed that once I met him everything would be solved. My strange feeling of longing would finally abate and everything would fall into place. Now that he's here in front of me, though, I feel it more than ever. I'm trapped in hollow longing and joy so bittersweet that I almost tear up right here on my chair. I wanted Robin to feel right; I wanted to feel like that familiar blanket I've always wanted was finally draped over me. Instead, I feel like my stomach is in knots and something close to grief. Why don't I know him?

"We'll be looking at alternative energy sources next time. See you then," Shane says. I uncurl myself, subtly checking my eyes for any moisture that may have escaped. After a few deep breaths I look over to Robin… and see that he's gone. All of the light hope that had been lingering around my head pops. Cold resolution settles into my chest.

"Come on," I say to Michael, getting to my feet. "Let's go."

"Saw you talking to Robin," Michael says out of nowhere as we pull away from the curb.

I give a flicker of a smile and shrug. "Yeah."

"And?"

"And what?" I stare emotionlessly out the window. Everything looks flat.

"You seemed pretty interested."

I shake my head. "No. I was… I mean, I might have been, but…" I trail off and lean my head against the glass. I don't even know how to begin to explain what happened in there. For a second there seemed like there was so much potential, something else going on, but… He left. "I thought he was cute, but that's it."

"Alright." We lapse back into silence until something that's been pressing at my brain bursts through my lips.

"Michael, how did Robin know who I was?"

"What?"

"He said…" I squint, trying to remember how the conversation had gone. "He said he's been asking you when I'll come and visit."

"Yeah. I've mentioned you and Pandy."

I run my thumb over the back of my hand and say, "Why was he asking about me?"

Michael shrugs, looking distinctly uninterested. "It's how he is."

"Oh." So that's the end of it then. A guy I thought I recognized asking about me because he's like that.

"Look, don't get too caught up in this whole thing, alright?"

I frown and look over at Michael. His eyes are on the road but his jaw is set. Is he being serious? "What?"

"This Robin thing. I know you have a crush…"

"I do not have a crush!"

"Whatever it is. I don't think he's for you."

Instead of agreeing with Michael—I don't think he's for me either—indignation flares. "I thought he was your friend."

"He is. But I think you should drop this little obsession."

"I am not obsessed!" I explode. All of the pent up uncertainty, frustration, loneliness, and bizarre hope that I've been feeling since I first saw Robin's picture are finally bursting through my seams. "Why are you going on like I'm in love with him? I *asked* about someone, okay? I just asked and you're making it seem like… like, I don't know, I'm hiding in a tree outside his window with binoculars or something." Michael opens his mouth, but I'm still full steam ahead. "And second, even if I *did* have some ridiculous, baseless, crazy crush on him, I don't get why you care and are being such a jerk about this. Do I have to run everyone I date past you, my lord? Is that what you want? Do I have to ask your royal permission every time I even look at a guy?" I stop talking and the car fills with silence except for the rumble of the engine.

The adrenaline of my outburst wears off. Michael's only ever been a good friend to me. There's no reason to have yelled at him like that. I know that I was yelling at myself, but Michael doesn't. I look over at him and open my mouth to apologize, but stop as soon as I see the expression on his face. He's sullen and his jaw is clenched. I know this look; no apology is going to change Michael's mood. Not yet.

I want to get out my camera and start looking at more pictures but the situation seems to call for me to stonily stare out the window. This is what I hate about stalemates; there's nothing you can do to entertain yourself. I've said my piece (yelled it, rather) and now I have to commit to the act and let Michael know that we are *not okay* until he feels bad enough to apologize, while simultaneously convincing myself that I'm in the right. This is going to be exhausting. I give an inward sigh and set my gaze firmly ahead. Once again, my life is a waiting game.

Michael doesn't apologize, even when we get back to the apartment. My desire to make things right has shied away in the face of Michael's rock-hard obstinacy. Now it looks as though we may never speak again. I mean, what could he possibly have said to defend himself? He is way too protective of me. And for what reason? It's weird, that's what it is. I want to hear him explain, but he won't because he's too stubborn and because there's nothing he can say to explain it.

I huff into the apartment, almost hitting Santa with the door as I fling it open. Pandy, who's sitting on the couch wrapped in a fluffy red robe, jumps and looks up from the book she was reading. "What's with you?" she asks, carefully inserting a bookmark in between her pages and pushing the book shut.

"Your boyfriend is a jerk," I sulk, pulling off my navy wool scarf with a scowl.

Pandy sighs. "What did he do?"

"He's acting weird about this Robin thing." About halfway into this sentence I begin to regret what I'm saying, but I keep going. Faltering would make it seem like there is something that Pandy can't know. Even though there is, or might be. Or maybe even there isn't. I haven't had time to sift through what I can and can't share. Sometimes I wish that when it came to Michael, Pandy was just my best friend. But it's never that simple, especially not after what I did. I made my bed, now I have to lie in it, and keep lying because I could never tell Pandy the truth. I take a breath and try to keep my face even.

"Well…" Pandy struggles with something. Please no, please no, please let her not suspect… "This whole thing with Robin *is* kind of weird, Katie."

I drop to the couch trying to hide my relief. Santa jumps up onto my lap and I begin to pet her, as I attempt to explain. "I know it's weird. It's the weirdest thing ever. But, now that I met him for real, I think… I think that it's over." Something breaks inside me as I say this, but my voice stays even. This crazy scenario is holding me back, keeping me bound to something that may never have happened. I need to moving forward. "Of course, it can't be over, because it never started, but I know now that nothing is going to start. Michael's just being mean about it."

"How so?" Pandy takes Santa from my lap and begins scratching the fur behind Santa's ears vigorously. Santa squirms and tries to jump to the floor but Pandy, who is immune to cat scratches, doesn't let go.

"Um." I run my hand across my bottom lip, picking at a crack as I go. Pandy's purse is sitting on the table and I rummage through in search of lip balm. "I'm sure that you both think I'm nuts, but Michael's being rude." I find some melon flavored Chapstick, pull the top off the tube and smear the contents across my lips.

Pandy sighs again, but this time it's sympathetic. "Men have no idea how to communicate." She puts her hand on top of mine and gives it a squeeze. "We just don't want you to go crazy, lovely, okay?"

I smile. "Babe, it's way too late for that."

"I know. Just don't go too far, okay?"

"Nowhere to go," I say, and click the Chapstick shut.

When I was eleven, I fell from a jungle gym and broke my leg. Ever since then, whenever the weather changes I can feel pressure where the break was. It drives me crazy because as much as I shift or squeeze it, the ache doesn't go away. It never hurts badly, just enough to remind me that something is off. Before I met Robin, his absence was an ache. I thought that once I met him the ache would either ease or turn into full-blown pain. Instead, I'm burdened with the dullness of dashed expectations and the infuriating itch of an unanswered question.

I remember him. I absolutely, completely, and totally remember him. If I close my eyes and sit for a very long time I can conjure up a shadow of recollection. A recollection somewhere with trees and water, but I can't take it farther than that.

I hadn't met Robin before the EA meeting.

Outside, the foliage has been stripped bare. I've been almost permanently glued to my computer screen, scanning every weather site for the first sign of snow. So far the skies have stayed clear, but I have a good feeling. Soon.

The meeting was two weeks ago. From the mass of blurry and underexposed shots, I've managed to select a few shots to show Geri. I hardly remember taking any pictures while I was at the meeting but here they are on my memory card. Some of them aren't half-bad. Was I really so distracted that I missed documenting some truly intriguing moments? There's Shane, face twisted in annoyance as he listens to his sister speak. One shows the projector illuminating the dust in front of it with a blue-white light. Half a dozen pictures show the EA members in various moods: laughing, exclaiming, and impatient.

If I could help it, I would have taken more time picking out the pictures I want to show. But I can tell that Geri's getting impatient, especially after my confused hack at the Halloween essay. I chose the picture she liked best but found I had nothing to say about it. Despite my attempt to remember the angle she suggested I take, most of my words were just there to take up space. I think she could tell.

Choosing which pictures of the meeting to show Geri was hard, mostly because the best one I got was of Robin. The lighting in the room wasn't great, so for almost anything to be made usable I had to spend a long time in Photoshop. It took hours of tweaking and adjusting just to get a few to surpass the look of a high schooler's digital camera. The one of Robin took the spotty lighting and used it brilliantly.

He's sitting in his chair, leaning back against the window. The top of his face is entirely covered in shadow but his nose and mouth are clearly illuminated, and he's smiling. He looks relaxed. It's a perfect counterpart to the flaming display in my favorite picture from Halloween. If I had any sense this would be my showcase piece for my meeting with Geri, but instead, I created an obscure folder among my mire of unorganized photographs and hope to forget about it.

As I tromp on over to Geri's, my snow boots laughing at the bare ground, I carefully rehearse. *I need some events shots to capture the mood… Outdoors would be better… You can't capture a complete feel for the group without seeing them in action.* When I get to the office, I notice that only her desk light is on, instead of the overheads. Cautiously, I peer inside and see Geri sitting in her chair, a tissue to her nose. She looks like a mourner, in a black ribbed turtleneck. Her loose hair looks like weeping willow branches covering her shoulders and chest.

"Geri?" I say carefully. I edge into the room, as if expecting a grenade. "Are you sick? If you are, I can come back tomorrow."

Geri sniffles and shakes her head, motioning for me to come in. I notice an empty carton of Ben and Jerry's leaving a thin milky ring on her desk surface. Uh-oh. "Are you okay?" I ask, pulling up my usual chair. The legs grind against the floor in an unusually noisy way. I wince, hoping it's not a hangover that's ailing Geri.

Geri sniffles, shakes her head, then nods and starts to laugh. As soon as she does so, her face crumples and she shakes her head again. "N-No. I'm sorry." She takes a deep breath before pulling another tissue out of her tissue box. "This is so unprofessional."

"What happened?" I ask.

As I reach out to touch her arm, the thought occurs to me that I've never been in this situation before. High school was spent with me wailing about my breakups and Pandy trying to soothe me. She always had every remedy available: movies, ice cream, chocolate, pictures of handsome celebrities, and even, once, a dartboard. She'd clean and bandage as much of me as she could, while murmuring, "He wasn't right for you." And always, after an hour or two of sobbing and cursing life, I'd end up agreeing. They weren't.

Is that what I should say now?

Geri sighs heavily and closes her eyes, a little more composed. "What always happens. But we're not here to talk about my love life. Do you have some pictures to show me?"

I nod, but don't move to pull my pictures out of my bag. Geri never gave any previous indication that she had a boyfriend, girlfriend, or any kind of love interest at all. I never saw any pictures on her desk. There weren't ever flowers, notes, or texts that she answered right away. For all I knew, she was a nun.

"How long had you guys been together?"

"Almost a year," Geri squeaks and I see fresh tears leaking from the corners of her eyes. Another deep breath. "It was time to have that conversation." She swallows. "He's not ready for the things I want. I told myself it was fine but…" She trails off and puts on a thin smile. "It wasn't. And I won't settle. You never know who's going to come through for you and who isn't. It's good to find out."

Is it? A memory of a cold emptiness fills my chest. I cough and shake my head, trying to fight it off. It was so cold that night…

"He just wasn't willing?" I ask, my heart filling with pain for Geri.

"Not enough. He said to wait. He said he needed time. But you have to make a decision, and I had already made mine." One last sigh before she looks firmly over at me. "But this isn't for you to worry about. Show me your darn pictures."

I walk home from the meeting subdued. Geri didn't say anything else about her crisis, but it's all I can think about. I can't imagine what it would be like. Sitting at work, going about your day, having the phone ring, thinking it's a regular business call and then… My stomach twists. It's always such an awful moment. That point when you hear the voice of the person who usually tells you how beautiful you are, suddenly saying that he can't be there for you. It doesn't matter how invested you were; it doesn't matter how long you had been together; it always, always hurts.

My pocket starts buzzing and I jump, feeling a strange foreboding, as if my thoughts are coming to life. *I'm not in a relationship*, I remember with some amount of relief. I pull my phone out of my pocket to see who is calling.

Of course.

"Jude?" Jude has an uncanny sense for calling at the absolute worst times. I haven't heard from him since he hit Pandora. I was hoping the silence would last for longer.

"Katie. Hey."

"Hello." I've stopped and am now standing staring blankly at campus's main building, noticing how dirty the stone looks.

"How is everything?"

"Everything is fine, Jude," I sigh, raising my free hand to my forehead. I don't have the energy for this. "How about with you?"

"Oh. Better. How's uh, how's Pandora doing?"

I squint. This is the first time that Jude has called Pandy by name. He usually just said "your roommate" or "your blond friend". "Her stitches are gone. She has a scar, though."

"Oh. Oh. Uh, are you around her?"

What? "No. I'm not. But you stay away from her Jude."

"I will, I will. I just wanted… I wanted to apologize."

What? "What?"

"I'm getting help, Katie. I need to tell Pandora I'm sorry. It was really good of her not to press any charges. She should have. It was good of her not to."

What is going on? Jude is actually getting help? Did Mom manage to convince him? I blink and blink again, unable to believe what I'm hearing. "Wow. Well, that's great, Jude. I'm proud of you."

He gives a hollow laugh. "I'm not. But I gotta start somewhere."

"Yeah. I can give you Pandy's phone number if you want."

"Thanks."

I recite the numbers to him and he thanks me. "Alright," I say, feeling a little dazed. "Good luck. I… I think this is great."

"Yeah. Hope your Turkey Day is a good one."

"Thanks, Jude," I say, tears pricking at my eyes. I wonder if my parents still have those Thanksgiving handprints that Jude and I made in elementary school. "I hope yours is too."

Chapter Eight

I spend a quiet Thanksgiving at school with Michael and Pandora. My family isn't that into holidays, Christmas being the one partial exception. I'm glad to have the company, instead of eating my turkey sandwich alone. Pandora's staying because parents are being fabulous overseas on business, and she didn't accept her sister's invitation to go skiing in Aspen. Michael didn't say why he stayed. He and I still aren't speaking. It's getting a little ridiculous, but I can't bring myself to care. The cold weather has turned me into a hermit. I've all but emptied my calendar, keeping only the most important of commitments (although I probably could push that dentist appointment back a month). I've decided to go Christmas shopping on my own this year. Pandy seemed disappointed when I opted out of our traditional trip with our building-mates, but she still went. It hasn't snowed yet.

I walk from campus down to the square where everything is decorated for Christmas. Our school, Travis University, sits snugly in the little town of Allensdale, Maine. Allensdale is small and far enough away from any major city that no one else cares about it. It's a sweet town lined with cafes and moose-themed boutiques. It's close enough to the ocean that on windy days you can smell salt in the air. The sea air enjoys bombarding all residents with more than our fair share of intense weather. Because of this, most people skip town for warmer climates once November hits, leaving the town delightfully deserted.

Hardly anyone is on the street. One or two couples meander around corners, weaving in and out of sight, but for the most part the sidewalk is deserted. I don't hurry with choosing a store. Instead, I wander about, enjoying the local decor. With Thanksgiving over, the whole town has blown up into a giant display of Christmas festivities. Holly and mistletoe hang over every door, and the shop windows are lined with candles and holiday bulbs. Even the more hipster coffee shops have put their employees into Santa hats—ironically, I'm sure. I smile as I walk past one.

After making a full loop around the square, I duck into one of my favorite little stores. It's a craft and home goods store stocked so full of fun trinkets that it makes me sore for a place of my own. Stacks of colorful plates, flower-shaped teacups, and owl patterned oven mitts grin at me from the window. They seem extra shiny, surrounded by tinsel and Christmas lights. The world is so perfect this time of year.

The problem, I realize as the bell above my head tinkles, is that Christmas shopping by yourself isn't any fun. Normally I'd be trying the hot cider samples set out by the store's sweet little owner and picking up everything that smells like Christmas. I'd hand them to Pandy to sniff too, being careful not to give her anything with patchouli. That soap had her sneezing for almost five minutes. Our laughter from that day echoes in my mind. I should get her something nice.

I wander through the store, looking at different cooking ware and fancy wine-laden tables, trying to come up with gift ideas. I find nothing. Nothing, that is, until I hear someone call my name from the back of the shop.

"Katie."

It's Robin.

He's standing in front of an essential oils display, his wind brushed expression warm. "Come here. I need your help with something."

He's oil on cinders. My body heats up.

"Hi," I say, feeling all breathy and messy from being out in the cold. Thankfully, I decided to wear my purple coat today. I straighten my gray beret over my curls and imagine that I might look a bit like Audrey Hepburn. Did she ever wear a beret? "What do you need my help with?"

I'm glowing. I'm needed.

"I'm trying to pick out a present for my little sister." He gestures toward the wooden shelves in front of him. "Think she'd like something like this?"

"How old is she?" I peer at a bottle of rose oil. Very sophisticated. Very expensive.

"Fifteen," he answers, picking up the bottle I'm eyeing. "How about this?"

I frown and take the little glass vial from him. "I doubt she'd use it. At fifteen, subtlety isn't necessarily what you're going for in perfume. I think this would go over her head." Robin nods and looks around the store, seeming lost.

"What's she like?" I prompt, delighted to have someone to shop with and for.

The chill that's been clinging to me since I walked into the store has finally lifted and my feet are prickling back to life. I slide out of my coat and remove my hat and gloves. Without thinking about it, I hand the pile to Robin. He accepts my coat, and laughs. "Typical."

"She's typical?" I rub my hands together, encouraging my blood to get moving. This never works. The iciness of my fingers seems to only keep my temperature down. But I never stop trying.

"No, I meant…" Robin looks down at my coat in his hand. "Never mind."

"Your sister," I prompt. He's running his thumb along the sleeve of my coat.

"She's smart. She's taking all honors classes and trying to finish high school in three years."

I give an impressed whistle. "What does she do in her spare time?"

"Reads, mostly." He slings my coat over his shoulder, and shoves my gloves and hat into his pocket. If I'm lucky, it'll all come back to me smelling like wool and cologne. I look at the shelf of oils.

"Does she want a new book?"

"I don't know what she's read."

A home store doesn't seem like the place for a nerdy fifteen-year-old. "I know!" I snap fingers with inspiration. "Not here. Come on."

I snatch my coat off Robin's shoulder, grab his sleeve, and drag him outside. Two buildings later we're in front of my favorite bookstore. As the overhead doorbell chimes, we're immediately engulfed by the wonderful smell of books. The interior of the store is similar to a library; as soon as I walk inside I always want to whisper. The only current occupant is the sweet middle-aged woman who runs the place. She smiles at me as we tumble inside. I smile back, ignoring her significant look toward Robin.

"This," I say proudly, picking a hardcover up off a rotating display. Robin takes it from my hands and flips it open.

"What is it?"

"It's a journal. Look, there's a quote from a different famous author on each page," I lean across his shoulder, pointing at the Dickens quote on the first page.

Even without physical contact, I can feel the warmth of Robin's body. I wish I could grab his arm and lean my head on his shoulder while snowflakes melt against my ear. His body is friendly, like the little bench that I used to cover with pillows before diving headfirst into an adventure story. I want to take Robin's hand and run into the streets. I feel like laughing and yelling, and pulling him so close to me that I worry he might snap.

Robin doesn't say anything. My stomach becomes a vacuum of disappointment. I was wrong.

"Perfect," he says finally, closing the book. "I think she'll really like this."

"Yes!" I leap joyously into the air. Robin laughs, holding the journal up and tipping his head in acknowledgement.

At the register, I beam proudly as Robin pulls out his wallet and pays. We're both puffed up with a job well done. But as soon as Robin is handed his receipt a realization springs on me like an annoying friend running up behind you and jumping on your back.

This is it.

We step back onto the street. The cold air slaps my face, making my eyes water. I cough and sniffle in resistance. I wish it would snow already, so the cold can serve a purpose instead of just abusing us.

Why aren't we best friends? Why can't I confidently invite him back to the apartment to watch something we both like—I don't know what we both like—and to have pizza, and to stay until it gets way too late? Why can't the pinch I feel when he's leaving be a normal crush on a normal guy that I have a normal friendship with? Why, even though he's right here in front of me, do I feel like he's missing?

"Cold?" Robin asks sympathetically as I run my hands up and down my arms. I nod and pull my hat (reclaimed from Robin and disappointingly smelling of my own shampoo) down further over my head. "Have you ever been to Beatrice's?" I shake my head, shivering now. "We're going there," says Robin decisively, leading me over to a silver corolla.

As I follow him, everything begins to dance again, but now my joy is mixed with panic. I was supposed to forget him. I was supposed to forget this whole stupid thing. I shouldn't be here, watching him hold open the door. I shouldn't be ready to climb in next to him.

"You…" I say, trying to think of something to stall. "I… I'm really cold."

He takes a step towards me and takes my hand. For a wonderfully terrifying moment, I think he's going to kiss it. Instead, after a moment's pause, he exhales warm air onto my fingers. "Ready to go?"

There's a callus underneath his finger.

I climb into the passenger seat and continue to shiver, even after we're inside and the heat starts whirring. "Are you okay?" Robin asks, glancing over at me.

"Fine," I gasp, kicking off my shoes and pulling my knees up to my chest. "I just get cold easily, and then have a hard time warming up. Ironic, isn't it?"

"Why?" inquires Robin. He throws the car into reverse and backs out of his parking space. Frozen pavement groans beneath our tires.

"Cuz of my name," I explain, looking out the window. I have no idea where he's taking me.

"Katie?"

"Yeah?"

"No, I mean, it's ironic cuz your name is Katie?"

"Oh!" Wow. Somehow I hadn't realized that he didn't know my last name. "No. No, my last name is Winters. So it's ironic that I'm not tolerant of the cold."

"Ah," Robin says slowly. "Yup, that is kind of strange."

"What's yours?" I ask. My window is fogging up. I rub my sleeve over the glass so I can watch the scenery flick by.

"What's my what?"

"What's your last name?"

"Valen," he answers.

"I knew that!" I snap my fingers, which are starting to tingle with warmth. I hate this part.

"Yeah?" asks Robin.

"Yeah. I guess Michael told me?" Valen. Where have I heard that before?

We're on heading south on the highway, nearing the state border. I don't usually go this way. The thrill of mystery ignites.

"What about you?" Robin asks. He reaches for the heat controls, and clicks the dial sideways. The roar of air subsides into a gentle hiss.

"What about me what?" I take off my hat and shake out my hair, finally starting to warm up. The combination of the heat and the rumble of the car is strangely soporific. I lean my head between my seat and the window, settling in for the ride.

"Do you have any siblings?"

I snap back to alertness. Do I have siblings. Ha. "One," I say with a brief, uncomfortable shrug. "A brother." He doesn't need to know anything more about Jude. "What about you? Any brothers?"

"Yeah, one younger brother."

"How old?"

"He just turned seventeen."

"Uh-oh."

Robin chuckles. "He's the good one. I was a lot more trouble when I was his age."

"You didn't have an older brother to keep you in line," I tease. "Troublesome older brothers are very character building."

"Your brother cause a lot of trouble?"

Ah, no, shouldn't have mentioned that. I don't want to bring Jude here, not into this car. Not now. "You can say that," I say dryly, hoping to end the line of questioning. "You're the oldest, then?"

"I am."

"You know what they say, 'first is the worst'," I cackle. My body is going haywire and I have no idea what I'm saying. I want to be sassy and sexy, and somehow lash out with this electrifying energy. Instead, I'm stuck with a childhood rhyme.

"Nay, come again good Kate. I am a gentleman." I look at him blankly and he explains: "Shakespeare. *The Taming of the Shrew.*"

My energy crackles into laughter. "Are you calling me a shrew?"

"You just called me the worst," Robin counters. His eyes are on the road but I notice that his head is inclined toward me. I like his ear.

"I was quoting," I explain.

"So I was I, and I was quoting Shakespeare. I win."

I stick out my tongue, my heart rate slowing. "Well, it doesn't apply. No one calls me 'Kate'."

"You lie, in faith, for you are called plain Kate,
     And bonny Kate and sometimes Kate the curst." Robin recites musically.

"Michael, right?" I quip. Robin looks confused. "Nothing," I clarify shaking my head. "I just think if anyone were to call me 'Kate the curst' it would be Michael."

Robin looks like he wants to say something more, but doesn't. We're quiet for a bit before I ask, "So what kind of trouble did you cause when you were younger?"

Michael's warning about Robin echoes in my head. It's a good idea to ask in case he's planning on taking me somewhere to kill me. Of course, if he is, it's a bit too late to do anything about it.

"Anything. Everything. I'd break whatever I could get my hands on."

My seat belt cuts into my throat. I try to pull it away, but the belt is locked in. After letting the strap snake back into its holder, I ask, "Why?"

"I used to be angry all the time."

I smooth my seatbelt back over my chest. "Angry at what?"

Robin doesn't answer right away. Instead, he drums his hands on the steering wheel, beating out a rhythm that I almost recognize. "I don't know," he finally says. "Probably my parents' divorce."

I wince. "Was it ugly?"

"No, not really."

"Oh." We're cut off by a red sports car. Robin slows. The red car zips ahead, and Robin lets another car in before returning to his previous speed. That would have gone much differently if Michael was behind the wheel. "What changed?"

"I joined the EA. It wasn't the group that you saw at the last meeting, back then. It was Shane, trying to create some semblance of order while the rest of us went around setting trash cans on fire."

I let out my second low whistle of the day. "How long ago was that?"

Robin continues his car-part drumline. "Four years ago? Yeah, when I started my part-time classes at TU."

Four years ago would mean... "I can't see Michael setting trash cans on fire." I tap my finger against the window, quietly trying to join in on Robin's performance.

"Michael was always a good boy." I stiffen, waiting for a snide tone. Good Boy Michael. Too good for any real fun. Robin, instead of sneering, starts to laugh. I want to join in, but the faraway look in his eyes is like a dead bolted door. I don't have access to what's causing his laughter. "He was one of the first members. He helped Shane get the rest of us under control. People like to listen to him."

I let this sink in. Of course. Of course he respects Michael. Just like I do. I'm beginning to fill with warmth for Michael when his warning about Robin comes back to me. Why, if Robin trusts Michael so much, is Michael wary of Robin? It doesn't seem like Robin's a troublemaker. Not anymore. I don't understand it. "Did it work?"

"For most of us." Robin's rhythm slows. "Not everyone."

"Are you sure the wild child is all out of you?"

"Nope."

I laugh, feeling delighted and out of control.

We pull into a parking lot. In front of us is a small white house with a large sign reading "Beatrice's" in loopy brown lettering. I figure it's a coffee shop, but as soon as Robin and I step into the wood paneled room, I realize that it's not.

"Is this heaven?" I ask, looking around me in wonder. I'm immersed in every version of chocolate imaginable. There are pretty little wrapped boxes of chocolates, chocolate sculptures, chocolate powder, mugs reading "hot chocolate" on the side in lettering matching the sign out front, chocolate cookies, chocolate recipe books, and even giant pods of cocoa beans—sadly only for display.

"This is my favorite place," Robin says, leading me to a room on the left. We enter an elegant little dining room full of small tables with white cloths. To my right there's a counter with a glass display case full of chocolate pastries and cheerful-looking cashiers ready to take my order. I glance up at the chalkboard displaying the menu, expecting to see the usual display of coffee drinks. Instead, I'm presented with a list of hot chocolate flavors. At least, I think they're flavors.

"Start with the hot chocolate," Robin instructs, "but next time you're here get a pasty. They have the best ones here. They get them from this bakery in Boston."

"The chocolate is all from different places," I say in fascination, reading the list. Ecuador, Madagascar, Venezuela… "I haven't even heard of Grenada."

"The Bolivian is the best if you like really dark chocolate," Robin suggests, pointing to the last option on the menu.

"Is that what you're getting?"

"Yeah. It's my usual."

"Then I'm getting something different," I declare. "A small Grenada hot chocolate please."

The girl behind the counter smiles in acknowledgement, then turns to Robin. "And for you?"

"Small Bolivian."

"Nine seventy-four please," she requests pleasantly.

"This stuff ain't cheap," I murmur, pulling out my wallet, but realize too late that Robin has already paid. "You don't have to do that!" I protest, sheepishly putting my money away.

"I do," he replies certainly, moving to a nearby table and sitting down.

"Why?" I follow his lead, taking the chair across from him. Brown paper is clipped neatly over the tablecloth—a smart move for a chocolate shop with a preference for white linens.

"Because I don't want you to waste your money if you hate it," he explains. I see his point.

A minute later, two hot chocolates appear in front of us. The cocoa beans' parent country is written across the plastic lids in red pen. As soon as the waitress walks away, Robin and I swap cups. I pick mine up, remove the cap, and dip my tongue into the froth on top.

"Wow." My eyes widen. "This is good." The drink is rich and so dark that I feel as though I'm drinking liquid baking chocolate. A tiny hint of spice plays at the back of my tongue. I wonder if it's the Grenadian influence.

Robin sticks out his hand. "Alright, pay up."

I reach into my purse and start rummaging around for my money, and Robin starts to laugh. When Robin laughs, he doesn't do it in the obligatory way that most people do it. Every smile and chuckle from him is full of delighted sincerity, like some impish little creature from a fairy tale. I can't help wondering if he's been sent to trick me into some terrible fate.

"I'm teasing," he explains, waving away my hand.

"Oh. Good," I reply, taking an embarrassed sip of my drink. "You know," I dip the tip of my finger into the chocolate and stir the foam. "I don't drink coffee, because it's gross, but I feel like this cocoa is making me feel the same way coffee drinkers do when they claim to get a really good cup."

"It's not cocoa," answers Robin, swallowing a mouthful and shaking his head.

"Huh?"

"It's not cocoa. Hot cocoa is made out of chocolate powder but hot chocolate is made out of chocolate itself. Not a lot of people know that, but it's important."

"Interesting." I take another thoughtful sip. "That explains why it's so rich."

"My chocolate is richer. My chocolate is so rich that it has a yacht."

"Well, my chocolate..." I can't think of anything. Damn.

"Taste." Robin hands his cup over to me and we trade, each taking an appraising swallow out of the other's cup.

"That is rich," I say, nodding and handing him his drink back.

"Yours is good too," Robin answers, wiping chocolate foam from his lip with his thumb.

"Oh! Oh I have it!" I say, snapping my fingers. "My chocolate is so smooth that it stole your chocolate's trophy wife!"

Robin laughs his enchanted laugh again. "You win."

"Yes!" I smile triumphantly and settle into my drinkable confection. Robin and I chat about absolutely nothing until we're finished (his cup empty, mine still half-full). Then we stand, bellies full and tongues singed. Robin nods goodbye at the woman behind the counter, and holds the door for me as I step outside. As soon as my eyes adjust to the bright outdoors I gasp, let out a delighted cry, and run out from under the awning to stand in the parking lot. I see Robin still standing on the porch, and I turn to him, giggling gleefully.

"Snow!" I shriek, jumping in circles as the small flakes dance around me. "Snow! Lots and lots and lots of it!"

"Well, Miss Winters," Robin says, stepping out to join me in the cold, "maybe your name isn't so ironic after all."

Chapter Nine

I didn't buy a single Christmas present, I realize as I stand in front of the closed door to my apartment. Oops. Oh well. I'm flying too high from Robin and the snow to mind. I push our apartment door open and smile at Pandy. She's at the table with her laptop open, her blue eyes framed by enormous round reading glasses. Seeing me, she pulls her spectacles off and looks at me seriously. My smile falters.

"Where are your bags?" she asks, nodding to my empty hands.

"I didn't find anything I wanted to buy," I answer, heading over to the couch and flopping down.

"You were out for a long time," comments Pandy. I nod, not offering any more information. Why do I get the feeling that she knows about my afternoon with Robin? It's not possible; we didn't see anyone we know, but still…

"I actually ran into Robin." There. Now that I've said, it I don't seem guilty. Surprise spreads over Pandora's face and her eyebrows draw together as she looks at me with concern.

"Katie, no…"

"It's not like that!" I snap. My memories from the afternoon sit in me as warmly as my hot chocolate. I won't defend them. Not to Pandy, not to anyone. "We ran into each other, he wanted help Christmas shopping for his sister, I chose a journal, and we went for hot chocolate."

"Where?"

"Where what?"

"Where did you go for hot chocolate?"

"To this place called Beatrice's," I answer smugly. I bet Pandora has never heard of it. Finding things that Pandy doesn't know about is a guilty pleasure of mine. Sometimes I feel like she and Michael don't understand that I have a life outside of them.

"Oh." Pandy doesn't say anything more for a while; she just looks at me thoughtfully. "I talked to Michael about why he's acting this way about you and Robin," she says finally.

Guilt washes over me. "What did he say?" I ask, looking at the floor, and licking my windburned lips. They taste of sweat and chocolate.

"He said a lot of things. He does like Robin. They're actually pretty good friends, but he worries about the two of you together."

I think back to Robin's declaration of trusting his friends—much more than I've been doing lately—and breathe a little easier, knowing that it's not entirely one-sided. But that begs the question…

"Why?" My stomach clenches, maybe a result of too much chocolate. I move onto my side, sticking our oversized pillow beneath my head and bringing my knees up to my stomach.

"He says Robin's a workaholic who never does more than casually dates."

I don't like the sound of that. I don't like the sound of "casual dating". A slew of images of gorgeous girls in low-cut dresses fill my head. I see them all lining up, spending an evening, a night, with Robin and then leaving because even they are unable to hold his heart. He's not supposed to be like that. He never used to be... *Or maybe he did*, I amend mentally. I don't know.

I look down at my legs. My jeans are damp from the snow. They've stretched throughout the day to fit a little less perfectly than they did when I put them on this morning. I feel sloppy and young. An afternoon distraction for a man who casually dates.

I can see him being a workaholic. I imagine him at his computer late at night, typing furiously to get something done. I picture the faraway look that he must get in his eyes when someone is talking and all he can think about is the next step of his project. I don't care about the EA. He'll know that.

Anger prickles my skin. Of course his work is too important. Of course it is. "He didn't seem that way when we were hanging out today." This protest is more for myself than for Pandy.

Pandy shrugs and lets out a loud squeak of a yawn. "It's just what Michael said. I don't know, even though they're friends, I get the impression that they can get competitive."

"Guys," I sigh. Maybe Michael's concern comes from having known Robin before he calmed down. But even so, he saw the transformation. That alone should speak for Robin's character.

Even though I'm practically sick from our trip to Beatrice's, I grab Pandora's purse and root through until I find half a Milky Way. I pull it out along with a small container of orange scented hand cream. "Can I have this?" I ask. Pandora nods and I unpeel the candy with one hand and my teeth while cracking open the hand cream with the other.

"What I don't understand," Pandora says, watching me distractedly, "is why Michael is so competitive with Robin. I mean, the EA used to just be a hobby of his, which was fine, something to get him some experience in the field. Even though I think it's kind of dumb, but whatever. He likes it. But it his involvement is growing at a pretty shocking rate. And the stuff he's been talking about is starting to sound borderline illegal."

Robin's description of when he first joined the EA squirms in my belly. But Robin trusts the group, trusts Michael to keep the group in line. Instead of voicing my concern, I shrug and break off a hunk of chocolate. "I doubt they'll follow through on anything too bad. They're environmentalists: melodramatically passionate by definition. Plus, Michael was never that rebellious in high school. Maybe he's going through that phase now. He wouldn't do anything to risk his future, especially considering how close he is to being done with his Master's."

"I guess…" Pandora chews at the end of her glasses. Bright blue argyle dips in and out of view.

"Robin trusts the group," I grandly pronounce. To punctuate, I take a massive bit of chocolate. My stomach groans.

"Katie, don't take this the wrong way…" The phrase that precedes all great compliments. "But what has been up with you lately?"

I pause mid-chew. "What do you mean?" I manage once I've coaxed the nougat-y clump down my throat.

Pandy sighs and tucks her glasses into her case before closing it with a snap. "You're hardly ever here anymore, you have the weirdest fascination with a guy you hardly even know, you always seem like you're thinking about something else, and you've been tense around Michael. He told me, you know."

I feel like a child caught in a lie by a parent. My face heats up as I pick at the aluminum—or is it cellophane?—wrapping on the chocolate bar. I don't know how to answer. Today with Robin wasn't supposed to be anything. An indulgence at most. But now here I am, wanting to explain the whole thing to Pandora. But if I do, then what? Maybe it'll all suddenly be real. Maybe it will suddenly all seem like a plastic play set. I don't know.

"Everything has been so weird lately," I admit finally, still avoiding Pandy's gaze.

"With Jude?" Pandora's voice is gentle, and despite my best efforts I feel moisture begin to collect in my eyes.

"Yeah Jude. And…" I sniffle, trying to discreetly wipe the tears away. Pandora's hawk eyes catch the gesture, though. She leans in and wraps her arms around me. Then I'm gone, sobbing into the shoulder of my best friend. Her comforting smell joins her in hushing me. I still feel like a child, but this time one that's in the lap of her mother. "Everything is so messed up," I sob.

"I know," says Pandora soothingly, running a hand over my hair. "Things have been crazy."

"There's not even a reason to be this upset, but I feel like I'm already in over my head." I don't know if spending time with Robin got me to the point of no return; maybe there never was a way out.

"Because you like him so much?"

I sniffle. "No. Because… Because he burnt his tongue."

That one bizarre moment. We were sitting at the table and our hot chocolates had just been delivered. My body had calmed and I almost convinced myself that it was a regular meeting of two people. I took a careful approach to my drink, blowing on it and testing the temperature, but Robin poured the drink straight into his mouth. Instantly, his face twisted in pain. "I thought it would be cooler," he moaned.

I said, "You always do that."

He had answered, "I do."

And for a moment it seemed like I knew what I was talking about.

"He burnt his tongue?" She sounds like she's asking about my imaginary friend. Maybe she is.

"He burnt his tongue, and I knew he was going to do it. He always does it."

"Did he have coffee at the meeting?"

"No." He didn't. "And I didn't like the group," I add sullenly, straightening up and wiping my eyes. "That's why Michael and I fighting."

Doubt flickers in Pandora's eyes, but I ignore it. She leans forward, reaches into her bag, pulls out a small pack of tissues, and hands it to me. The lotioned kind, of course. I gratefully take one and blow my nose.

"Do you really feel like you and Robin have a connection?"

I nod resignedly. "It's more than just thinking he's cute or having a good time with him. It's like I *know* him. Really know him. He had this…"

He had the callus on his finger.

I shake my head, and forge onward, "And when I'm with him it's great, but when I'm not I feel like he's going to break my heart, Pandy. It's scaring me. I almost feel like he already has. I almost remember him, I remember things about him, but I don't know where I've met him before."

Pandy takes a breath as if to say something, but exhales wordlessly.

"What?" I ask, glancing up at her face.

"I was wondering. This might be a stupid question but… is it possible that it's all because of Michael?"

"You mean because of the stuff he's said about Robin?" I ask cautiously. "No. When he says things like that, it just feels like my suspicions are being confirmed, not like it's any new information."

"I don't mean like that," Pandy says quietly. "I mean, do you think your history with Michael is why you're convinced Robin will break your heart?"

I feel as though someone has just dumped a bucket of ice water over my head. I sit up with a sharp inhale and shake my head furiously. "No." I say firmly. "No, no, no."

"Okay," Pandora says quickly and I can see a pink flush creeping into her cheeks. "I mean, I didn't think so, it's just, he's so close to you…"

"I love Michael. And I love you. I love you and Michael. I've never wanted anything more out of him, believe me." The words are so emphatic it's even hard for me to tell that it's a lie. For a moment, I believe that I certainly never kissed Michael and that I never even wanted to. I was the best friend to Pandora throughout all these years. I can keep that up. I know I can.

Except it isn't true. If I want to be the kind of friend to Pandora that she is to me then there's something that I have to do. I lick my lips in preparation, and glance at my best friend. She's looking at me with a mixture of apprehension and patience. Oh god. I can't do this to her. I can't. But I have to. It's time.

"Pandora, Michael and I kissed." I say this so quickly that it sounds like one word.

Pandora stares at me for a couple seconds then asks, "Just the once?"

"Yes, just once."

"I know."

My jaw drops. "You know?"

"Three years ago. Right?"

I nod, not entirely sure of what's going on. "How do you know?"

"Michael told me."

Something slimy slides around in my stomach. Of course. Michael. "I should have told you. I shouldn't have had to tell you. There should be noting to tell. I'm so, so sorry, Pandy." I gulp and look down at my hands, trying not to remember how they touched Michael's face. He had had a little acne on his cheek. The memory makes me queasy.

Pandora smiles tightly. "It was a long time ago."

"That doesn't make it okay. At the very least, I should have told you." Michael did.

Pandy stares at me, her expression calm and calculating. "So why didn't you?"

I crinkle the colorful plastic of the tissues. "I didn't want it to have happened. I really didn't. So I convinced myself it didn't. Michael and I never talked about it again, and it just sort of... went away."

"Why bring it up now?"

It's a good question. I squint down at the tissues as I consider. "I couldn't lie to you." I feel her starting to say something but I hold up a hand. "Not directly. I could convince myself that it never happened, but you just asked me... and I couldn't. I'm so sorry Pandy."

I hear Pandora sigh and out of the corner of my eye see her stand. Expecting her to leave the room, my head snaps around and I prepare myself to stop her. Instead of walking out, she drifts to our bookshelf and idly starts pulling out books and examining the covers.

"I kissed someone that weekend too," she says finally. A huge fissure runs down the center of my world. *Pandora* kissed someone? Pandora *kissed* someone? I blink repeatedly, seeing if refocusing my vision will help me understand the situation any better.

"What?" I finally gasp.

"This guy I met at the wedding. A friend of the groom, I guess. I told Michael not to drink too much that weekend, but I knew you guys were going to that party. That meant he would, so I drank too."

"That's the same reason Michael drank. He knew you were going to be."

Pandora smiles without humor. "I know. The drink of the Magi. Anyway, we were so close to graduation, and I was thinking about everything and all of a sudden being with Michael seemed so…" Was she going to say boring? "Scary. Like, once we started college, it was going to be real. And my drunk brain wanted to try something else for the night."

I nod. It makes sense. Her logic makes total sense, but I just want to start crying again. She was supposed to be perfect.

"So," I say, trying to keep my voice steady, "that explains why you didn't get mad at him, but why didn't you get mad at me?"

Pandora shrugs, flipping through my copy of *Ana Karenina*. I want to read her expression, but her back is toward me. "I couldn't get mad at you and not him. So I didn't get mad at either of you."

"Why didn't you talk to me about it?"

Pandora turns and flashes me a sad smile. "I wanted to pretend it didn't happen."

"Like me."

"Like you."

The smile slides from Pandora's face, and she looks bereft. For the first time, I notice how small she is. A little girl in a big, empty room. "I didn't want you to know that about me. I didn't want to admit to being that kind of person."

"Pandy," I say, locking eyes with her, "I know exactly how you feel."

I hate that moment before my phone connects. No matter how well I know the person on the other end, no matter how many times I've called them, the second the ringing starts always sends anxiety through my body. Finally, Michael answers. "Katie?"

"Hey Michael."

"What's up?"

I stare at my door, my eyes tracing the outline of the dark fairy poster I've had since seventh grade. I don't know how to have this conversation. I don't even know if it's okay to have. But it's time to get this all out into the open. "I talked to Pandora."

"Yeah?" He sounds distracted. Oh well. He won't be once I tell him what I talked to her about. I shift my torso, as if the change in position can make this conversation less uncomfortable. From the scrambling in my head, I try to pick out the right words for this encounter. Before I can say anything, though, he speaks. "Listen, there was something I wanted to talk to you about, too."

"There is?" I pounce on this lifeline, happy for little extra time to think. "What's up?"

"I wanted to say that it's cool if Robin hangs out with us more."

I pause, momentarily forgetting about the reason why I called. "What?"

"Pandy talked to me. I've been a jerk. I'm sorry."

"Thanks," I say, taken aback. "But I don't think I want to see Robin anymore."

"You don't?" Michael sounds surprised. "Why not?"

"He's just…" I tuck my feet under myself and wiggle my toes. I can't explain this by explaining what's wrong with Robin; I don't know what's wrong with Robin. "I'm not interested," I finally say flippantly. I'm an alcoholic turning down a drink.

"Are you scared?" The whole concept of men being oblivious to what women are feeling is a lie. Michael proves this repeatedly.

"I am," I sigh, sitting down on my bed. "A lot. He makes me feel out of control, and not in the good way. With him I don't feel like I'm flying, or even like I'm falling, I feel like…" I run my hand over my face trying to come up with the words. "I feel like I'm tied up and being force-fed heroin."

"Sounds like love," Michael remarks. I stay quiet. *But does love also make you feel angry?* I switch my phone to the other side of my head and wait for Michael to fill the silence. "You should try it," he says finally. "If you're having such strong feelings for the guy, might as well see if it leads anywhere."

"You knew this whole time." I run a hand over my face.

"Yup."

"Mike..." I don't know what to say. Finally, I take a deep breath and say, "I'm sorry."

"I know you are, Katie-cat." The nickname is a ruffle to my hair. I settle back into bed feeling softened and cared for.

"I don't know what to do about Robin, though," I tell Michael. A tug on my duvet brings it up over my shoulders.

"I do," Michael states. "I'm inviting him to hang out with us all tomorrow."

Pandy calls my feelings a "dichotomy". I know because she told me. I'm lying in bed with a blanket over my head, trying desperately to get back to sleep, even though it's already 10:00 in the morning. I don't want to see Robin. The laughter of our afternoon Christmas shopping has faded and slowly been replaced with anger. Remembering our time together is like scratching a rash; it's a relief to do, but as soon as I stop I hurt so much worse. I don't want to see him. I don't want to like him. I can't.

But no matter how hard I try, the thought of him makes me warm and scrunched up. I want to know him. I want to know his favorite food, what music he listens to, and how he ended up here, in Maine, ready to meet me. Pandy's gotten a bit impatient with the whole thing ("Do you like him or not?") but Michael has stayed gentle, figuratively holding my hand through each mood swing.

He came over last night after our phone conversation and sat with me as I tried to make sense of my acidic extremes. Pandora gave us a bit of a look, but then moved into her bedroom and nothing was said on the matter. I've relaxed a lot now that Pandy knows what happened. I don't have to pretend that my relationship with Michael is something that it isn't; we're all on the same page now and can finally move forward.

"Is he at all like Jude?" Michael asked, tossing a pillow up in the air and catching it.

"Not that I've seen, but that's a good point. Maybe I hate all men because my brother sucks."

Michael caught the pillow again. "Maybe. But you don't hate me."

"I used to," I told him with my eyebrows raised.

Michael paused from his pillow throwing. "You're weird."

"Because I didn't like you at first?"

"I mean…"

"I know what you mean." I rolled my eyes at Michael's arrogance. The idea that a freshman girl that Michael Lombardi started hanging out with wouldn't like would seem so foreign to him. He resumed his pillow toss.

This talk, I could tell, was going nowhere. I eased myself off the couch, leaving Michael alone with his game of catch.

I insisted that Robin only come over under the pretense of seeing Michael. Michael suggested that Robin come over to do some EA work while I hang around looking casually cute. I liked this idea at first, but now that the time is here, I'm regretting every decision that ever led me to this point.

Time to get out of bed. I drag myself up to a sitting position and swing my feet over the edge of the bed to the floor, feeling around for my slippers. I find them and slide my feet into the purple fluff, yawn, and traipse over to the bathroom. Michael, I see, is already in the living room, sitting on the couch with his computer open. He's clicking rapidly, his gaze locked and focused. Without looking up, he gives me a nod good morning. I respond with a tired scowl.

Pulling my robe tighter around me, I pad into the bathroom. I brush my teeth slowly, eyeing my selection of perfumes. There are so many, and I hardly ever wear them. Would spritzing myself now be inauthentic? I pick up the rectangular bottle of licorice spray that Pandora bought for me and give my arms an exploratory dab. I sniff. That does smell pretty fantastic. I nod confidently at myself in the mirror.

After a moment I stop brushing, realizing that not everyone likes licorice. *Still*, I reason, chewing on the brush's plastic bristles, *if he doesn't like it, then he can deal. Never change yourself for a guy.* And with that I spit confidently into the sink, trying to ward away unpleasant thoughts of a relationship doomed by licorice.

I have selected the best outfit in the entire world. It's absolutely perfect: gorgeous, expensive, and flattering, but still true to my own style and not obviously dressy. I'm wearing a sea-green cashmere cowl-neck sweater that's tight and soft enough to wear as a shirt, and my best-fitting pair of dark blue jeans. They cost more than I care to admit, but they've been worth every cent. I've donned a thick dark brown leather belt, and my hair has been tamed into two finely-crafted braids that end just past my shoulders. Perfect.

"Maybe I'm too dressed up," I fret, twisting in front of my mirror as Pandora watches me skeptically.

"You spent forever on this getup and you claim to not even like the guy. Get over it."

I sigh. "Do I look like I'd be wearing this even if he wasn't coming over?"

"Would you be?"

"No."

Pandy rolls her eyes. "Step away from the mirror and go flop out on the couch casually with your book. What's the point in trying so hard to look like you don't care if you're not there to look like you don't care?"

I see her point. Obligingly, I pick up my copy of *A Portrait of the Artist as a Young Man* and convince myself that I might actually get some of my reading for class done today. In the living room, Michael is where I left him.

"When is he going to get here?" I ask casually, settling myself down on the couch and making sure not to touch Michael.

"Dunno. We said sometime in the morning. Knowing Robin that could be as late as one o'clock."

I shoot Pandora an annoyed look and she shrugs helplessly. Great. Just how long am I going to have to sit here on the couch, looking pretty, not mussing my hair, and reading James Joyce? Footsteps sound, and in a second there's a knock on the door. Not long, as it turns out. I look at Michael expectantly and he grunts, "C'mon in."

As the door handle turns it occurs to me that it makes absolutely no sense for Robin to be meeting Michael here; Michael has his own place and Robin must too. Why, oh why, would Michael suggest his girlfriend's apartment? It's too late though—the door is pushed open and Robin stands in the doorway, looking windswept and tired.

"Hi Mike," he says, dropping his bag to the floor. "And Kate too! Hi Kate."

I smile at him, then look back to my book, only to realize that I haven't opened it yet. Dammit. I hurriedly flip open to approximately where I think I am and start to read, desperate to minimize obvious searching time. The words skim by me nonsensically. Great.

"Scoot over," Robin orders. I move my feet to make room for him. "Whatcha reading?" he asks, tipping the book toward me to look at the cover. Seeing the title, he nods in recognition and says, "I've never read it."

"You should," I say with an authoritative nod, even though he really shouldn't. No one should.

"Do you want to get started?" he asks Michael. I give Michael an expectant glance behind Robin's back. He isn't looking.

"Sure. I've been doing some research and…"

Oh my god. Michael isn't going to help me out. He's actually going to work. I glare at him then stalk into my room. I close the door behind me, and flop onto my bed. I cast Joyce aside and stare at the ceiling.

I've always been a driven person and I'm unused to vagueness in my own desires. That I don't know what I want with Robin is eating away at me just as much as anything else in this whole crazy scenario; if I can't make up my mind, what am I supposed to work toward? I sigh and turn over onto my stomach, pulling my blanket up to my chest. The baby blue material clings to the sheets and I look down at it sadly.

I've always wanted a special blanket of my own. I never had one when I was little. There was no "blankey" to carry around and cry about when I left it at home. The closet thing I got to that was lying in my parents' bed, and feeling each of them breathe on the other side of me. I was never able to capture that experience on my own.

I want something with wonderful meaning from someone special that I can wrap myself up in when I'm cold and feel cozy and loved. I've always bought my own blankets, and none of them have any kind of meaning. I've tried, but they never do.

I reach over to my bookshelf and pull off the one thing that I do feel connected with: a book of Grimm's fairytales that Jude gave me for my twelfth birthday. It was one of the few times that he didn't forget my birthday, and it happened to coincide with a time when I was starting to feel particularly distant from my family. I've always loved fairytales, but I was starting to feel like it was time to outgrow them. This realization broke my heart, but I wanted to connect with my friends, none of whom watched Disney anymore. The stories themselves were doing less for me, too. Singing teapots and happy endings were now falling flat against my pre-teen ears. I was just about to throw away every sign that I ever dreamed of castles when Jude came into my room and dropped the wrapped package on my bed.

"Happy birthday, kid," he said, giving me a two-fingered salute before heading out to cause God-knew-what kind of trouble. I unwrapped the parcel and stared at the cover, entranced. The spiraled writing seemed enchanted, and I traced my finger over the letters again and again. *It's from Jude,* I thought to myself. *It would be rude if I didn't at least look at it.* So I opened the front cover and fell in love.

These stories were *dark*. They weren't the simple tales of girls in pretty dresses who were rescued by a prince. These were tales of vengeance, heartbreak, murder, and suicide. I could read these. I could love these. I began collecting more, professing a love of literature rather than of fairies, and soon possessed many more books of lore, including a whole collection Hans Christian Andersen.

The Little Mermaid was my favorite. I read and reread the part where she finds the prince asleep with the witch until my eyes filled with tears that splashed upon the page. I assumed it was a silly teen thing to do, but in all these years the heartache has stayed sharp. The feeling of complete dissatisfaction was the closest thing that I got to feeling fulfilled by a story, so I kept looking, ever more hungrily, for new tales.

I read ones with happy endings, sad endings, beautiful endings, and terrible endings. Each tale would hit me in a different way, but nothing struck the exact chord I was looking for. I've kept looking throughout the years, hoarding stories of my own, hoping to find the ending that made me say, yes. Yes. This is how the story should end. No ending has been right though. So I keep coming back to The Little Mermaid, and let it break my heart over and over again.

I left that one at home. That decision probably had something to do with Jude, but I don't want to bother figuring that one out. I open the front cover of Grimm's Fairytales and begin paging through, captivated by the pictures as always. I'm about to start on the first story when there's a knock on my door. I look up from the book in my lap. Michael is standing in the doorway, an expectant look on his face.

"Are you coming out?" he hisses.

I close my book. "I thought you guys were working."

"I had to show him something. Come on." He jerks his head toward the living room.

I oblige, setting my fairytales down and picking Joyce back up. This time, I find my place before reentering the living room. Robin's reading a thick stack of printed pages and only glances up briefly when I come out. He's taken up most of the couch, so I move to the kitchen and take a soda from our fridge.

"Want one?" I offer. Robin doesn't look up, apparently not having heard me. Feeling foolish, I crack open my soda, and wince at the assault of bubbles on my tongue.

"Here's what I don't get," Robin says, turning another page and staring at the back intently. I wait quietly for Michael to answer, but then look around to see that he's not in the room.

"What?" I prompt.

"Our group—the Earth Avengers -"

I unsuccessfully stifle a giggle. "That's such a stupid name!" I sputter, holding my soda can up to my face to try to hide the hilarity. Hearing it aloud gets me every time.

"It's a really stupid name," Robin agrees without missing a beat. "But anyway, the EA—"

"You should add words to the name that start with RTH and then you guys can be EARTH."

Robin thinks about this, squinting into space. "Robin the Handsome," he says finally. I choke on my mouthful of soda.

"Sold," I say, wiping my bottom lip with my thumb. "So anyway, the members of the Earth Avengers: Robin the Handsome…"

He nods. "Thank you."

"What don't you get?"

"Well," he frowns down at the papers again, tapping his pen rapidly against the stack, "we have a lot of things we want to get done."

"Like getting the project with Velke Corp going," I say knowledgeably, repeating the one phrase I remember from the first meeting.

"That's one of them. But the problem is, there are still a lot of group members who think they know better than anyone else." He knocks his fist on the table in frustration. "This proposal is made up entirely of protest ideas. Which is fine." He indicates this with a palm-up hand gesture. "But we're not going to make any difference if we don't also try to work with official channels. We're shouting, not talking." Stress emphasizes his words.

I frown and take a seat next to him, looking over at the papers even though I don't understand a thing they're saying. "Have you brought this up with them?" I ask. "Maybe Shane could help."

Robin leans back and closes his eyes. "Shane's more of a figurehead at this point than anything."

"He runs the meetings," I point out. I remember the room respecting him. It certainly seemed like he was in charge. There was, however, the grumbling. Lots of grumbling.

"That's it. We talk ideas." Robin straightens and looks at me intently. "He has great ideas. No one listens, though."

"Who do they listen to?"

Robin's gaze shifts as Michael comes back into the room. He's holding a stack of papers that he's sorting through.

"We need to get some of this in motion," Michael asserts. Robin takes the paper from him. He stands, stretching and yawning. He moves his arms around, tugging them this way and that before settling back on the couch to resume his reading.

"One second," I say. I run into my room, grab my camera and come back out and click the button just as Robin turns his head toward me, switching his attention over to a second page. I glance at the result and grin. Picture perfect.

Robin puts a hand self-consciously in front of his face. "I hate posing," he protests.

"You weren't posing. That was candid."

He grunts in agreement. "It's better than having to sit for a painting that you're doing anyway."

"I don't paint," I tell him as I flip back through my recent pictures, deleting all the blurry ones.

I hear a moment's hesitation. Robin finally says, "I thought you did."

"Nope. I used to kind of want to, but I suck. My camera's the only thing for me."

"I see," Robin says, looking back down at his papers, but I can tell that he isn't fully convinced.

Robin refuses Michael's invitation to join us in town for lunch, saying he has stuff to do at home. *Of course he does*, I think moodily watching the door close. Every time he leaves, I feel like it's over. I remember hearing my mom explain to me once that babies see life as a train going by. When their mother leaves the room they have no concept that she might come back.

"I can't explain it," I say, curled up on the couch as Pandy undoes my braids. "When he's here everything feels right and like it's in place. It's not anything he says or does; it's his presence. Like when you're a kid and your parents come back from a trip. Even if you're not interacting, it feels good that they're there. But when he leaves I feel like he's not coming back."

"He's coming back," Pandy says soothingly.

"I know. It's just...I feel like I'm already in love with him, even though I'm not, or maybe I feel like I was. And in some ways it feels like something is starting, but it also feels like it's over and has been for a long time. He was never even mine in the first place. I don't get it, Pandy, I feel like I've skipped all of the steps in-between."

"Love at first sight?" she suggests.

"No." I shake my head. "I don't think so. It's different from that. I *know* him, Pandy. And he broke my heart. I just don't know when."

"But he came back, didn't he?" Pandora is looking at me reassuringly, and I nestle close to her, trying to still my spinning thoughts.

"Yeah," I say closing my eyes. "I guess he did."

Chapter Ten

"Who is this?" Geri asks, holding up the picture of Robin. I blush just looking at it, but I'm careful to keep my voice neutral.

"He's a member of the group I'm doing my essay on."

"This is a powerful shot," Geri says, nodding with approval. She hasn't mentioned what happened in our last meeting, and neither have I, even though I'm dying to know how things worked out.

"I like it a lot," I agree.

Robin is gazing at the sheet in his hand, his face focused. You can see passion in his eyes and a hint of excitement around his mouth. Just by looking at the photo you can tell he's in love with what he's holding. Every time I see the image, my insides twist. I printed it in black and white so it almost looks like a shot from an old movie. Despite my complicated feelings, I love it.

"Tell you what," Geri says, swiveling her chair to face her computer. She begins typing and clicking, clearly looking for something. "Here it is." Another click and her printer jumps to life. I look at the freshly printed piece of paper I'm handed. After reading it over, I glance at Geri, wondering what she's implying.

"I think you could win this," she says, interlocking her fingers and resting her chin on her hands. Her words accelerate my heart rate. I listen dumbly as she continues. "The deadline isn't for a few months. That'll give you time to get your portfolio together. The winner is going to be featured in a gallery in Portland."

I take the sheet from her and read the guidelines more carefully. Phrases like "featured with some of the country's top photographers" jump out at me. My picture. One of my pictures up in a gallery, up on the wall next to. The exposure I'd get.

"Go for it," Geri urges. "You have some real talent. It could be fun to see what happens." Her eyes are lit up in a new way. I can tell she's imagining me, a student of hers, winning a contest and being featured in a gallery. "It's for the New England area. The judges are all from around here and want to help young photographers move forward. Will you enter?"

"I will." I can't think of anything else to say. I'm dumbstruck at the prospect.

"How is that photo essay turning out?" Geri asks, as I button my bag closed.

I think of the hacked up slew of unrelated paragraphs that comprise my "notes". "It's coming along. They're not meeting again until January, but in the meantime I've been doing research. I'm probably going to start the first draft of the written part over vacation." I don't want to tell her that I've already started and have, so far, been failing.

"In the meantime, work on your portfolio. See if there are any pictures you already have that you might want to submit. You can take more, and you should, but take a look through what you have."

"I will," I say again. I'll do as Geri says and look through what I have and probably take some more, but I already know the picture that I want to submit. Halloween, and the girl with the fireworks.

I haven't been to the bridge in a while, so I decide that it's time for a visit. As my feet walk the now-familiar path I wonder why I'm continually drawn back here. I think it's that it was the scene of my most honest moment. I want to revisit those letters again, written months ago, and explore the feelings that are stirred up.

As I approach, I begin exploring my disconnect. It was just a couple months ago, but somehow the girl who drew those words on that wall seems like a little sister instead of me. Still, there's no harm visiting. The emotions have smoothed over and I feel as though I'll be able to look at the bridge with a more artistic perspective instead of an involved one.

Here it is. *I MISS YOU* right there in big bold letters and, of course, the *TOO* that was mysteriously added. I smile and snap a picture. When this bridge is torn down or redone, no one will remember this, or even care. But I have the photograph, so no matter what, this bridge will always belong a little bit to me.

And what's this? I look at the sloppy writing below and raise my eyebrows in surprise. My hasty addition—*I can't believe you went*—is still there. I forgot that I had written that. I put my camera to my eye again and zoom in, ready to take another picture but once everything is focused I stop. There, beneath my second fit of frenzy, is a new set of even tinier lettering. I hold my breath and step closer until my face is almost touching the words. I crouch down and run my eyes over the phrase again and again, hardly daring to believe it.

"I thought you didn't paint."

It couldn't be. The words from the bridge slam around in my head so hard that I barely even notice that it's getting dark. I'm aware that my body is shivering but I don't feel cold. I tingle with exhilaration and dip sideways, detouring toward town instead of back to the apartment. I'm not yet ready to submit to light and the conformity of my normal routine.

It's Robin. Robin wrote the answer on the wall. He knows. He knows just like I do.

I shouldn't be so convinced. We can't be the only two people who have had this conversation, but still… This doesn't even count as painting. Who would use that line in a situation like this if it wasn't…? The spark in my step fizzles out. Yes, it's a possibility, but things like this just don't happen. Maybe by "paint", the writer meant "paint graffiti". Maybe someone else had the same conversation. It seems unlikely, but the world is a big place. I have no way to prove that this message was for me. But neither do I have a way to disprove it, so maybe, just for this nighttime walk, I'll keep it for my own.

The streetlights come on. Snow swirls at me through the air, landing on my shoulders and head. I can't tell if it's new or the old stuff being blown around, but I'll take it. Michael would be upset with me if he knew that I was walking alone at night. He's always been too protective. He thinks that anything could happen to anyone at any time, even though Allensdale is one of the safest places I've been. I don't get why Michael is so scared all the time.

I turn the corner and see our little town gleaming in front of me. The windows of the two cafes are lit, offering respite from the cold. I choose the one on the left, a cute little place with a mostly wooden interior, and quicken my pace. I'm almost there when I see him standing in front of the shop, a takeout cup in his hand, gazing at the signs on the window. I stop and look. He seems to be standing in a spotlight, bathed in the orange glow of the street lamp, and for a second I take it in. But in a moment he's going to turn and either face me and see me, or move away. Neither option is what I'm looking for tonight. I give his back a nod of recognition, then turn back toward campus. Not tonight.

Tonight is a night for fairytales. I get back into my room, slip into my biggest sweatshirt, and climb into bed with my Grimm's collection. I made myself a cup of tea on my way in, and now am curled up with my book in my lap and my mug in my hands. Steam wafts into my face as I page through the book, interested, as always, more by the pictures than the words. Once I reach the Wedding of Mrs. Fox I stop browsing and begin to read. I may as well be reading the end of the Odyssey in terms of the plot, but something about the idea of these sneaky woodland creatures catches me up every time. I watch the widow refuse suitor after suitor after suitor, ending up alone but unwilling to forfeit her standards.

I finish the tale, and then stare pensively at the poster on my door. I'm blanketed by a wonderfully heavy melancholy. Not the right ending, but a good enough for tonight. I throw back my last sip of tea, pull on a pair of pajama pants and crawl under the covers. The hot liquid lies in my stomach and the story on my chest. They join forces and together carry me off into a sad and peaceful sleep.

It's so cold out here. It's cold and I've been waiting and waiting. Where is he? It's cold, so cold. The grass is making my feet damp, which will make everything more difficult. They wouldn't be so damp if he was here already. Why isn't he here?

I open my eyes and look at the red letters on my clock. 2:30 in the morning. He should be here by now. I rub my hand over my eyes. Who should be here? A familiar panic is rising up on me, and I sit up, trying to shake my dream. I'm here. I'm in my bed. I'm not waiting for anybody. Nothing has happened to anyone; everyone is safe; everyone is as they should be.

Heat spreads through my chest and something is rising in my throat. I feel like I did when I was a kid. I'd fall asleep waiting for one of my parents to come home and wake up to find them still gone. A million awful scenarios would rush through my head and I'd dive beneath my pillow, hoping to block out my fear, but unable to fall asleep until I saw the glint of headlights through my bedroom window.

There are no headlights to relieve me now. I can't even pinpoint the root of this anxiety. What if this is intuition? What if I'll wake up in the morning to find out something's happened to Pandora or Michael? Or Jude? Oh god, what if it's Jude?

It's not Jude. It doesn't feel like Jude. Jude can take care of himself.

I roll out of bed, keeping my blanket wrapped around me, and walk out of my room and over to Pandora's. I push the door open and am relieved to find her alone, sleeping soundly and looking like the angel she is. I crawl in next to her and she stirs.

"Katie?" she asks sleepily.

"I had a bad dream," I say, cuddling in close. Pandora reaches over and pats me on the head.

"It's okay, you can stay here."

"Thanks."

She's already back to sleep, and I lie for a while, soothed by her warmth and steady breathing. I know that soon I'll be back to sleep, then wake up annoyed by Pandy's regular thrashing and cover-stealing. But right now I'm exactly where I should be.

I wake in the morning overheated and with a crick in my neck. Pandy is still dead asleep and heavy as a rhino—a fact I discovered in my attempt to steal more room. It's time for me to go back to my own bed. I bring my blanket out into the living room and the early morning light. I'm not tired. I change my route and end up curled under my blanket on the couch, watching the light and shadows change around the room as the day heightens. At one point, Santa jumps up on me. I let her join me under the covers but she doesn't stay for long. Even my cat can tell that my bedding lacks magic.

I don't think I doze off, but Pandora emerges from her room before any time at all has gone by, so I must have lapsed into some sort of trance.

"What was your bad dream?" asks Pandy, plopping down next to me and kicking her foot. Santa runs up and begins batting at the pom poms on Pandy's socks.

"It was more a feeling than anything else," I explain, searching for the details. "I was waiting for someone. I woke up freaked out and panicked; you know how it is."

Pandy nods. "Usually when that happens to me, I'm dreaming about Michael."

"But then you wake up and he's there."

Pandy smiles. "Usually."

"Thanks for letting me come in with you last night," I say, feeling childish.

"Any time babe." Pandy gets up off the couch, and gives me a passing kiss on the top of my head. She pads to the kitchen, grabbing some leftover pizza from the fridge, and shoving it into the microwave.

"Pandy…"

"Yeah?" she asks, bending over and retrieving a paper plate from below the sink.

"I think I want to see Robin today."

"Okay."

"Just to…" I lick my lips. "Just to see if he's okay."

He answers on the first ring. "Hello?" His tone is short and formal. I must have caught him at a bad time.

"Hi," I squeak, "It's Kate."

"Kate, hey!" Robin's voice warms instantly and I smile, relaxing into the couch.

"Actually, it's not Kate. It's Katie, but you don't seem to get that," I scold, hoping he can hear the grin in my voice.

"I know who you are."

A jolt runs through me and for a second I don't know what to say. Taking a deep breath, I say slowly, "I'm calling because… I miss you." My tone is light, but he'll hear the meaning. If it is him.

"I miss you too." I'm back with those words on the bridge. Blue and red scream for my attention, pressed up against the wall like illicit lovers.

"Do you want to do something about it?" I challenge, running my fingers through my hair, working out the knots as I go.

"I'd love to, but I have a ton to get done. What about tomorrow?"

My romantic haze lifts, leaving my cheeks pink. Disappointment battles with humiliation. I don't flirt like this. I don't get rejected. "Tomorrow's Sunday. I'll probably have a lot I need to do," I say simply.

"Okay." Robin sounds disappointed, but I roughly shove any guilt aside. I made the first move. He rejected it. If he wants to hang out with me again, it'll be up to him. I'm done.

"I'd better get going," I say crisply, getting ready to hang up.

"Wait, Katie?"

"Yeah?" I don't know why I'm still on the phone.

"I really do want to hang out sometime."

I nod sadly without him there to see it. "Me too."

I kind of miss him calling me Kate.

It seems as if Michael has the answer.

"Get over it and invite him to the matinee," he orders impatiently after I relate the story to him the next day.

"But I don't want to have to make the first and the second move," I complain, digging my fork into the school's excuse for lasagna. Michael shakes his head.

"Guys don't keep score. He said he wants to hang out, right?"

"Yes…"

"And he mentioned today?"

"Yes…"

"That was the second move."

"But…!" I protest as Michael shoves my phone firmly toward me.

"Call," he instructs.

"Fine," I pout, finding my call list. I wince as I select the number, and wait with a pounding heart as the line rings.

In a second I hear, "Hello?"

"Hi, Robin?" I stammer. "It's Katie."

"Hey there," he says, sounding distracted. Again. I stab my food in resentment. "What's up?"

I can't do this. If he says no I'll never try again. Ever, ever, ever. With anyone. "My day's cleared up, and I was wondering if you wanted to come to a movie with me and Michael and Pandy. We're going to catch a matinée of the new werewolf movie and make fun of it. Do you want to join?" I speak a little too quickly and run out of breath just before the last few words. They come out as a croak.

There's a pause that lasts a lifetime, during which I jump headfirst off an imaginary cliff. "Sure," he says finally, and I hear clicking. He's on his computer. That's what the distraction is. He can't put his computer down for two seconds to talk to me. "Sounds fun. What time?"

I glance at Michael and mouth the question to him. He holds up three fingers. "Three," I answer, cutting off another piece of lasagna and separating the layers.

"Can I meet you guys there?"

"Yeah. We'll probably get there around 2:30. Pandy is picky about seats."

"A queen needs the right throne," Robin laughs. This description conjures up the image of a royally decked-out Pandy on Halloween. He must have seen her. I recall the image of his hoodie flitting through the crowd.

But if he saw Pandy, why didn't he say hi to Michael? I look across the table at Michael, chewing away at a piece of broccoli on his fork. A piece of green gets lodged between his teeth, and he uses the tines of his fork to free it. He said the EA wasn't there. He's always had trouble lying.

"That she does," I answer, before I lose the thread of our banter. "We'll make sure to put your name on the list." I hang up and Pandy gives me a patronizing look.

"Now was that so hard?" she asks.

"Yes, Your Majesty. It was." I sulk, thrusting my fork into the top of my food.

"But," Pandy points out, "you get to hang out with Robin."

"You're right," I say, breaking into a grin. "I do."

Chapter Eleven

I don't know what happened. I opened the door to Robin with one invitation, and now he's everywhere. I can't turn around without seeing his mess of brown hair, walking next to Michael, sitting on our couch, or reading over Pandora's latest essay. The seamless transition has me reeling. Usually whenever one of us would bring in an outsider—a date of mine, a friend of Michael's, a relative of Pandora's—they never exactly clicked. Robin, however, feels like he's always been here. Or at least, like he should have been.

It's the last day before we all leave for Christmas. We're sitting in the apartment, working through the perishables in the fridge as the TV blares laugh tracks.

"I don't sense any synchronicity here at all," deadpans Pandora as we watch the stars grab hot wings and yell at their own TV screen.

"We're watching a show about people watching TV. I think we've hit rock bottom." I take the last gulp of orange juice and toss the container into our trash pile. Michael's brought beer but only he and Pandy have partaken, another plus for Robin.

I've trained myself out of the baseless anger and pulled myself away from any pitching-over-the-edge crush I might have been developing. I look at Robin now, laughing at my joke and shaking his head and feel safe. We don't need to kiss or hold hands. He doesn't need to tell me he loves me or think that I'm special. As long as he's around and smiling, I'll be happy. It's not the over-the-top reveal I was waiting for, complete with an explanation for my crazy feelings and reciprocity from Robin, but at least everything has settled.

The episode ends and I stretch, fighting off lethargy. Robin's phone rings. He excuses himself and goes into the hall to answer, leaving me alone with Michael and Pandora.

"Either of you guys want to go for a walk?" I ask, standing up and wincing as feeling begins to return to my feet. They shake their heads in unison.

"Ask Robin," Michael says, taking a swig of beer and selecting the next episode. "He's the one you're dating."

I inhale quickly and start to cough. "We are not dating!" I gasp. My eyes are watering and I wipe them with the back of my hand.

Pandy snorts. "You so are! He's here all the time, you guys spend every spare moment together, and he pays for you when we all go out."

"It's the twenty-first century, Pandora," I say haughtily, gulping around the tickle still in my throat. "It's not about gender roles; it's about who can afford it."

"And you can't afford it, so he pays. Ha! Got you." Pandy rubs her hands together wickedly. I open my mouth to respond, and close it again. The way she says it, it sounds like it's true. But Robin and I aren't dating. I can't have missed that.

Robin rejoins us, looking down at the diminishing pile of chips. "I'm going to make a snack run, anyone want to come?"

"Katie does," Pandora volunteers. "She was just saying she wants to go for a walk."

I strike Pandy with a lightning glare, then pick my coat up off the couch. No getting out of this one. Robin, distracted by his phone, doesn't look up as we leave the apartment.

"To the market, good sir!" I cry. I seize his arm, and we stumble toward his car. Robin, likely so he can stay upright, finally shoves his phone into his pocket. I grin. We laugh as we nearly crash into the side door, skidding to a halt, inches away from the metal. Robin opens up the passenger's side for me with a little bow. "My lady."

"Thanks." I'm aware of how clunky my response sounds. It's out of line with the playful environment I just created, but Pandy's words have just come back to me with force.

There's drizzle coming down from the sky, which is the same gray as Robin's Corolla. The trees lining the parking lot are bending sideways in the wind, nature's sympathetic head tip. Pandora's statement swirls in my head, causing my stomach to churn.

We get into his car and Robin turns on the radio to a rock station. We launch into gear to the sound of Led Zeppelin.

"Robin…" I say, working hard to build up my nerve. I wish nerve was something you could build. Take enough time, put everything together like Legos, and suddenly you're brave.

"Yes?"

"Just so you know, we're not dating."

His cheerful expression tightens. "Good to know," he says after a moment.

That didn't come out as intended. I desperately try to back pedal. "No, no, that's not what I meant. I mean, we're not dating yet."

"Why not?" His tone is even but something is off. I don't know what I just did.

"Because!" I kick the floor covering in front of me in frustration. Tiny plastic teeth bite into my shoe. "Well, first of all, do you even like me?"

"Yes." Robin says. "I do."

"Oh." My face flushes and I don't say anything as I process this.

"Do you like me?"

I blink hard, trying to figure out how we got here so quickly. Five minutes ago everything was normal and fine, and now we're suddenly admitting that we have feelings for each other? Everything is changing—why? Why did I have to bring anything up? "I—I think so," I stammer, nervously pulling the sleeve of my hoodie down over my hand.

"Is that it?"

"Is what it?"

"You don't know how you feel about me. That's why we're not dating." His voice is low, almost soothing, as he tries to coax out of me what I mean. As if it's only what I think that matters. *Expect something out of me!* I want to scream. *Ask me… Ask me to…*

I kick the floor again. "No! Well, maybe. But I do like you. I like you a lot. I just don't know if I should." I press my palms over my eyes and wish for the car ride to be over.

"Why not? What, exactly, did I do?" I know what he's talking about. He knows what I'm talking about. The anger, the coursing anger that sometimes takes hold of me that I've sometimes been unable to hide. He remembers my moodiness from that very first day. He knows that I blame him for something.

"I don't know." My eyes heat up and I take a few deep breaths trying to calm down. The hands that are folded into my lap, the photographer's hands, are shaking. I can't calm them.

Images and recollections are swirling nonsensically in my head, making me feel sick. I want to say yes to him. I should say no. I want to say yes. I fling my shoes onto the floor and pull my feet up under me, trying to warm them. "I don't know. I do like you…"

"So why?" His voice is back to gentle, and I feel some of my tension ease.

"This isn't how a relationship is supposed to start." It's only a fraction of the truth, but it's the only one I can grab and drag to the surface. "Call me old-fashioned or whatever, but I think both people should *know* when they're going on a first date. I thought we were just hanging out. I would have done things differently if I had known that this was dating. Which it wasn't. But, if you *do* want to date, I'd be open to it. But we have to do it right." That's the best I can do. I settle back and look at Robin expectantly.

Robin smiles then his mouth opens into a laugh. His spritely laugh. The dangerous one. "Fair enough," he says, pulling into the grocery store parking lot. "So, we're not dating."

"No."

"Then you're buying the chips."

By the time we return to the apartment, I'm giddy. What a backwards way to start a relationship. It's about time for something to happen. I've been spending so much time being terrified of what being with Robin would mean that I never realized how much I wanted it.

Pandora shoots me a questioning glance as I walk in but I grin, shake my head, and mouth *I'll tell you later.* We settle back into place. I prepare myself for Robin to make a move—put an arm around me maybe, or take my hand. But as the new episode starts, Robin stays where he is without any indication he wants to touch me at all. I hint a few times, moving my hands to make them easy for him to take, giving a little shiver to invite some cuddling, but to no avail. Robin remains unmoved by my invitations, moving only to dip a chip into the salsa. That I paid for. This sucks.

As the episode progresses my frustration builds. I told him that we weren't dating *yet*, not that we shouldn't. It was pretty much a free pass at starting something up. But he's not. *Well, who needs him anyway?* I think, leaning past him and taking a chip of my own. I've been fine not dating him up 'til now; we can continue like this forever. I don't care. The anger comes crackling back.

The episode finishes and I let out a noisy yawn. "I'm getting tired. Maybe we should stop for the night."

"Good idea," Pandora agrees, getting to her feet, and stretching her neck. I hope she's not really tired, because I have a lot I want to talk to her about.

"Time for the men to get moving." Michael also stands up and wraps his arms around Pandy's waist, lifting her off the ground with a squeeze. She shrieks and kicks her feet until she's safely back on the floor, then turns around and gives Michael a kiss. Jealousy aches in my chest as I imagine the goodnight kiss I could be giving to Robin right now. Stupid, *stupid* rules.

I shove my hands into my pockets and rock in agitation as Robin packs up his stuff, shoves another loaded chip into his mouth, and pulls on his shoes.

"Walk me out?" he offers, and I see a glint in his eye. Oh my god. Oh my god, it's now. Am I ready? I've never anticipated the start of a relationship before. As I walk toward the door I'm terrified. I know he's going to kiss me.

The air outside is mild. The dirt in the parking lot has thawed, causing mud to trickle through tire marks and splash up against our shoes. We get to his car and he turns, looking at me as though he knows something I don't.

"What?" I ask. I realize there's a dot of salsa on the corner of my lip and I lick it off, trying to get my mouth as clean as possible. This is it.

"Thanks for the chips," he says, then leans in and gives me a tight one-armed hug.

I'm so distracted by the feeling of his arm against my shoulder that I don't realize what's happening until he pulls away. I lurch forward, as climbs into his car. The door slams, leaving me speechless in the parking lot. He backs up, waves, and moves off, his car bumping up and down over the speed bumps security just installed. Then he's gone, and the only light that's left is the porch light of our apartment. I breathe out.

Turning around, I head slowly inside, not sure if I feel disappointed or relieved. I could feel either but I want neither. I guess I just want to sleep. Up the carpeted stairs, back into the apartment and to Pandora's questioning stare. She'll want to know everything. Sadly, there's nothing to tell.

The second Monday after break, Michael informs me that there will be an EA meeting that afternoon. I tell him I'm sick. I've wrangled my notes into something of a first-draft format, and I'm starting to be able to imagine showing it to Geri. I've got about half a dozen usable pictures so far. All of this helps extinguish my guilt over bailing. I just really, really don't want to listen to an argument on if wind energy is worth destroying our view. Especially when I can't kiss Robin.

Geri is focused on my contest entry, anyway. I've already told her that I know which picture I want to use, but she's still pushing me to keep looking. I don't know how she thinks I can top the one I have.

"Inspiration is all around you," she pressed at our last meeting. Her eyes were bright and I noticed that she'd tacked the contest flier onto her bulletin board. "Go, look, develop your skills. You might end up surprising yourself." *Commitment,* she might as well have been saying. *Have some commitment.*

I'm in my favorite antique store in town. The shop spans two levels joined by a spiral staircase smack in the middle. It feels like it should be a museum more than a store, but I'm not complaining. I started taking pictures here my first year at Travis U, and by now all three of the employees know who I am. They're okay with me bringing my camera, so it's become my go-to spot for inspiration. Sandy, a tall, freckled girl, is currently on duty. Since things are slow, she's leaning against the staircase railing and chatting with me as I snap away.

"How's your project going?" she inquires as I dust off a dark blue vase with my sleeve. I frown and lean forward, but can't get my reflection to appear in the glass. I switch to a set of opera glasses that are featured in the window display.

"Which one?" I ask, holding the mini binoculars up to my eyes. The store slips out of focus. I crank the knob back and forth but the image remains blurred. I put the glasses back onto the display.

"You were entering a contest?" Sandy is amazing at remembering everything her customers tell her, a quality I suspect she got from her mother, the store's owner. Isabelle Jordan can tell you not only when every piece in her store was made and what it's made from, but also when she got it, who sold it to her, and what it costs. It's remarkable.

"I want to win. So badly that it's scaring me. But my boss is almost more intent on it than I am, and I don't think she likes the picture that I've chosen." I slipped into calling Geri my boss right around the start of our intensive and now it's stuck.

Sandy nods, slipping her foot back through the wooden bars of the stairwell. "Why doesn't she like it?"

"I think she would if I wasn't so set on it. She's afraid I'm ruling out better options. 'Don't settle' has pretty much become her slogan."

"Kind of like my mom about my boyfriend." Sandy cracks a grin.

"What's your boyfriend like?" I like hearing Sandy talk. She has a soothingly simple way of looking at life. All of the things that make my head feel like it's going to shatter seem to fit perfectly in boxes in her world.

"Sweet. He's tall, like me, and goofy. We like to watch Disney movies together."

I smile at the image. Sandy, with her springy hair and freckled face, singing along with an equally lanky fellow to "A Whole New World".

"What about you?" she asks. "Do you have a guy?"

"Not one I can watch Disney movies with yet," I answer, looking through my viewfinder and capturing a brass salt and pepper shaker set.

"He doesn't like them?"

I sigh and delete my last shot. "I don't know. There's a lot I don't know about him." I try to picture Robin watching *The Lion King* with me, and can't. I can only picture him working.

I pick up a glass vial that looks like an exaggerated coke bottle and wipe away a smudge with my shirt. "This is cool."

"It was my grandmother's," Sandy explains, smiling with pride.

"And your mom is selling it?"

"My grandfather gave it to her and neither of them liked him that much."

We laugh and I put the bottle down. With inspiration is running short I turn off my camera and put the lens cap in place.

"I think I'm..." I trail off, spotting a tin harmonica sitting unassumingly on a windowsill. I walk over to it and pick it up gently, irrationally afraid that it might break. "Wow," I breathe. Turning it over in my palm, I see loopy letters across the bottom, so faded that I can't read what they said. My hand closes automatically over the instrument and I ask Sandy, "How much?"

"Sixteen dollars," she answers, after looking over to see what I have.

"I'll take it," I say, all excitement and smiles. This is perfect.

I wrap the harmonica as soon as I get home and it sits in its shiny red wrapping paper for days before I get up the nerve to text Robin.

"I have a Christmas present for you," I finally send, four days after the purchase. We've been back from break for almost two weeks, but who's counting? As soon as I see that the text was sent I close out of messaging and set my phone down, determined not to check it for at least three hours. My phone lights up before I take my hand off it.

"What?" That was quick. I bite my lip, trying to decide if he's asking what the present is or if he's generally confused by my message. I clarify, "I know it's late, but I think you'll like it :)"

Now I can allow myself wait for the response. Since I know he's with his phone. I sit on my bed with my phone in front of me staring at it patiently until it lights up again. This time it takes nearly five minutes and by the time my phone buzzes I'm ready to throw it out the window.

"I have one for you too."

I squeal and jump up off the bed, spinning around my room in excitement. Laughing, I flop back down on my stomach and hastily type back, "When do you want yours?"

In less than a minute he answers, "Now?"

"Come on over ;)" I send this, then run into the bathroom to fix my hair. Once I'm in front of the mirror I freeze. *What am I doing?* I'm acting like an idiot accordingly, I answer myself, and everything is as it should be. Nothing wrong with that. But instead of doing my hair and changing into something cuter, I walk out of the bathroom and over to the couch. I only have a few minutes before he comes over and I think I need to sort some things out in my brain before I see him again.

I've been trying to ignore it, but I've known from the get-go that if I fall down this rabbit hole I'm going to get hurt. Maybe even broken. It's been reflected through the cracks in my sanity and my own persistent doubt. Intuitively I know that there's something more going on here, and intuitively I know that it's not somewhere I should go.

It's so self-indulgent. My words from class that very first day come back to me, softly pushing me toward the sensible answer.

I lie down on the couch and draw my knees up to my chest. The image of that red wrapped present in my room fogs up my vision and I take a deep breath, heavy with melancholy. I wanted so much for this to happen but I've always known that I won't let it.

There's a knock on the door, then Robin steps in. He's wearing a green ski cap and I notice that his hair has gotten a bit longer. It now pokes out of the bottom of his hat. I like it this way. I shove down my urge to jump up and give him a hug. Instead, I greet him with a standard smile.

"Hey," I say, uncurling.

"Hey," he says back, dropping his green bag onto the floor. God, he always looks so happy to see me. "Do you want your present?"

Of course I want my present. What kind of stupid question is that? "Sure. I need to get yours though." I head toward the door of my room, needing to get away from him so I can clear my head and get back onto the right track.

Because no matter how hard I try to get around it, the fact remains that he left me waiting.

I pick up the harmonica and shake my head rapidly. I feel like I'm fraying around the edges and something is bleeding through. Waiting. Waiting for what? I want to remember but as soon as I try and catch it, it fades away.

Clutching the harmonica so tightly that the wrapping crinkles, I stride back out to the living room and find Robin sitting on the couch, poking mischievously at Santa's tail.

"Here," I say, offering the package. He takes it and looks at it, turning it this way and that before pulling at the paper. I stay standing as he runs his finger along the seam, breaking the red apart. What a stupid gift idea. He's never mentioned music, ever.

But I know he's going to love it.

The paper is off and he's staring down at the harmonica, completely silent. I hold my breath. He hates it. He's trying to figure out why I gave it to him. He's trying to think of something nice to say since no obvious compliment comes to mind. I'm an idiot.

"Where did you get this?" There's something in his voice that I've never heard before, and he's looking at the instrument as if it's an alien.

"At the antique store in town," I croak. I don't understand this reaction. Why won't he look up?

"I love it," he says finally, turning it over in his hand. "How did you know?" He looks up at me holding the harmonica tightly in one hand. "I had one exactly like this when I was a kid. My dad gave it to me for Christmas when I was about six. I lost it when I was on a train coming back from visiting him when I was thirteen."

I sit down beside him. "I didn't know that. I just saw it and… Well, you came to mind." Feeling as if strings from the ceiling are guiding me, I rest my head on his shoulder.

"This is awesome." He's smiling now, the shock gone, his gaze back on the harmonica. I wait for him to put it to his lips and play a few notes but he keeps looking at it. "What I have for you isn't nearly as good," he says, finally getting to his feet.

I tip my head up again and he pulls out of his bag a lumpy package. I grin at the poor wrapping job, imagining him struggling over it by himself after having refused the gift-wrapping option during purchase. The Santa-print paper (Clause, not the cat) tears easily, and as soon as I see the contents of the present I stop. Soft, midnight blue material slithers into my hand, heavy and warm. I look up at Robin, my mouth open although I don't know what to say.

"You got me..." He got me a blanket. He got me a special blanket. He didn't know. I never told him. I look back down at it and run my hand over the material again and again, fighting the tears that are threatening to fill my eyes.

"Because you're always cold," he explains. I can't say anything. There's nothing to say. So, instead, I lean in close and press my lips to his.

There's no surprise. He responds right away, gently putting his hand to the back of my head, pressing me closer to him. A moment later, I have to break away because I feel a euphoric giggle bubbling up inside of me. It escapes, and soon I'm flat-out laughing. I look over at Robin and the nervous look on his face causes me to laugh even harder.

"No," I say, waving my hand and trying to regain composure. "No. I'm just really happy." I fall into laughter again and this time Robin grins and tugs me toward him.

"Come here." He kisses me again. We kiss, and we kiss, and we kiss until the light has changed and I begin to wonder if soon Pandora will be back from her afternoon with Michael. I pull away.

"Pandy's going to be back soon," I say. Robin nods, understanding, and gives me one last gentle kiss before getting up to go.

"I love the harmonica," he says, picking it up off the couch where it had been sitting next to us.

"I love the blanket," I answer, shaking it out and pulling it over me.

"I'll see you soon?" he asks as he heads for the door.

"So soon," I promise, watching him go. The door closes and I'm left alone, nestled safely under the blanket.

It's not going to work out, that same voice inside me warns, but this time I'm not put off by it. *I know,* I silently answer, *but I'm going to see it through*. I don't want to miss out on knowing Robin.

Chapter Twelve

I don't tell Pandora what happened when she gets home. She knows something is up. I can tell she does. I'm not making a huge effort to hide anything, but I'm also not inviting her to ask. She doesn't, not even about where the blanket came from. I don't mind. I'll tell her later. The less I use my mouth the better I'll be able to save the kisses. I want to spend the evening curled up replaying the whole thing over and over again.

His shirt was soft and his face was scratchy from not shaving. I had to get used to the green in his eyes and the gentleness of his jawline. His nose went out farther than I expected, and the experience was much more alien than I anticipated. I didn't remember anything about him.

I've moved off the couch and into my bedroom, comfortable and safe beneath my new blanket. It's been rare lately that anything has seemed right, but everything feels softly in place now. I'm not sure how long it will last, but I'll take it. There's no point looking for trouble when I'm sure there's plenty to be found. It'll find me soon enough.

My feet are so cold. So cold and so wet. But he'll come, I know he will. He's never left me waiting before and he won't do it now. Not when it's so important. But doubt is creeping in like the cold; I want to shake it off, but I can't. I know he'll come. I know he will. But I'm afraid he won't.

There's a nearby sound and I turn, my heart leaping. Warm delight is tainted by guilt. Of course he would come. I always knew that.

But he isn't there.

A bird flies out of the bushes and the world around me grows quiet again. Where is he? Do I see lightness in the sky? Am I looking east? I don't know where I am anymore. Where is he?

I don't think he's coming. I don't want to, but I fear he's not coming. He's not coming. He's not…

I wake up and wince at the harsh light that has entered my room. I feel hungover. My teeth are coated with something thick and my tongue is sticking to the roof of my mouth. Pink lines cover my skin where my clothes from yesterday pressed into me and my neck aches in a way that I hope won't worsen. I feel like I was painted with trash. But as soon as I turn over and feel the softness of the blanket on my shoulders, the events of yesterday come back to me, bursting like fireworks in my chest.

We kissed. Robin and I kissed. I have a boyfriend.

Do I? Did that count? I've never been one to kiss men at random, but what does a kiss mean to Robin? Of course, with us it wasn't only a kiss; there were the presents, and the conversations, and… Whatever it is. There's that. But still.

As I swing my legs off over the edge of the bed and force myself into an upright position, determination takes me by the shoulders. I need to find out. My cell phone is in my hand now and before I even look at the screen I start to dial Robin's number. Right before I enter the last digit, I stop. It's eight-thirty in the morning. Robin probably isn't up yet. I set my phone down on my nightstand and deliberately close my eyes. I won't think about how crazy I'm acting. I won't. People always act crazy at the beginnings of a relationship. It's what romance does. This isn't a sign; it's just early morning confusion. I'm going back to sleep.

I can't fall asleep. I'm not tired. I sigh and pull open the drawer of my nightstand. Foregoing my required reading for class, I pull out my copy of Grimm's Fairytales. This time I don't make it past the table of contents. For once, I'm not in the mood for fairytales. It's not a night to search for the right ending. I place the book back inside the drawer. Maybe a cup of tea will do the trick.

It's not until I've already pulled my favorite mug out of the cabinet that I realize Pandora is sitting at the kitchen table. When I spot her I jump so high I nearly drop my mug.

"You scared me," I gasp. "What are you doing up?"

"Nothing," Pandy shakes her head, her ponytail swinging from side to side. With her hair up, I'm surprised to see how dark her roots are. I'm about to turn and resume my tea making when the image on her t-shirt catch my eye. She's wearing an oversized gray t-shirt with the different phases on the moon shown curved over her chest. I remember this shirt. She got it on a trip to the planetarium that we took in eleventh grade. This can only mean one thing.

I sit down beside her. "What's wrong?"

She shakes her head again, and this time I see tears leaking from the corners of her eyes. "I…" she squeaks, "I think Michael might have feelings for somebody else."

Everything cracks.

"What?" Question after question slam into my skull and I blurt the first one that bangs into the foreground. "Why?"

Pandy presses her palms into her eyes. "He's been acting different lately. And it's scaring me to death." I see her shoulders moving up and down but her voice is remarkably even. I swallow and bob my head up and down in understanding while fixing my gaze on the table top.

"How has he been different?" I want to hear it from Pandora.

Her hands slide up so they're resting on her forehead. I ready myself to hear her list the things that I've already noticed: the absences from hanging out with us, how poor his temper has been, and the strangeness of his dedication to the EA, especially now that we've discovered its chaotic past. Instead Pandy murmurs something that I'm unprepared for: "He doesn't look at me anymore."

"I…" There's nothing to say. I close my mouth and instead wrap my arms around my best friend and feel her soften into my shoulder.

"He's changed. I know he's always had this…" she struggles to find the word. That's unusual for Pandy. She always has the words. "This power of people that he liked to use. But most of the time it's been harmless. Now I think he's using it on the wrong people."

"You mean the EA?" Relief bubbles up in me so abruptly that I almost laugh. "Pandy, Michael's the one who's keeping everyone under control. Robin told me. Michael's got everything on track."

Instead of brightening, Pandy's expression drops even further. "You have so much faith in him," she whispers.

"You do too," I urge, trying to get her to remember the feeling. "It's Michael. We've known him forever. There's nothing going on."

Pandy's face crumbles. "I don't want to lose him, Katie. I don't. But it's Michael. I'm not supposed to be s-scared." She's crying now, hiccupping for air and sniffling quietly. I want to say something to take the pain from her but I can't think of anything that could help. I'm scared too.

"It's Michael," I repeat eventually, watching the second hand on our kitchen clock move sluggishly by. "He loves you. He'd never do anything to hurt you." At these words, Pandy stills. I realize my mistake too late and quickly try to rectify. "No. Pandy… no. That wasn't… No…" Guilt grips my throat and for a second I'm afraid that I'll start crying too. "That was a long time ago. It was different. He never meant…"

Pandy straightens and after she wipes her eyes lays a hand on my shoulder. "It's okay." I've always marveled at Pandora's ability to regain composure. I've never seen her hysterical or unable to be calmed; within a few minutes she's always back upright and ready to move forward.

"It's not okay," I say miserably. Pandy pats my shoulder. The kettle begins to whistle and I get up to attend to it, glad for something to do. After I pour us each a mug of tea I sit down with her again and begin the interrogation. "So. Why are you feeling like this?"

"It's…" Pandora runs her finger around the rim of her mug, looking down into the cup. Her face is angled away from me but her posture looks stronger than before. "It's hard to explain. Intuition, I guess." She lets out a small laugh. "I wish it wasn't. I really wish there was a reason because then I could reason it away, you know? But intuition is hard to ignore."

I nod, thinking of Robin. "Yeah. I know."

She sighs and straightens, pulling out her hair tie and letting her curls tumble over her shoulders. "I guess I'll have to wait and see."

What an awful solution. My mind races desperately, trying to come up with something, anything, to help her. "I could talk to him."

She shakes her head, primly raising her mug to her lips and taking a sip of tea. "He won't tell you."

"I wouldn't flat out ask, I'd…"

"Katie." She cuts me off with a stern look. "He won't tell you."

"The EA really is a stupid name," I comment, adjusting my scarf using Robin's rearview mirror.

"But we came up with a better name, remember?"

I grin. "Of course: The Earth Avengers: Robin the Handsome. It's much better." I finally get my scarf even and open the car door, double checking my camera before I get out. As much as I'm smiling and trying to look relaxed, I can't ignore the worry that's chewing at my insides.

It's the last week of January and the ride over here was the first time that Robin and I have seen each other since we kissed. I'm still not sure where we stand. We kissed hello so it seems that whatever this is has solidified, but I don't know how to act in the meeting. I try hard to remember if I saw any other couples when I was here last time but nothing comes to mind.

I wait for an anxious second to see if he's going to take my hand, but his arms are loaded with posters that he made. I walk ahead on my own. I get to the door before him and hold it open, closing it behind me after I slip in. Shane is in front of us almost immediately. He scoops Robin's posters up in his giant arms, and disappears within a matter of seconds.

"Wow," I blink, "he must have really wanted them."

"They're really good posters," Robin says seriously. I laugh and shove him. He grins and pulls me in for a hug, briefly nestling his head in my hair. "I'm glad you're here."

"I'm glad to be here." I hear footsteps and pull away. Bizarrely, I'm afraid it might be Michael. *Only because I haven't told him yet,* I reason. It would be a pretty lame way for him to find out that Robin and I are official... ish.

It's not Michael. It's a tiny girl with massive amounts of thick brown hair and a sleepy smile.

"Hi Rob," she says, giving Robin a hug around his waist.

"Hey Vin," he replies, smiling as he hugs her. "How's the arm?"

"Still on."

Jealousy jumps up in my stomach. I stand patiently waiting for someone to introduce me, but after the hug is over "Vin" floats away and Robin turns his attention back to me. "Shall we get some seats?"

I nod, put off by the encounter. I let Robin walk ahead of me and take a moment to adjust my camera's settings.

Once we're seated, Shane begins to talk. I watch for some sign of what Robin was talking about—that Shane is only a figurehead now—but everyone is listening to Shane with rapt attention. I shrug inwardly and flick through my most recent batch of EA pictures. I have a lot of good ones from the last meeting I attended but documentation of their field work is lacking. I look over at Robin to ask when the next event is, but he's leaning forward, looking like he's getting ready to speak.

"That's not a good idea," he says, snapping up the first pause in the conversation. I lift my head. in an attempt to ascertain the discussion subject. Unfortunately, no light is shed from the following response.

"Shut up, Rob." The girl from before is playing lackadaisically with the ends of her hair. "You don't think anything's a good idea. Remember Boston?"

"Boston wasn't a good idea!" somebody shouts, and the whole room laughs.

I'll ask Robin after the meeting. I'll ask him when the next activity is too. My interest in the words being called from both side of the room begins to wane. I look around the room, hoping to catch a glimpse of Michael. There he is, standing by the door, listening with a serious expression. I catch his eye, and smile. He holds up his hand in acknowledgement, then turns his attention back to Shane. He looks so solid, standing there in the doorway, just like the Michael I've always known. He can't have feelings for anyone but Pandy. It wouldn't make sense.

But what gave Pandy the idea that he does? She's never been prone to jealousy, rational or otherwise. There has to be something serious going down to make her so worried. He's been tense lately and around less, but when he has been with us he's been as warm and interactive as always.

He doesn't look at me anymore, Pandy said. So what, or who, has he been looking at?

I gaze critically around the group. Most of the girls here, save Jessica, aren't exactly beauty queens, but Pandora's own beauty renders competition in that field redundant. If Michael was looking at someone else there'd have to be something special about her. The EA certainly has a strong family vibe. They're all still teasing and nudging one another as they remember Boston. Their mass-scale inside jokes don't seem open to newcomers. Not a single person is looking at me, much less offering to fill me in. My mind flickers to Vin and the hug she gave Robin ("Rob") when we came in. I bite my lip, imagining if Robin saw her every week all by himself. For a long time, he did.

Stop it. We'll get to past partners, romantic trysts, and one-offs in due time. We'll have to have that talk. I glance at Michael, as he stands in the doorway, working at a hangnail with his teeth. Oh god. I'll have to tell Robin about that.

By the time the meeting ends, my head is swirling with doubts. I sigh and shove my hands into my hair, trying to pull myself together. All in due time, all in due time. As I sit, trying to compose myself, Michael walks over and crouches down next to me.

"How's it going, Katie-cat?"

"It's going," I sigh, extracting my hands from my mane. The bracelet I'm wearing catches, and I spend a moment trying to untangle it. Robin is across the room talking to girl, well, a woman really, and together they're bent over a map. Behind them hangs a picture of a rainstorm over a lake. It's beautiful with tiny indentations where the raindrops meet the water, and suddenly I want to be there, standing in the open with rain falling onto my head. *Take me there,* I think. As if he can hear my thoughts, Robin glances up from the map and smiles. I grin back and he gives me a wink before looking back down at what's before him.

"What happened in Boston?" I ask.

"Boston? Oh, we, uh…" Michael breaks off with a smile, shaking his head at the memory. "They had an exhibit on 'Industries of America'," he holds up his fingers as air quotes, "in the Museum of Science. It was supposed to be this positive thing, but really it was bull. It was a lot about mining." Michael gives me a significant look. I frown and nod, pretending I get the importance. He continues. "We got this idea to post a bunch of facts around the exhibits about tailings. We had all of these printouts and Ducky built a 3D model. It was a powerful way to show the damage that's being done."

"And Robin didn't think it was a good plan."

"No. Thought it was too risky."

"But he went along anyway?" I look back at Robin, still preoccupied with the map and the girl. "Why?"

"Robin shows up, whether he likes the plan or not. And so he could play on those piano stairs. He kept running up and down them until we made him stop."

We laugh together. "How did it turn out?"

Michael shoves his hands into his pockets. "We managed to get everything set up before we got kicked out. We were written up for vandalism and attempted theft." In explanation, he subtly tips his head toward the girl from before. Vin. "Someone wanted a souvenir. They won't let any of us back in now."

"And Robin can't play on the stairs anymore." I nod, pondering.

"Nope. So you guys are...?" Michael tilts his head toward Robin.

"Yeah," I say feeling a warm squirm of excitement.

"Huh. He must have told you about Vin then," says Michael, and before I can say anything he gets to his feet and leaves.

No. No he has *not* told me about Vin. I'd never even heard of Vin before today. Even her name makes me feel sick. Vin. Vinnie. How cute. How different. How obnoxious. I'm pacing in front of the house and kicking rocks gloomily. There's a detached part of me that wonders if Robin will notice, but he's talking with Shane so I don't hope for much.

We get back into Robin's car, and without thinking I reach over and place my hand on his. To my delight, he flips his hand over and gives mine a squeeze before taking it back to start the car. The sweetness of this gesture spreads over me like butter on toast. For a while I sit, letting reassurance knead its way into my knotted body. It's fine. We're fine. There's nothing to be afraid of.

Once we're on the road, he speaks.

"So. Valentine's day is coming up," he says in the clunky way that men have with introducing new topics.

I nod. "Sixteen days."

"What should we do?"

It takes all of my willpower not to throw my arms around him. The way he asked that—so matter-of-factly—makes me want to dance with joy and relief. We're not stuck in that awkward place where neither of us is brave enough to ask the other one. There will be no uncomfortable inquiry of "What are your plans?" No carefully constructed, "I'm not entirely sure yet. You?" Whatever we're doing, we're doing it together.

"Let's see a movie," I reply, feeling wonderfully decisive.

"In theaters or at home?"

"Home. It'll be cozier."

"Home," he confirms. I love the way it sounds when he says it. Home.

I'm too busy grinning to notice right away that we're not taking the usual route back to campus. In fact, we're heading in the entirely opposite direction. "Where are we going?" I finally ask, once I figure this out.

"If we're seeing a movie at home, I thought I'd show you were home is."

"Alright, show me where home is," I answer, interlocking my fingers in my lap. Valentine's Day at Robin's. Valentine's Day without Pandy and Michael darting in and out of the living room, mouthing, "sorry" at us each time they need to come out and get something. Robin is going to show me his place. I'm going to get to see where Robin lives. "Hey Robin?"

"Yeah?"

The questions from the meeting build inside me like helium and finally the most important one escapes. "What… What are we?"

"Humans," he answers confidently, and I playfully swat his arm.

"No, I mean… what are we to each other?"

"What do you want to be?"

Dammit. I was hoping that he'd have the answer but here he is, turning the question back on me. What do I want us to be? I want us to be in love, truly and passionately, with eyes for no one else, even when we've fallen into the lull of comfort that comes after the first few months of any relationship. I want us to be best friends, closer to each other than we are to anyone else. I want to know why I want this;

I want to know why I feel like it will never happen. "I don't know."

"I can wait." This response, this simple, simple response causes my heart to explode in my chest.

"I want us to be together," I blurt and my ears ring in the silence that follows.

"Are you sure?" he finally asks.

"Yes," I say firmly. "If I need to have my heart broken, I want it done by you."

"I'm not going to break your heart," he says.

I love his apartment. It's not as big as the one I share with Pandora, but it's a lot cooler. The walls are brick and the windows are small, giving the whole thing a vintage coffee shop feel. Robin has coated almost the entire thing with maps: of different countries and continents, new maps, old maps, and, it seems, a few maps of imaginary places.

"Wow," I say, looking around in wonderment, "You live here?"

"That's what the lease says." Robin throws his coat over the back of a chair. "I don't hang out here much. I usually am just here to work."

"Where do you hang out?" I ask, following him back into what I assume is his bedroom.

"Anywhere. Campus. Town. Friends' places. Work."

"Where do you work?" I ask with a frown as I lean forward to examine a map of Middle Earth. It's strange to think I don't know this about him. I don't know much about his life at all, except that he's part of the EA.

"Wordy's," Robin answers, slipping his hands around my waist and tugging me back to be close to him.

"I love it there!" I cry, thinking of the charming bookstore-cum-coffee shop a couple blocks from the town square. I spin to face him. He reaches forward, brushes some hair back from my face, and kisses me.

"I want to know everything about you," I murmur after our lips lose contact.

"No you don't," he says, running a finger along my cheekbone. He turns to continue the tour.

"I do…" I start to say but then quiet myself. Maybe I don't.

Vin.

"I don't know where you're from," Robin states. He pulls out his phone, briefly checks the screen, then plugs it into the charger on his kitchen counter.

"Hartford," I answer.

He looks up at me. "I knew that. Cuz you're from the same place as Mike."

I lean against his dark gray ottoman but don't sit. "We went to high school together."

"I visited him there once. It's a nice city." Robin nods as he speaks, flipping through a pile of papers before dumping them into the trash.

"You were in Hartford!" I exclaim, delighted at the prospect that I might have seen him. That would explain so much. "When?"

"Let's see." He pauses in his sorting and squints at me. "Two summers ago. August."

I deflate. "I was already back here." I mentally kick my long-ago decision to be an RA that year. Stupid early return.

"I was excited, because I thought we were going to be able to get some EA stuff done." Robin drifts back over to me and takes my hands, rocking them back and forth as he looks down at them thoughtfully. "We made this cool model that we were going to show at a high school to get people interested in the group."

"What happened?" My palm brushes against his callus.

"It was dumb. On our way there, we ran into this guy who ended up smashing it."

I look up at him, startled. "Out of nowhere?"

Robin gives a quick shrug, then flips my hand over and starts tickling my palm. "It was the brother of one of his friends. I guess there was some bad history there."

I jerk my hands away and stare at Robin in horror. "Michael never…" I trail off, feeling like I'm going to vomit.

"Michael never what?" Robin looks concerned.

"He never told me that you visited. That's all." The room swims in and out of focus. I smile weakly, and change the subject. "So, do you want to finish the tour?"

"Sure. Over here is my room."

He leans through the doorway that we're standing in front of, and flips on the light. I look around approvingly. It's clean for a boy's room. A fresh scent is wafting in from the open window, making the air crisp. His sheets are a simple blue, and he has a desktop computer set up against the wall facing his bed. The only obvious chaos is the stacks of book that surround his bed. Robin stays standing as I look around, so, as soon as I'm done taking everything in, I feel comfortable flopping down on his bed.

"I like it here," I say with a nod.

"I'm glad." He continues to stand. I roll onto my stomach and look at the books he has piled by his desk. Most of them are historical nonfiction, with titles do dramatic that I want to giggle. I pick up one about Alexander the Great and examine the cover.

"This is your light reading?"

"A lot of it's for credit," Robin explains, finally sitting next to me on the bed. "I'm almost done with my history minor."

"Read to me," I say handing him the book.

"What?"

"Read to me."

"Okay," he answers. "From where I am or from the beginning?"

"Anywhere," I answer, yawning and rolling onto my back. "I just like being read to." Robin moves up until he's sitting next to me. Leaning against the backboard, he opens to where the dust jacket was tucked inside the pages.

"A man so remarkable that he was known for establishing loyalty among those that he had defeated, Alexander explored widely diverse cultures. His life was one full of exploration and expansion, beneficial to almost all. The one thing for which he lacked the foresight was producing an heir; a grievous problem when illness felled the king at thirty-three."

"Sad," I murmur, rolling onto my side to face Robin. As he continues reading, I stop hearing the words and instead just listen to his voice. It's even yet expressive with all of the gentle slopes of the road into my hometown.

I want to keep it for myself, I think, reaching forward and tangling my hand with his. *I want to lie here forever and listen. I want to keep him for myself.*

Chapter Thirteen

I'm in absolute, giddy, head-over-heels love. I'm pretty sure Robin is, too but of course I can't tell anyone because it's way too soon. I love him. I love him so much that I can't even believe how fast I've fallen. It's only been a day since I saw his home and already I feel like it's mine. I feel like he's mine. And I still don't know anything about him.

I've been infatuated before. Plenty of times. I've liked guys so much that being around them made me dizzy, been kept up all night thinking of them, that sort of thing. This is new. Being with Robin is… easy. It's beyond easy. It's as if we're scripted and have memorized every line perfectly, getting each scene down with only one take. It's like waking up early on Christmas morning. It's like being in love.

Last night after we got back from his place we went for a walk. It was Robin's idea—I was getting ready to say goodbye for the night when he pulled me away from my front door and off toward a street light illuminating the snow. We held hands; I was wearing mittens and he was wearing gloves and I felt warm despite the January wind.

There wasn't anywhere to go—campus is small and so familiar that nowhere feels like a destination. So we followed our feet, watching our footprints appear and wondering where the curved path was going to take us. We ended up in front of the Alumni Hall. Before we considered if it was time to go back or if we wanted to forge ahead into town, I flopped backwards into the snow pulling Robin down with me. The snow pillowed around us, flying up and landing gently on our coats. I giggled and inhaled, smiling upwards at the stars.

We didn't talk. We held hands, kissed a little, and laughed a lot, but we didn't talk. We didn't need to. We lay, side by side, until we shivered and had to go inside.

Of course, I'm all stuffed up today. But it was worth it. More worth it than anything has ever been.

I want to tell Pandora about last night, but she's in her room with her door closed. Before I make my way over to knock on the door, I talk myself out of it. What is there to tell? How do you say, "We lay in front of the Alumni Hall and it was perfect?" And there's still something off about her and Michael. He hasn't been around much in the past week, and Pandy's been more and more withdrawn.

I stop at her door and listen, trying to hear if she's awake. She is and, by the sound of it, Michael's here too. I hear his low rumble as he speaks, although I can't make out what he's saying. I smile and step away from the door. Michael is in there with Pandora, just as he should be, and I want some breakfast.

I walk into the kitchen and am about to see if we have any cereal left (Pandy eats ridiculous amounts at once, usually mixing many different kinds in one bowl) when my phone rings. I grin and pick it up, not even bothering to look at the caller ID.

"Hello?"

"Hey." A male voice, but certainly not the one I was expecting. My insides drop.

"Jude." He sounds drunk. I close my eyes.

"What've you been up to?"

Images of him throwing Robin's model to the ground stab at my brain. "Nothing, I'm actually busy right now so…"

"Got a boyfriend?" How can he always sense this? Every single time I've started seeing someone, no matter how secretly I've kept it, Jude has known. No sense lying to him.

"Yes. You'll meet him sometime," I lie. There is no way that I am ever, ever going to introduce Robin to Jude.

"He's no good for you, Katie. None of them are." My skin prickles.

"You don't know anything about it." I realize that I've opened the cabinet and am now staring at three brightly colored boxes of cereal. I close the door.

"This one is worse. I know it, and you do too."

"You just found out about him!" I shout in disbelief, growing cold. Remembering that Michael and Pandora are in the next room I lower my voice and hiss, "You don't even know who he is."

I don't either. The words and a chill run through me, starting at my shoulders and ending at my feet.

"Doesn't mean he's good for you. I got a feeling that this guy is trouble."

"You're trouble," I snarl. My inner mantra of *it might not be him* has shut off and now all I hear is an angry ringing. "Leave me alone, Jude. Just because there's a guy in my life now who *doesn't* screw everything up doesn't mean that you can assume that he's bad for me. If you want me to stop seeing people who are bad for me then stop calling!" I hang up the phone.

I stand shaking, staring down at the phone in my hand and feeling the tears build. Jude's words have knifed their way into my skin. But why? He doesn't know what he's talking about. He never knows what he's talking about. He's the bully, the antagonist, the worst of the worst. But somehow...

My thoughts are interrupted by Pandy's door opening. I blink hard, trying to rid my eyes of moisture but this only causes some to leak over my lids and down my cheeks. Great.

"Hey…" I say, trying to sound normal, but I stop when I see who it is. "Michael."

"You," Michael says, pointing a finger at me, "do not look good."

"Jude called," I explain feebly.

"Ah." Michael's answer is short but understanding. He regards me with concern, waiting for me to explain, or not.

"He doesn't like Robin. How he said it rubbed me the wrong way."

Michael walks over and gives me a hug. I take a shuddery breath and lean into him. His hand moves to my hair and we stay like that for a moment, until I hear the door to Pandy's room open. I leap back. Pandora stumbles out, looking sleepy and content, and blows us each a kiss. I let out my breath and subtly wipe my eyes, not ready to put this drama on Pandy.

"I'm going to go out," I say, looking to the sunshine on the lawn.

"Have fun with loverboy!" Pandy calls as I walk to the door. Funny how she knows that some Robin time is exactly what I need.

"Can we move our Valentine's Day plans to earlier?" Robin asks right after I finish pouring myself a cup of tea. My mug stays on the table.

"Why?"

"EA business. They need me that night. I was thinking we could do something in the afternoon instead."

I don't answer. Valentine's Day is not for the afternoon. Valentine's Day is for nighttime. It's for dinner and romantic movies and cuddling under heaps of warm blankets and kissing. It's not for lunch; it's not for a date squeezed in before the more important work plans; it's not for the EA. "Who all will be there?" I finally ask.

"Can't say," replies Robin, shaking his head after he tosses back the last of his coffee before helping himself to another cup. I watch critically as the brown liquid fills his mug.

"Why not?"

"It's not my place."

"Whatever," I say, turning away and leaving my drink on the counter.

"Are you okay?" I hear concern—and confusion—in Robin's voice, but I don't turn around.

"Fine," I answer as lightly and dismissively as I can. I pick up one of his books from a nearby table and begin flipping through it without seeing any of the words.

"We can watch the movie in the afternoon," he says gently. I hear his chair push backwards, and a second later I feel a hand on my shoulder.

"Sure. Fine. That'll work." I squeeze my eyes shut as I feel Robin's arms slip around my waist just like they did yesterday. This time, though, it's very different. "The afternoon is fine." I'll have to make other plans. But with whom? Pandy probably has plans with Michael. Michael wouldn't ditch Valentine's Day for the EA.

"We could do it a different day…"

I soften. He's trying. In his silence I can hear his uncertainty, and finally I turn to face him. I should try too. "Let's do it a different day."

"You look nice," I say, smiling at Pandora from my perch on the edge of the tub. She finishes dabbing on her cherry red lipstick, and smiles back as she clicks the tube shut.

"Thanks," she says, twirling to show me the full effect of her outfit. She's in a puffy red dress that looks more like it's meant for Christmas than Valentine's Day, and has a red bow clipped into her curls. She's donned a shade of lipstick that matches her outfit exactly. The whole getup makes her look adorable and painted, like something you would see in a shop window. "Are you ready to go?"

"Yup," I say, getting to my feet. My outfit is significantly less impressive: I'm wearing black slacks (admittedly my best-fitting pair) and a crimson loose-sleeved cowl-neck top emphasized by a heart shaped necklace that Pandy gave me when we were fourteen. I've straightened my hair for dramatic effect, but besides a little mascara I decided to go au natural.

Pandy gives a jump and a clap, then skims out into the hallway. I laugh and follow her, feeling encouraged but unable to muster up her level of enthusiasm.

Michael, it turns out, also has EA business tonight. Administrative stuff, he claimed as he gave Pandy a kiss on the cheek. They need him there while the others go out. No one has told us what's going on, but Robin did ask to borrow my memory card. I've tried to make something of this clue, but can't.

Instead of moping, Pandy has taken Michael's absence as a challenge. She's drawn out an exciting plan for the two of us, spanning from the moment Michael walked out the door until possibly two or three a.m. day after tomorrow. I'm grateful for her company—as well as her enthusiasm—but I'm doubtful that I'll be able to keep up. My mind keeps wandering (more like missiling) back to the EA's mysterious Valentine's Day project. For all of Robin's claims that he likes to stay out of the sketchy parts of the group's missions, I find it interesting that he can't tell me what's going on tonight. But I'm determined to trust him so trust him I will. All thoughts of moonlit liaisons with Vin are firmly banished.

"Come on!" Pandy calls over her shoulder.

I pick up my pace and join her at the door. Pandy slides on her black satin Mary Janes and I stuff my feet into my new chocolate ankle boots. Step one, Pandy has decided, is to go to as many of the local college haunts as we can think of, see who we can get to feel sorry for us, and score as many free drinks and treats as we can. We decide to start with Café Labrador: a favorite of the TU crowd.

Walking in is a disappointment. There are only a few people there, which is a little surprising. I guess most people are above bringing their Valentine's date to a coffee shop. I see only a few couples and one group of three guys sitting around a table, deliberately drinking coffee while typing on their computers.

"This place is dead. Let's go," I say, jerking my head toward the door.

"Nope," Pandy answers with a shake of her head and flounces over to the guys at the table.

"Pandy…" I hiss, snatching her by her wrist, "they're studying. They don't want a distraction."

"Oh, they want a distraction," she assures me. She takes the last few steps until she's right in front of them. Despite my mortification, I can't help but smile. This reminds me so much of how things started with Michael. "Felix!"

The shortest of the guys looks up. I vaguely recognize him from a class I took with Pandora our second year. He's skinny with blond hair, a wide mouth, and intelligent eyes. "Hello, Pandora," he says formally.

"My friend Katie and I were abandoned by our men tonight. Do you boys mind if we join you for some studying?" She's addressing the whole table now.

Felix nods and moves his chair toward the wall to make room but one of his table mates, a big, dark haired guy in a Game of Thrones t-shirt, holds up a hand. "Two gorgeous women such as yourselves shouldn't be studying tonight."

"Especially since you're all dressed up pretty," says the third contestant, a brown-haired hipster who might be trying to come across as gay, but is obviously straight.

"We don't want to bother you," I say quickly, marveling at how quickly Pandora works.

"We want to be bothered," replies the big one, and he rises and pulls two chairs forward.

Half an hour later, we're at a karaoke bar with Mr. Game of Thrones (Garth) watching the definitely-straight guy (Thomas) perform "Man, I Feel Like a Woman". Felix elected to go home after our venue change. Pandy has selected Garth to be her date, and Thomas volunteered to be mine. Pandy is flirting and teasing, and I'm laughing so hard that my stomach hurts.

"How do you do this?" I gasp, wiping tears from my eyes.

"You just gotta want it," Pandy says with a grin, taking a sip from her mug of beer.

"I guess you do." I shake my head and move in as Thomas rejoins us.

"That was magical," Garth tells him somberly.

"I know," Tom answers. I look at Pandy to see if she wants to do California Gurls with me (a perfect choice for winter in New England) when I see her reach into her purse and pull out her phone.

"Hey baby," she sings. "I miss you. But guess what we've been up to?" She pauses for a moment and her expression goes from delighted to puzzled.

"It's for you," she says, handing me the phone.

"Mike!" I cry, leaning back into the plastic of the booth. "What's up my brother?" I probably sound drunk. Maybe I'm drunk by osmosis.

"Katie. Listen." I listen. After he's done talking I hang up the phone.

"What?" asks Pandy, paused in her smile to see what I'm going to say.

"We have to go," I say, pushing my way out of the booth to get to my feet. Pandy, understanding the urgency in my voice, gives a quick nod to the guys and follows me outside.

"What's going on?" she asks, her voice sober.

"We need to get downtown. Robin's been arrested."

Chapter Fourteen

I've never been in a police station before. I was expecting something solemn and maybe a little dramatic but this just feels... bureaucratic. Pandy and I are sitting on uncomfortable slippery chairs while Michael stands at the front. He's talking quietly with the man behind the protective glass. I strain my ears to hear what's being said, but I can't make out any distinct words. Eventually, Michael comes back and sits beside us.

"They're bringing him out," Michael says. He reaches over and gives my hand a reassuring squeeze. I nod and take a deep breath, trying to process the last half hour.

Michael picked us up outside the karaoke bar. It wasn't until I was inside the car that I noticed that Pandora's coat was around my shoulders. And that I was shaking. It took me a bit to find my voice.

"What happened?" I finally managed to ask. Michael pulled quietly onto the highway, his headlights strong against the falling snow.

"He got picked up for trespassing." He wouldn't tell me anything more and we all spent the ride to the police station in silence. Now, I'm leaning against Pandora's shoulder feeling exhausted, scared, tired, and sad.

"Do we have to pay bail?" I have my wallet with me but I don't have much, only a couple hundred on my card. Will that be enough? How much does bail cost for someone on trespassing charges?

The door opens with a mechanical groan and Robin walks out escorted by a cop who hands him a plastic bag with a wallet and cell phone it in. Robin takes the bag.

I stand uncertainly, not at all sure what to do. I want to run over and hug him and tell him everything will be okay. But I don't recognize the way he's standing, or the expression on his face. He's looking at the door.

"Let's go," says Michael. He puts an arm around Pandy's shoulders and heads for the door. I wait for Robin but he walks past me without pausing. I quicken my pace to catch up.

"Are you okay?" I ask, breathless from the speed and the cold. Robin doesn't answer.

We gather in front of the car and wait for Michael to retrieve his keys, but before he can pull his hand out of his pocket Robin grabs him by the collar and punches Michael in the face.

Pandy screams. Michael staggers backwards, unable to regain his balance with one of his hands compromised. He falls back against the car, hitting it with a thud. He struggles to straighten, wrenching his hand free from his pocket. He's holding his keys. Pandora and I stand for a shocked second, waiting to see what will happen next. Michael unlocks the car.

"Let's go."

Robin turns and strides away, disappearing at an alarming rate. "I have to…" I say, turning helplessly to my friends.

"Go," says Michael, and I break into a sprint, finally catching up with Robin.

"Hey. Hey!" I grab his coat sleeve and he finally stops. "What happened?" Robin finally looks down at me. I grab onto his gaze, silently pleading with him. *Tell me what's going on. Let me in.*

"Have Michael explain that to you," he says eventually.

"Robin…" He starts walking again. "Stop!" I yell, stomping my foot. "This isn't fair. Tell me what's going on!"

Robin stops and I see his shoulders slump. Once back in front of me, he bends down and kisses my cheek. "I'll call you later," he says, and lopes away, leaving me alone in the snow.

I don't know how long it is before I feel Pandora's hand on my shoulder. I feel bad. I should be comforting her; we should both be comforting Michael. I'm stunned into paralysis by Robin's display of violence. He wouldn't tell me anything. He was violent and angry. He had just been arrested and he strode away without giving me a second thought. He hit someone I loved without a reason, without an explanation. He hit someone because his own mood was off base.

Familiar. Everything is familiar again. But this time, it's not in the way that's been haunting me since before our first meeting. I sink down to the ground and let the snow cover my pants.

It's familiar because of Jude.

"I'm sorry," I say. I realize that I'm crying. I pull my knees up to my face, letting my bones dig into my eyes. My chest begins to heave as my throat, eyes, and nose, clog up with confusion, anger, and grief. "I'm so sorry. I don't know what happened. I don't know what he... I don't know anything. I'm sorry."

"Shh." Pandy's hand is on my head. I feel her crouching next to me. Her dress must be in the snow. She must be cold and wet but still, here she is down on the ground next to me because I'm crying, even though it was my boyfriend that hit hers. I raise my head and see that Michael is standing on my other side. He extends a hand and I take it, letting him pull me to my feet. I cough and shudder, then wipe my eyes with numb fingers.

"Are you okay?" I can't see any bruising or swelling on his face; the cold must be keeping it down. I see that his mouth is bleeding.

"Still kicking. In a line of work like the EA, you take a few hits."

I shake my head numbly. Snow falls onto my neck. "Not like this. I mean, you went and you bailed him out of jail and he–"

"It's not the first time." Michael cuts me off with a jerk of his shoulder.

"What?" Horror snakes through me. I snatch Pandy's hand, as if my friend can fight off whatever it is that Michael is telling me.

"Not with Robin, don't worry." He laughs softly and puts his hand on my head. "The EA can be tougher than people expect. They want someone to blame."

"Emotions must run pretty high after something like this," Pandy explains, returning my squeeze.

"Has he hit anyone before?" I'm sad and shaken like I just fell from a bike. I don't understand. I don't understand any of it.

"No." Michael puts an arm around my shoulder and I fall into it while Pandy strokes my hair.

"I don't want him to be like Jude," I squeak as new tears form.

"He's not," Pandy says soothingly. "He's not."

It's not until the following morning that I feel ready to hear the whole story. After getting home last night, I stumbled into bed and slept the heavy sleep that follows tears. Unfortunately, true to form, I woke up today with my whole head pulsing. After a breakfast of aspirin, I sit down on our couch with a mug of tea and wait for Michael to explain.

He's leaning forward and resting his wrists on his knees. A bruise developed overnight and now the left side of Michael's face is mottled with red and dark purple. At least he's washed his mouth so the dried cracks of blood are gone. "How much do you know about last night's project?"

"Nothing," I say, shaking my head. "Or, no, actually…" I remember the request Robin made, the day before Valentine's Day. My one clue. "He asked me for a memory card for his camera. It involved taking pictures?"

Michael nods. I sip my tea, stalling my speech until my feelings can rush by. I'm the EA photographer; if it involved pictures, why didn't he ask me? Did he know he was going to get arrested? Probably not, by the way he reacted, but he must have suspected some element of danger. Why did he go? I swallow my tea.

"I'm not going to get into details but basically we were collecting evidence."

"Evidence for what?"

"There have been some less-than-safe chemicals showing up around town. We're trying to track it, get the guys that are leaving the dirty trails, and find out what's in them."

I balk. "Do you have any suspects?" The question is cartoonish. I imagine myself with a blonde bob, leaning in breathlessly to see what Michael knows. *Oh do tell me, detective.* Of course, in that scenario, I'm probably the culprit.

"I can't tell you that. Not yet. It turns out that they're all owned by the same parent company. That's what last night was about."

"And you're planning a lawsuit against them?"

Michael cracks his knuckles. I flinch at the popping sound and shift my hair to cover my ears. "Nothing we've collected so far can be used in court, but it's becoming increasingly evident that we have to do something. Last night proved that."

I nod. It makes sense. I take another sip of my tea and after the taste of chamomile has faded I ask, "Why does Robin blame you for his arrest?"

"I was back at headquarters. He didn't get my message that cops were heading that way until too late."

"That's not fair." I shake my head. "You spend your Valentine's Day on this thing and end up coming down to jail to bail him out then he punches you because he didn't check his phone soon enough? No. No. That's unacceptable."

Michael reaches forward and puts a hand on my knee. "Drink your tea." I oblige, swallowing too much at once and wincing as the painful bulge works its way down my throat.

"It's not fair to you." I protest once I can speak again.

"Getting arrested wasn't fair to Robin."

I sit for a long time, staring at the tea bag sagging at the bottom of my mug. "Okay," I say finally, putting my mug down onto its coaster. The couch is soft, and I'm tired. The throbbing in my head has lessened, but my whole body still aches. I lean back and close my eyes, blocking out the sunlight and the sight of Michael's bruised face. "Okay."

He said he'd call me, so I wait. I wait, and wait, and wait until I am ready to throw my phone at the wall, scream, and swear that I'll never speak to Robin again. Then I wait some more. Finally, as the day is drawing to a close and I've given in to my more pressing homework assignments my phone begins to buzz.

About time.

"Hi." I'm not sure how to manage my tone; I'm angry and relieved all at the same time so my greeting comes out strangled and flat.

"Hey there, Kate!" His voice is warm and charming. There isn't a hint of apology to be found. I scowl and put my hand over my face.

"What?" I ask crankily.

There's a moment's pause then he asks, "Are you okay?"

"Am I okay?" I sit up, my blood pounding furiously in my head. "Robin, you get arrested last night, punch Michael when he bails you out, then take off without telling me anything about what's going on! Yeah, I'm just dandy."

Silence. My adrenaline lessens and I flop backwards again. "Listen…" I begin, but he interrupts me.

"I'm really sorry."

I nod, swallowing. "I know."

"The whole situation is just a lot more messed up than you know."

"I guess. I talked to Michael. He filled me in a little." I'm winding the blue fringe of my blanket around my finger watching the material be pulled up and then slip away over and over again.

Robin doesn't answer right away. Then, "I'm guessing Michael didn't tell you everything."

"No, he didn't. But he explained why you were upset."

I hear breath on the other end of the line, static-y and unnatural. "That's one I'd like to hear."

"He said that you blame him for the arrest."

"It's one way of putting it."

"Do you?" The blanket slips out of my grasp and slithers back down onto the bed.

"Yup." We're both quiet. Finally, Robin says, "We need to do Valentine's Day."

"No, don't worry about it," I say automatically and I watch my inner martyr crawl out. I bite my lip. I do want to do Valentine's Day, but at this point I don't know what we can do that will be any fun. I'm feeling wronged and sad, and don't want to use my energy pretending that everything is okay. "I'm not big into Valentine's Day anyway."

"Alright," Robin says, and I feel my chance at romance click shut. "Do you want to come over later anyway?"

"Sure." My phone beeps to let me know that the call has ended. I pull my feet under me, trying to warm them up.

Despite my exhausted mix of disappointment and anxiety, as soon as I step through the door of Robin's apartment I feel like I'm home. Robin, or the idea of Robin, had been collecting strangeness in my head ever since the arrest, but the moment my eyes land on him standing at the stove and stirring something in a pot, everything settles. He turns and raises his eyebrows in delight as he licks sauce off a wooden spoon.

"What are you doing?" I ask, walking over and looking down at his concoction. It bubbles and hisses menacingly at me, sending up a splash of tomato that nearly hits my shirt.

"I'm making us dinner." He puts the spoon into my mouth and it's my turn for my eyes to water.

"This is good! Did you make it yourself?"

Robin nods. "Pasta isn't the most original meal but it goes with the theme."

"What's the theme?" I ask, looking around the apartment. I notice that he's pulled out some hardcovers from his shelves and left them in deliberate stacks around the room. I walk over to the nearest one, searching for clues in the title. *The Davinci Code.* Uh oh. This could go over my head pretty quickly.

"I didn't have much time to get decorations," Robin explains, his hands sheepishly in his pockets.

"For what?" I pick up *The Davinci Code* and start flipping through.

"What do you notice about all these books?" He guides my hand back down to the nearest stack and I examine it again.

"They're all…" I'm stumped. Beneath the next book in the stack is *Emma.* "Classics?"

"Maybe I should have stuck with just one theme. They're all either red," He brandishes *The Davinci Code*, "or love stories." He holds up *Emma.*

"That's…" I look around, trying to find the words. "That's… Wow." I see it now. There's an old copy of Catcher in the Rye, and over there a hardbound copy of Romeo and Juliet. I pick up *Emma* and hug it to me. "I love it."

Robin grins in the way that he has that lights up his whole face. Nothing is held back or calculated; it's a pure expression of joy. He pulls me to him and hugs me tightly, and I return the gesture, wrapping my arms around his waist.

"The food," he says abruptly, and drops our embrace to run over to the stove. I laugh as I watch him turn off the gas, and dip the wooden spoon back into the mixture. He pulls out a heaping spoonful, sticks his tongue right into the middle, then drops the whole thing. "Hot!"

After he tips his head and runs water over his tongue I ask, "How does it taste?"

"I can't tell cuz my tongue got burned off." He straightens and wipes his mouth with a dishcloth.

"Let me try." I retrieve some of the mixture from the pot, then carefully sip a little into my mouth. "Perfect. I think it's done."

Robin gets out two bowls, fills them to the brim with pasta and pours his steaming red sauce over them. It smells heavenly. After giving us each a pair of chopsticks (an ill-advised choice, I can't help thinking), Robin leads me to the couch where we're surrounded by stacks of DVDs.

"Are these decorations too?" I ask, flipping through the first pile.

"These are our options. There's Netflix too, but I wanted to make sure we could watch something you like."

"Where did you get all these?" There are classics, action, romances, movies I love, movies I like, movies I hate, movies I've never seen, and even a photography documentary.

"All over. I had some already, and borrowed most of the others."

"That's..." I try to speak again, and fail. I pretend to be examining the cover of *Robin Hood* while I collect myself.

"I didn't know what kind of movies you like. I wanted to make sure you had a good Valentine's Day."

I lean onto his shoulder and close my eyes. He smells like spices and salt and somehow like ink. "I like you," I murmur.

"I like you too," he says, kissing the top of my head.

"Let's watch this one." I hand him a movie picked up at random.

"Good choice."

The movie turns out to be an old comedy starring a young Peter Sellers. I laugh hard through the first part but by halfway I find my eyes growing heavy. Before I know it, Robin is gently shaking my shoulder and asking if I'm awake.

"Is it over?" I ask, straightening up and rubbing my eyes. My neck aches from leaning against Robin's shoulder. My mouth feels sticky and swollen.

"Yeah."

"What happened?"

"You'll have to see it yourself." The screen glows blue and starts letting out an almost inaudible hum. When I was a kid, the TV would crackle after a movie. I used to run my palm over the whole thing until all of the static was gone.

"Not tonight," I yawn. I lift my arms above my head and stretch, willing energy to come back to my body. "I don't know why I'm so tired."

"Poor little Kate," Robin says, running a hand over my hair. This doesn't help my fatigue at all. I shake my head and struggle back to alertness.

"I don't want to go outside," I groan, thinking of the cold walk out to the car.

"You're welcome to stay," Robin offers. I blink, now wide-awake.

"Would that be okay?" I ask uncertainly. I don't want him to think I was fishing for an invitation, but if he really wants me here...

"Sure. I can give you something to sleep in."

"Okay." He gets up and rummages through some plastic drawers before pulling out a button-down shirt and a pair of sweats.

"Thanks," I say. I pause for a moment, then head out to the bathroom to get changed. When I return, I am wrapped safely in what seems like yards of his clothing, and he's changed into a t-shirt and a pair of shorts. I climb happily into bed, nestling close to him and pulling his arm beneath my head as a pillow. He chuckles and rests his hand on the back of my head for a moment before reaching over and turning out the light.

He falls asleep before I do but it doesn't take long for exhaustion to get to me. I fight it off for as long as I can, watching Robin sleep. It doesn't seem real that he's here. It feels like he could just disappear. I want to stay awake and watch him so I can be sure that he's still lying next to me, but before I can help it, sleep overtakes me and I plunge into oblivion.

Chapter Fifteen

Where is he? I jolt awake, breathing hard as I ascertain my surroundings. That same nightmare. I burrow my face into Robin's shoulder, breathing deeply and clutching his shirt. He's right here. He didn't leave. He's right here. Robin shifts and I release my grip to avoid strangulation.

"I'm going to go get some water," I whisper. He responds with a snore. I crawl out from the warm sheets and pad into the kitchen where I help myself to a bottle of water from the fridge. I crack it open and sip, trying to force myself back into a sleepy state. The kitchen clock reads 4:13; I'm going to hate myself if I don't go back to sleep. I take another gulp of water, but my body stays tense and jittery.

I rise from the stool and begin looking through his books, left out from earlier. They cover nearly every subject and the whole collection is almost entirely nonfiction. I look at title after title, fascinated by Robin's wide field of interests. I wonder how many of these he's actually read. I browse through the titles until I come across one that stops me in my tracks.

Untold: The Lost Story of Lady Katharine Valen. Valen. Robin's name. I reach forward to touch it but before my hand can reach the spine a sound makes me jump away.

"What are you doing?" Robin is standing sleepily in the doorway to his bedroom. I give a guilty shrug. "Come back to bed," he yawns, walking past me toward the bathroom. He gives me a kiss as he moves by. I realize I've shifted so that I'm blocking the book's title from view. The door to the bathroom clicks shut and I snag the book from the shelf before obediently walking back into the bedroom and climb back into the sheets. Sleep seems even farther away than before.

I reach down and shove the book deep inside my purse. *Tomorrow,* I think. *Tomorrow I'll get Robin to read it to me.* Yes, that seems like a good idea. And now sleep swoops over me, and my eyes fall shut. I'm gone before Robin comes back.

Sure enough, I'm almost too exhausted to make it to class in the morning. Robin, unfortunately, seems to be a morning person. His belligerent pillow-whacking on my head forces into consciousness. I groan in protest but rise, my internal time calculations telling me to get moving. As I stumble around, collecting my things, I spot the corner of last night's book sticking out of my bag. Before I muster up the words I need in order to ask if I can borrow it (speaking in the morning is nearly impossible), a piece of toast is shoved into my mouth. The next thing I know, I'm being shepherded out the door and into the car. The cold air rouses me, bringing me out of my sleepy shell. By the time I get to my apartment, I'm starting to feel like I might be a human again.

"See you," I say, giving Robin a kiss through the window. He waves to me as he drives away and I head inside, desperate to warm up. "I'm home!" I sing as I step through the door.

"Where have you been young lady?" Pandy is walking through the living room with a towel wrapped around her hair.

"Robin's," I say smugly, walking into my room for a fresh pair of clothes. Pandy follows me in and I see that she's grinning.

"Tell me," she commands, "what happened." Her eyebrows are raised expectantly.

"Nothing like that," I say, taking off my shirt and pulling on a new one, "We did Valentine's Day. We watched a movie and by the time it was done I was tired so I stayed over."

"Boo," Pandy pouts. I toss my discarded shirt playfully at her.

"I'm not that easy."

Pandy rolls her eyes. "You are the opposite of easy. Hey, question, what did Michael end up saying was the reason for Robin's attack?"

I stall, straightening my sock. "I guess just that Robin feels like Michael should have kept him safe. He was back at base or something." I pull my hand away from my foot and begin to fidget with the buttons on my shirt. I'm still not sure how I feel about this. Last night with Robin was amazing but… he punched my best friend out of his own emotional weakness. It's too similar.

"Huh." Pandy's tone catches me off guard and I look over at her. She's leaning against my door frame, examining her nails. Her red Valentine's Day manicure is still pristine.

"I know it's stupid," I say quickly, rising to Robin's defense. "I know it is. But I think he shaken up, and wanted someone to blame. He's never been arrested before…"

"I don't think that's what happened."

"What? What do you think happened?" I eye her nervously. She lifts her head and shakes her curls back before fixing her calm gaze on me. I shrink back, not wanting to hear why she thinks Robin did what he did to Michael. I don't want to know.

"I think Michael called the police."

"What?" I hit my bed, hard. The wooden post knocks into the back of my thigh and I rock back in forth, pain battling shock and confusion. "Why?" Pandy doesn't say anything. I try again. "Why would Michael call the police?"

"That I don't know," she says thoughtfully. "It seems strange to sabotage your own mission."

"Uh, yeah," I scoff. Ouch, this is going to bruise. "Why would you think that? Did he say something?"

"No," answers Pandy, her voice mild. Her thumb is to her lips and her blue eyes are fixed on the poster over my bed. "I just think he did."

"I gotta get to class," I say, forcing myself to my feet. My leg groans in protest and I limp over to my dresser to grab my purse.

"Okay." Pandy's still looking at my wall looking lost in thought.

"I don't think he did it," I say as I walk by her. Pandy shrugs, breaking out of her reverie.

"Maybe. I'll see you after class?"

"Yeah."

Pandy plants a kiss on my cheek then floats into her room before closing the door gently behind her.

As many pictures as I take, and no matter how many I look at and edit, the one from Halloween is still the best. Every time I look at it, I can feel myself receiving the letter, email, or call, telling me I've won. The girl in the picture is beautiful, mischievous, dynamic, holding a lit firework over her head, her face halfway obscured in shadows. Her hair is flying in every direction, reflecting the explosive light. It's trouble, beauty, sexuality, and power all wrapped into one. But there's something relatable about it. The parts you can see of the subject could almost be anyone. I imagine looking at it hanging on the wall next to a photograph by Annie Leibovitz as agents from the art scene discover that I'm the next big thing.

"It's great, but I don't think you should stop trying," Geri says, after I tell her yet again that this is the one that I want to enter. "It's smart to try as many times as you can before you settle on your final choice. You might surprise yourself."

I already did, I think, slipping the print back into my bag and getting ready to go.

"How is the EA essay coming?"

"Fine." The strap of my camera bag hangs loosely around my shoulders. I tighten it, feeling ready to leave. I'm trying to conceal my anger at the EA. I joined, hoping that they would help me forward. As it is, they've forced me to sit in that dark little room again and again. Then, when something is actually happening, something that needs pictures, I'm left alone. "I still need to get them in action."

"Time is ticking away," Geri reminds me. "I want us to shift our focus to the contest."

"We will," I assure her. I don't tell her that mine already has. Almost every night is spent looking through my pictures, trying to visualize which ones I'll put in my first published photo book. I always return to my winning piece.

I check the time, give Geri a pleasant wave, then I dip out the door and go to find Robin. He's sitting by the lobby door in one of the school's famous plush chairs. His laptop sits open in his lap. I smile at his look of concentration.

"Whatcha working on?" I ask, plopping down next to him and looking over his shoulder. He tips his computer away from me.

"EA stuff."

I scoot half an inch over. He scoots half an inch away. "Stuff I can't see?"

"Sorry," he takes my hand and kisses it, his eyes still on the computer.

"It's okay. I do need to get some shots of you guys in action though."

"Yeah." Robin's keyboard is louder than his voice. He's typing so rapidly that I wonder how his brain can keep up. "Almost done," he says distractedly.

While I wait, I pull out my camera and start reviewing some of the recent pictures I took of the beach to see if anything might be contest-worthy. After a couple minutes I feel someone standing in front of us. Robin and I look up at the same time.

"Vin." He shuts his laptop and stands up to offer her a hug. She returns it and I massage my wrists until they're done.

"Hey, you." Vin smiles lazily at me. I'm pretty sure that she doesn't know who I am.

I give her a tight wave, then look at Robin. "Ready to bolt?"

"Yeah, just one second. Vin."

Vin looks up at him. "Hm?" God, she is so *tiny*. She can't be more than five-one and looks like I could break her in half. Her hair is long in the way that adds artificial beauty points. I watch it swish across her lower back, the chestnut version of something a prince could climb up.

"You did good work with the summary. Were the pictures anything we can use?"

"Um…" She tips her head to the side, tapping her foot. "I think so. They seemed pretty good."

"That's something, anyway." Robin's face echoes the anger I saw on Valentine's day. Vin watches him blandly.

"Gotta go." She graces us with another slow smile and saunters out the door. *Her hair.*

"Robin," I say casually as I watch him gather his stuff, "what's her deal?"

"What do you mean?" Robin straightens, offers me his hand, and slings his bag onto his shoulder.

I take his hand and focus on indifference. "First of all, what kind of a name is 'Vin'?" Despite my best efforts, a cranky tone is slipping through.

"It's short for Virginia." Robin gets the door for me and I walk through, waiting for him once I'm clear of the frame. "Anything else?"

I know it's not a good time to bring up Michael but I don't know of any other way to ask the question that's been bothering me. "Did anything ever happen between you two?"

"Nope."

No way around it. "So, why did Michael say...?"

"What?" Robin stops abruptly and looks at me. "Michael said what?"

"Nothing!" I blink in surprise. "He didn't tell me anything. He just mentioned something about how you have something to tell me about Vin."

Rolling his eyes, Robin begins walking again. I hurry along with him. "Michael doesn't know jack. He says stuff just to get people going."

That doesn't sound like Michael to me. "What's going on with you guys?" I insist, catching his sleeve. "Will you slow down?"

"Sorry," Robin drops his pace. "Don't worry about Michael." The mixture of the half-run I just did and the unseasonably warm weather prompts me to remove my sweater. I slip out of it and Robin takes it from me.

"I'm not worried about Michael," I tell him, crossing my arms over my chest. "I'm worried about Vin."

Robin gently puts an arm around my waist. "Why are you worried about anything?" he asks.

Because... "Because it's a pretty girl that Michael hinted you have a history with!"

Robin shifts my sweater over to his other arm and adjusts his grip on my waist. "I never wanted to date Vin."

"That's good to hear," I say, breathing out. I can't relax completely, though, because there are plenty of things you can want to do with someone that isn't dating.

"We used to be close, though. Before things got complicated."

I frown. "Complicated in what way?"

"The EA pushes you. I was pushed to get it together, Vin was pushed the other way." I nod. She's sensitive. Fragile. Emotional. Things I was never allowed to be. She's the tiny girl with the porcelain heart and I'm the one with the frizzy hair and the brother that made me grow up too fast.

"So, what?" I ask flatly.

"It was hard to be close to her after that. I still try to be like a brother, though." I fight back a bark of laughter. A brother. I hope not. "How's your contest entry going?"

I can't help but grin at this question. "Perfectly. I have such awesome picture. Geri wants me to keep looking, but I know this is the best one."

Robin squeezes my hand in support. "When do I get to see it?"

"When it's ready." My phone in my pocket begins to hum merrily; for once I actually have the ringer on. "It's my mom," I say checking the screen. "Hi, Mom!"

"Hey, kiddo."

I stop. After taking a deep breath I make an apologetic gesture to Robin and duck off onto a side path. "What do you want, Jude?"

"Just want to see how things are." He doesn't sound drunk. Huh.

"I'm fine. Busy." I keep my tone clipped. Can't he drop his social calls?

"Figured."

I rub my hand over my stomach, trying to massage away the guilt. "You're at home now?"

"If that's what you want to call it."

"Give it time," I urge. I want him to think that I mean that everything will smooth over. He knows what I mean. Give me time.

"Call me sometime, kid."

"I will," I promise, or lie, and then hang up. I stare at a green little bug that's crawling over a leaf. It's at the very edge, and for a moment it looks like it's going to fall off. Instead, it begins to move along the underside. I take out my camera and snap a picture. Robin is waiting where I left him.

"Sorry," I say breezily. "My mom forgot her ATM pin."

"You know your mom's ATM pin?"

"No." My camera bag digs into my shoulders and I wiggle around, trying to straighten out the strap. "I have to go and do some homework."

"Don't do your homework," Robin catches my hand and spins me to face him. "Hang out with me."

"Later," I laugh, pulling away and smoothing out my hair.

"Fine." He gives me a kiss, then ambles off in the direction of his car. He waves at a couple people going by, then turns the corner and drops out of sight. I slide down against a nearby tree and close my eyes. It's easy to be charmed. It's easy for people to be nice. But how many times does a guy need to get arrested before I'm done?

Chapter Sixteen

I'm in my room, the door is locked, and my heart is pounding. The book from Robin's apartment lies in my lap. Valen. The story of a Valen. I wonder which one.

I shouldn't have taken it from Robin's apartment. It might be a special book, a family one. But I can't help being pulled in. It's a story for me. Another story. Another ending. I want to explore.

Lady Katharine Valen. Why does the name sound familiar? Did I learn about her in school? Read about her in one of my fairytales? The title of the book proclaims her story was lost. I wonder how she ended up winding around the world to fall into my lap. I stroke the cover almost protectively, before opening the book.

I pass by the beginning words. Beginnings never tell you much of anything, anyway. This one is probably telling me why the author is interested in this story. I don't care about that. I care about why I'm interested.

I turn the page and am greeted by a full, glossy print of a painting. A man and a woman, neither one's face visible to the viewer, are holding each other tightly. Starlight pours down into their hair, the woman's glistening red and the man's an oaky brown. I gasp aloud at the beauty of it, and run my hand over the page, mesmerized by the scene. Her dress tumbles freely past her waist and onto the ground, swirling in the wind and wrapping around the man's leg. They look complete together.

I hold the book up to my chest, embracing the picture before I turn to the next page. The second picture freezes my lungs. The third chills my body. I turn page after page, letting color and chaos fill my eyes until I can't look at any more. Then, I go back and read the words.

It was a love story and it ended in ice. There was no fire, no fairies, no witches, no spells. There was heartbreak and a woman who refused to accept it. So she painted. These are those paintings.

I hurt. I hurt all over, from my head right down to my soles. I read for hours and hours and then cried after that. Then I read some more. Soreness pulses behind my forehead and eyes and my neck complains from lack of care. My elbows are angry from having been leaned on and my hands are heavy from holding the hardcover. My chest simply aches.

Images from the story stir dizzily in my head like a fever dream. Stale air, skin, too much food, shouting, and paint. Paint on the canvas, bright and brash and naked. What is this? I'm sweating. My hands cling to the cover of the book and I pull them away.

Robin can't have read this; the pages had that new book shyness, sticking together and needing to be coaxed apart. I was probably more violent than I should have been, but my desperation for the words kept me moving quickly. I tore one of the corners.

I wonder where he got it. Was it a present? An impulse buy because of the name? One of those things that shows up and you never quite know how? I bet he hasn't read most of his books. What other kind of information is hiding in that room full of maps?

It's dark. Maybe midnight. I don't know. When I first moved here, nighttime was an impossible luxury that stretched out in hours of anonymity. I could use the time for myself and feel as though I was no closer to morning that I was an hour ago. Now I feel lost. Do I sleep? Can I?

My phone answers the question by bursting into song. Robin. It's late. It's one o'clock in the morning. Why is he calling? Blood pumping, I answer in a panic.

"Hello?"

"Kate? I need the memory card that I borrowed."

"Now?" I wrinkle my face in confusion.

"Now. We're working all night to try and get ready for our next event."

"What's the next event?"

"Can't tell you yet, but it might be a good time for you to take pictures."

About time. "Do I need to bring the card to you?"

"No. I'll come and get it."

I hang up my phone and look for the SD card, which I find wedged between some books on my desk. I decide to kill some time while waiting for Robin by looking through what's on it.

Most of the pictures make no sense to me. There are pipes and puddles and signs that seem to be telling me to be careful. I spot one with Robin's shoe in it and another with someone's coat. My pictures come after, light, colorful, and almost childish compared to the implications behind Robin's set. I open up my contest picture and fiddle with the lighting.

Robin knocks softly on the front door. I tiptoe out to let him.

"Do you have it?" he asks. I nod and hand it to him. "Thanks," he says.

I see him raise the black piece of plastic to the light, making sure it's the right one. Then, without a moment's hesitation, he snaps it cleanly down the middle.

"What are you doing?" I shriek. Then, remembering Pandy sleeping in the next room, I clap my hand over my mouth. "Inside," I hiss, shoving Robin through the door to my room. "What are you doing?" I demand again.

"Some of the pictures I took have evidence of who was there. I needed to get rid of it."

"My pictures!" I splutter in outrage. "That was mine! You can't, you can't just-" I'm too angry to form complete sentences.

"You have them elsewhere, right?"

"That was my card! You can't borrow it, then come in and break it!" Anger shakes my body. I want to hit him.

Robin pauses, and I see his demeanor change. "I'll buy you a new card," he promises, running a hand through his hair. He slumps onto my bed. "We messed up, and got some shots that we shouldn't have."

"You could have asked me!" No, I do not want to start crying. I will not. I won't. I take a few steadying breaths and force my voice into a calmer register. "You can't borrow, contaminate, and then break my stuff, Robin."

He puts his face into his hands, and I use the opportunity to wipe away some of the moisture that has collected around my eyes. "I didn't think. I'm sorry. We were looking through those pictures tonight, and I saw something that shouldn't be there, and I panicked."

"I get it." I slump down next to him. The shattered pieces lie forgotten on the comforter. "They're not expensive." I wrap my arms around myself.

"I'll buy you a new one," he says again. I feel his hand on my shoulder, and jerk away. I don't want him to touch me.

"If they already knew you were there," I say, more to keep him distracted than because I care, "then what do you need to hide?"

"What's that?" Robin's tone changes and I see he's staring at my computer screen. I reach over and snap my computer shut, feeling suddenly self-conscious.

"My contest entry."

"You have to delete that."

"What?"

"That's Vin. You have to delete that."

"I'm not deleting it!" I move so to stand protectively in front of my computer and glare at Robin.

Robin picks his coat up off the bed. "I have to get back. We'll talk about this later. Don't show it to anyone, okay?"

"Just go," I say, shoving Robin out the door. He ducks out and I collapse onto my bed, shaking. I've never seen him like that before. What's going on? I roll my head to the side and stare at my sleeping computer. That picture isn't Vin. Even if it is, why would it matter? She's delicate, fragile, unable to deal with things, sure. But Robin's reaction didn't seem like he was trying to protect a camera-shy friend. What the hell is going on?

I wake up the next morning to the Revenge of the Headache. I can't think of anything worse than forcing myself to get out of bed, get dressed, and walk across campus to sit in class. Except, it turns out, lying in bed on my own with my thoughts hammering away at me. I drag myself to my feet, and, somehow, manage to keep myself upright, all the while cursing everyone and everything. This has to be worse than a hangover. Not only do I feel like I was run over by a bus, but I also feel as though I could, and probably will, burst into tears at any minute.

I get to class a couple minutes late. Luckily, everyone is still rattling around so I dart in unnoticed. I slip into an empty seat at the back, hoping to slide into a bored trance and numb some of this energy that's been crackling over me all night. Sit and listen.

My brain refuses to accept any of the jumbled words that are being spoken. Nothing anyone says is making any sense to me. I'm so tired…

"I think a great example of this is how in Pride and Prejudice Mr. Darcy goes to bat for the Bennet family after the scandal with Lydia." Of course Jemmy's voice makes it through the cotton fog that's strangling my brain. Something in me stirs and I watch her sitting at her desk, fluffing her hair and blinking expectantly at Davies.

"He does exhibit some classic hero behavior," Mr. Davies says, nodding and knocking his knuckles on the desktop. "Why do you think he does it?"

"Because it's the right thing to do," Jemmy answers without missing a beat. I roll my eyes.

"That's a good one," I snap, and Jemmy and Davies both look at me in surprise. The energy is changing, jumping from my skin into my blood and pushing me to speak. "Darcy only helps the Bennet family because he's in love with Elizabeth. So many families suffered scandal back then and I'm betting Darcy didn't help a single other one. Yes, it was the right thing to do, but no, that's not why he did it. He did it so that he could bang Lizzie without having to deal with a smear on her family record."

"He doesn't care about her family," insists Jemmy. "He even said so earlier."

I snort. "He does care about her family. He lists all the reasons why they're unsuitable and tells her that he loves her despite them."

"But is that so bad?" Davies cuts in, moving around from the back of his desk, brought to life by a good class discussion. "Darcy lived in a time when there were clear-cut conventions. Acting from that was actually the most powerful way he could have helped Elizabeth and her family. And don't you think a good way to show someone you care by helping one of their loved ones?"

"Maybe," I shrug, "but I still say that he wasn't doing it for her. He wouldn't have helped any of them if there hadn't been something in it for him. Back then, men used duty as a way of getting into what they wanted and getting out of what they didn't." As I speak, I feel my argument gathering steam. Last night's story stabs into my stomach and I speak even faster, trying to dispel this emotional knife. "Elizabeth's future would have been ruined because of her trampy little sister if a rich and powerful man didn't *happen* to be in love with her. I don't think making Darcy out to be some romantic hero makes any sense at all."

"Love is a powerful motivator," Davies agrees, "but is that something to be condemned? Is a beneficial gesture less beneficial when coming from a place of apology? Or honor?"

"Let me tell you something about honor," I say scathingly. I'm leaning forward on the table now and the wooden edge is cutting into my gut, but I don't care. I slip off my shoes and pull my feet under me so I'm sitting higher up. "Honor should mean devotion to that which is most important. But men like these don't see honor as sacrificing all to be with the person they love—they see it as a guaranteed way to get people to take them seriously. It's all about public opinion. It has nothing to do with doing the 'right thing'."

"How do you know that that was his motivation?" protests Jemmy, turning to glare at me.

"Oh, I know." I realize that I'm shaking, but I'm too angry to care.

"I think that's enough for today," Davies says quickly, and I feel my shoulders slump.

What. Was. That? On my way out the door I nearly collide with Geri, who is standing and clearly waiting for a word with Davies. "Sorry," I mumble, not catching her eye. I can't talk about pictures today. I don't want to tell her that I've been looking at other photos when I haven't, and I don't want to tell her that Robin doesn't want me to use my very best photo.

Keep looking, she's told me, again and again. And what, end up losing what I really want, like she did with her relationship? I don't want to deal with any of it right now. I feel her stance shift as she recognizes me and prepares a word of hello but before she can present any of it I slip forward into the crowd. I'll see her tomorrow. I'll tell her I didn't recognize her. Right now, I need to get home.

When I burst into my apartment, the first thing I see is Robin kneeling on the floor playing with Santa. I stride over to him, only barely registering Michael and Pandora in my periphery.

"We," I say grabbing onto the shoulder of his shirt, "need to talk."

Robin stumbles to his feet as I continue to tug and follows me out. I ignore Pandy's startled expression and the look of curiosity on Michael's face and slam the door behind us. Robin looks concerned.

"Let's walk," I tell him, and stride toward the exit of our building. Once we hit the cold air outside I turn to face him. "Why did you break my memory card?"

"I already told you why." Robin has his arms across his chest and I notice that he's just wearing a hoodie. The one I stole.

"You can't call someone up in the middle of the night, then come over and damage their property!" I stamp my foot, sending a spray of slush and pebbles into the air around me. Robin backs up, barely avoiding getting his jeans wet.

"I know. I know. I shouldn't have done it like that."

"No! You shouldn't have!" My voice is high with all of the tension of the day, but even though I'm shaking, the threat of tears is gone. "You can't do that Robin. Ever."

"I won't. I promise. I'm sorry."

"And why," I continue, beginning to pace, "can't I use the picture for the contest?"

Robin puts his hand on my arm to try and still, me but I jerk away and glare at him until he answers. "It's Vin in that picture."

"So you said," I snarl. "Why does that mean that I can't use it?"

"Because it could get her arrested."

I stop moving. "What?"

"Katie." For the first time I'm starting to hear impatience creep into his voice. "The EA was behind the disturbance on Halloween."

"Well, that…" Click, click, click. Everything begins to make sense. "That isn't my problem. It's a damn good picture. Why would it get Vin arrested anyway? Fireworks aren't illegal here." My mind flits back to the news after that night. There was some property damage: singed grass, and a scratch on one of the security cars. What else did I read about?

"I can't tell you that." Robin's voice and face tighten.

I stop pacing. "It was a diversion." Snow begins to sprinkle from the sky and I impatiently dust the flakes from my jacket. "You guys did something else."

Robin doesn't answer; instead he puts his hand to his forehead. "Vin has a tattoo. It's right below her shoulder. It's visible in the picture; she'd be identifiable."

My lungs fill up with too-cold air. "Robin. Was it something else?"

For the first time since I've known him, Robin looks very young. "Things got out of hand that night. We didn't have anything planned. I heard about the fireworks at the school; I thought it would be fun to watch. Vin heard about them too. I thought she was just going to do a protest, like the one you saw at the school. I wanted to make sure it didn't go farther than that. It didn't, so I went home. It wasn't until later that–" He breaks off.

"That what?"

He closes off, again. "It's better for everyone if you don't know. But please, please do not use that picture." I've never seen him look so desperate. His whole face is a plea for mercy. I feel my structure weaken. I could use something else; I'm a good photographer. After all, I wouldn't want to get Vin in trouble. But, trouble for what?

"It's not better for me! You're keep asking me these favors and not telling me why. No. I won't do it. Not without an explanation." Extreme scenarios are forming in my head involving me going to the police and showing them the picture just because I can, just to spite Robin, and Vin, and the whole stupid lot of them. But then… I don't want to get Michael in trouble. He wasn't part of the thing on Halloween. He was with Pandora and me the whole time.

"I don't want to get you into trouble," Robin sighs, dropping his hand away from his face. He unzips his hoodies, slides it off his shoulders, and hands it over to me. "You're shivering." I jerk away from his offer.

"More like you don't want to get Vin in trouble. But fine! Don't tell me what you guys did that night. But *please* let me use the picture." I don't know why I'm asking his permission. I stare at him desperately, willing him to tell me it's okay.

"You take so many great pictures." He's turned the look around and is now using it on me. "Why do you have to use one that could get my friend into trouble?" I feel the situation freezing up in the cold air. We're not going to get anywhere today.

"I need to talk to you about something else, too." My voice drops and I take a deep breath. I know this isn't a good way to start the conversation, I can see it on Robin's face, but I don't know how else to broach the topic. "Hold on."

I run inside, sprinting up the stairs and banging back into the apartment. I don't look at Michael or Pandora;

instead, I run into my room, grab the book, and fling myself back into the hallway. By the time I'm outside again, less than a minute has passed.

"What...?"

"We need to read this book. Together." I tell him, holding it up. He looks at the cover.

"Isn't that mine?"

"Yes." I'm nodding my head like a maniac. "Yes, it is. Can we go back to your place and read it?"

"Okay." Robin takes my hand. He must think I'm crazy, but there's understanding in his gestures as we walk over to his car together. I lean my head on his shoulder.

We get back to his apartment and I lead him over to the couch, where I sit and turn to face him. I brandish the book. "Have you read this?"

Robin shakes his head. "No. I haven't."

"Why do you have it?" It's an important question. I'm not sure why it's important, but it is.

"I saw it in Wordy's a few months ago and picked it up. I was curious about the name." He's speaking slowly and calmly, but his gaze is wary.

"Do you like fairytales?"

"No."

"I do."

"I know."

"Okay." I take a deep breath. "Okay. I don't want you to read it. First let's look at the pictures."

"Alright." The wariness is still there. I want to reassure him, but I can't. I have to forge forward. I open the book.

Twenty minutes later, Robin leans against his brick wall, tossing a pen between his hands. "It's probably something archetypal. You know, something that everyone relates to."

"Maybe," I say doubtfully, looking back over the pages of the book. The written description offers me frustratingly little of what I want to know.

"Tell it to me again," he requests, sitting down next to me on the couch and peering over my shoulder. The pen cap jiggles as Robin continues to fidget.

I turn back to the picture section. I should start with the first picture, start with the couple, the love. What's at stake in this story. But I don't.

"There was a king." The man on the page radiates up at me. Light shines from the middle of his chest so brightly that his face is washed out. The picture exudes royalty. I imagine laying down allegiance for such a king.

"See," Robin interrupts. He points at me with a pen. "Archetype. Even the picture." He leans over and taps the image. "You can't even see his face."

"That's because she's portraying impressions," I snap, feeling disproportionately defensive. "And she probably would have gotten in trouble if he was recognizable." An uncomfortable recognition passes between Robin and me. A story anyone can relate to. I look again at the king's covered face.

"Keep going." Robin straightens and reclaims his spot against the wall.

"There was this king, and even though he was happy with the queen he liked… side dishes." The next picture: a bawdy one, with the king grabbing a maid and pulling her onto his lap. The colors in this one are garish and brash. Looking at it makes me queasy. The king's face, I note, is still hidden, this time behind the squealing maid.

"Great way to put it." Robin throws the pen at his left hand, where it smacks into his palm.

"Thank you." I remember the explanation at the beginning of the book, and continue. "The queen was okay with it, and she even sometimes helped suggest his next..."

"Course."

For the first time, I see something in the background. I look closer, past the gropings of the king, and see the queen standing in the shadows. Her crown glimmers, but the rest of her persona is dark. "Companion. It was a big step up for the women selected. I guess if she had a kid, it pretty much secured her position for life."

"As the king's..."

"Companion," I say, speaking over the vulgarity that Robin offered. "Yes. So a lot of people aspired to it."

"Good for them." Robin's voice is dry now. I take a deep breath and move along with the story. I turn to the next picture. The woman from the first picture, with her red-brown hair and a flowing skirt, grins widely up at us. It's the first painting to show a full person. Her joy is startling.

"At one point the queen suggested her best friend, a noblewoman." That feels strange to say. "But her friend didn't want to go."

Robin exhales and drops the pen to the floor. My mouth is getting dry from all this talking. It's time to go back to the first picture, the one so important that it's used for introduction. The one that drew me in. I turn to the picture of the lovers.

"She didn't want to go because she was in love with a knight." Robin isn't looking. His gaze is fixed on the gold that's flashing between his hands. I hold the book closer and continue talking. "The queen didn't know that, though, so she suggested her, the noblewoman, to the king, thinking she was helping her friend out."

An unconvinced puff of air escapes Robin's lips, and he picks the pen back up. I watch as he starts yanking the cap off then shoving it back on repeatedly, as if trying to pound out a result.

"She didn't want to go," I say quietly. "She turned the king down." My voice gets stronger. The next picture: rage and chaos. The king, surrounded by fire, his eyes still in shadows. "He wasn't happy. He wasn't used to not getting his way, so he threatened the woman, saying he would hurt her and sabotage her family if she didn't comply. But she didn't! She didn't comply. Instead…"

"She made that plan with her boyfriend to run away." This is the first part of the retelling that Robin has helped out with. I pause to see if he's going to say anything more, but he doesn't. Next picture.

"Yes. They made that plan to run away. But her boyfriend was a knight, and the night before they planned to leave, he was called away on a mission that would take him out of the kingdom for a year.

"The king did it on purpose," I explain, "because he found out about their plans to go. So, instead of meeting at the bridge that they agreed on, the knight left her there to wait, while he spent the night getting ready to leave." I can't turn to the next page. My hands are shaking and Robin reaches down, trying to soothe me. I can't turn to the next page. The water, the trees, the starlight, the bridge. I can't.

"He had to."

"He didn't." I shake my head and slam the book shut. "He really didn't. And she still went to meet him, but he didn't turn up, and she waited the whole night..."

"But what happened next?" Robin is staring at me with challenge in his eyes.

"He left." I answer shortly.

"And what did she do?"

I get up off the couch, and turn from Robin so he won't see the pride that I'm trying to conceal. "I think I'm going to go," I tell him, looking around for something to gather up. Unfortunately, I didn't even bring my coat.

"Wait," Robin pleads, getting to his feet. "She..." He looks down at his shoes. "She painted, right?"

I nod. "She painted. She painted her story. All of this." I raise the book half an inch, then let it drop heavily to my side.

"She painted." Robin keeps looking at the ground.

"It's probably not real," I offer weakly. "Just someone's analysis of a series of lost art." In answer, Robin walks over and kisses me on the cheek, before stepping back and letting me walk away.

Chapter Seventeen

"Whoa," Michael says, putting a hand up to his eyes. I jump, having not heard the door.

"Michael," I say, putting my camera down.

"You don't usually use flash," Michael comments, hanging his coat over mine.

"I'm not going for results right now." My camera screen shows a startled Santa, staring at the camera in fear. Her ears are erect and her eyes are wide; it looks like she's not such a fan of flash either. She's now hiding under the couch, waiting to make sure that the aggressive light is gone for good.

I walked home by myself. The trip was longer than I expected. By the end of it, my feet howled and I was angry at the darkness. Why are there built-in hours every day that are designed to prevent you from your goals? It makes sense in the summer when there's an abundance of sunlight to make up for it, but it's so hard to do anything in the winter. To resist this, I took out my camera, turned the flash on as brightly as it would go, and spent the next half hour snapping anything and everything I could.

I hold up the camera and aim it at Michael's face, but he holds up a warning finger. "No."

"Fine," I grumble. "Where's Pandy?"

"Tutoring. What about Robin?"

I'm distracted by the image of Pandy working, reading glasses on, bent over a student's paper, explaining in her enthusiastic way about varying sentence structures. I have never seen anyone that excited about varying sentence structures. "At home I guess." I yank the adjustment loop on my camera strap, then poke the little hill that's created.

"Is everything okay?"

"I don't know if things have ever been okay with us," I answer truthfully. "And I think I'm starting to figure out why."

Michael listens quietly through the story, not offering any comments or perspective until I'm done. "So she went to the king," Michael murmurs, nodding his head. And then, "Did she have a choice?"

"The knight wanted her to appeal to the queen. The king probably wouldn't have done anything if the queen asked him not to. When the knight came back he was heartbroken, but I guess he still wanted her back. She stayed with the king, though, and built up this externally great life. But she never got over the knight's betrayal, and she ended up painting all of these tragic scenes. That was how she spent her life after that. Some stories spun off from it; The Little Mermaid is even argued to be inspired by these paintings. Switch genders and put the whole thing under the sea and it's pretty close." I refresh my lung space, and continue. "But after a while the paintings got lost, and until now it's been left untold."

I think of my book, my little story without the right ending. My mermaid, piercing her own heart with a knife. Now, it seems, I've found the true ending. I hate it.

"So why is this story a problem for you and Robin?" Michael looks professionally patient, like a psychiatrist, or bank manager.

I bring my hands up to my face and speak into my palms. "Because I remember waiting under the bridge."

I hear Michael breathe out, and I pull my hands down an inch so I can peer at his face. He's looking right at me. "It was a bridge?"

I take my hands away from my face and nod. "It was a bridge. And my feet were getting wet, and I was cold, and I just remember it."

He doesn't ask me the obvious question ("Are you sure you're not remembering something else?"), and instead sits quietly, his knuckles to his lips. I wait for his response, but he doesn't give any.

"It's probably nothing," I say after a bit, hating myself for undermining the situation. I turn my camera back on and am lining up another shot of Santa—freshly returned from her hiatus under the couch—when Michael speaks.

"What does Robin remember?"

I lower my camera. "He didn't say. But..." I struggle to find the words that can describe the whole thing, the uncanny feeling of recognition we both had, the little points of familiarity, the words on the bridge... "He says maybe it's something archetypal. A story that everyone recognizes?"

Michael shakes his head. "It's too specific."

I swallow. "That's what I thought, too." The implication of our agreement hangs between us. "So, if it is..." I can't bring myself to say the word. "If this is what's been going on this whole time, then what do I do now? What's the next step with something like this?"

Michael takes my camera from me and looks me steadily in the eyes. "I think you know the answer to that," he says, then, with a gentle firmness, he puts his hand on my back and guides me to the door, moving me forward into what I have to do.

He's right, of course. I did hope that he would have a word or two in the other direction, something to at least start a discussion, if not entirely change my mind, but he's right. I shove my hands into my pockets, angry at myself, or life, or Michael, for another walk in this frigid darkness. The area of my chest left exposed by my sweater aches with cold even though there's a layer of coat covering it. I pull my jacket tighter, but experience no benefit. This walk is taking even longer than the last.

After what seems like hours I'm at Robin's front door. My hands hurt too much from the cold to bother knocking, so instead I call out. "Robin?"

Robin's face appears at the window. "Kate?" His cinnamon sprinkling of freckles is invisible in the low lighting, making him look older.

I step back, feeling suddenly shy. "Can I come in?"

Robin disappears, then reappears at the door, taking my hand and pulling me inside. "Did you walk all the way here?" he asks, taking off my glove and putting my cold hands between his warm ones. I nod. We stand together in the front hallway until I finally remember how to speak.

"I came here because…" I look around the hallway. I've never stood for long out here, only dashed through on my way into Robin's apartment. The hallway, like the rest of the building, has a dark but historical feel about, with its close together brick walls and low-hanging ceiling. I wonder who else lives here. "I talked to…" Again, I stop. "I thought about it and…"

Robin's eyes are patient. I can see his freckles a little better in this light but there's still a lot in his face that I don't recognize. And that, I realize, is it. "It's not the same." I whisper.

"It's not." Even though he's gripping my hand, I can't feel his callus.

"I don't want it to be." The images from the story swell in my mind again: the paint, the screaming, and the wrong skin, hot against mine. I close my eyes. "It can't be."

Robin waits. Again, it's me. It's up to me to make this decision, to say yay or nay, to push us over the edge, in either direction I choose. I fix my gaze steadily on the wall behind Robin's shoulder. "Can I come in?"

And so, I ignore Michael's warning. I drop my doubts and misgivings on the floor like heavy bags and let Robin pull me inside, kissing me and saying things. My name, I think. The door closes behind us and there, in the cozy antiquity of Robin's apartment, we relearn each other, bit by bit.

Chapter Eighteen

"I guess it was a pretty good career move." I lick the sticky sweet brownie batter off my fingers and pass the bowl to Pandora.

"How so?" Taking a more careful approach, Pandora runs her spoon along the inner rim of the bowl, emerging with the perfect spoonful. It was hard to pull myself out of the bubble that last night with Robin created. But I knew that I had to go home eventually and, when I did, tell Pandora everything. Between classes and Pandy's tutoring job, I wasn't able to snag her until almost eight p.m. She looked confused when I suggested we have a girls' night (Monday isn't an ordinary time for this), but I think she knew something was up, so she agreed.

I expected the process of explaining to be a difficult one, but once I started talking everything just rolled out. I told her everything, from my first recollections of the bridge, to how last night ended, making sure to include my conversation with Michael. Pandy seems to be taking it in stride; if she's skeptical of my story at least it isn't showing.

"The paintings showed quite the luxe life. She's pictured with jewels, and fancy clothes, and then a baby. She didn't look happy, but she looked set."

"How do they know that it's autobiographical, instead of just a story?"

I pick up our shared glass of milk and take a swig. Pandy likes the low fat stuff. We're in constant battle over that. Whenever Pandy goes grocery shopping, she brings back cartons upon cartons of this watery garbage. I like to get whole milk. Today, however, I'm glad for the dilution. The brownie batter is enough.

"She put herself in the pictures. Paintings." It's all theories; musings stuck in the world of scholars who can't agree on anything. A Google search showed me more possibilities for the story than I cared to know existed. Most of them made me want to laugh. "It looks like her son didn't get the throne."

"Mmm, too bad." Pandy helps herself to another spoonful then slides the bowl over to me again. "You could have tracked down the current ruler and claimed heritage."

"I don't think it works that way," I giggle.

"How much of this do you actually remember?"

"Not a lot." I stare down at the brown batter and watch as little bubbles pop on the surface. "When I saw the scene, I recognized it. I've been having this image come back to me of waiting by a bridge, and it's cold. It's a definite memory. And Robin remembers that I painted."

"Do you remember the king?"

I shake my head and dip my finger into the bowl. "No. I just remember a lot of anger, and an impression here and there. No clear images besides the one by the bridge."

"Hmm."

For the first time in two days I'm beginning to relax. Despite the bizarre nature of the situation, talking to Pandy somehow makes it all feel normal. Just some girl talk in the kitchen. Forget that the topic might have happened a thousand years ago. "How are things with Michael?"

Pandy shrugs before getting off her stool to rinse off our spoons. "Fine."

"Anything more on…?" I trail off and watch her back as she runs her fingers over the flatware as water splashes down from the faucet.

"No. It's all fine."

I flounder, trying to come up with a way to ask for more. "Do you think you were imagining it?"

"Who knows?" Pandy comes back with a roll of plastic wrap and covers up the bowl of batter.

"Did you talk to him about it?"

"And say what?" asks Pandora mildly, sticking our mixture into the fridge.

"That you've been getting weird vibes from him. Ask what's going on." I try to imagine how I would bring it up. It is a weird thing to say, especially if he's given her no reason to doubt his fidelity—at least in recent years—but if I was able to figure out this thing with Robin, Pandy should be able to talk about her issues with Michael.

Pandy shrugs again but this time doesn't say anything. Finally she yawns delicately and announces, "I'm heading to bed."

"That's the best idea I've heard all day," I reply, suddenly realizing how tired I am.

"Goodnight," she says, giving me her customary kiss on the cheek.

"Dream sweet," I reply as she walks away. After all the adrenaline, rage, joy, and shock of the past few days all I can feel is exhaustion. Maybe tonight I'll sleep.

"You've got to be kidding me!" The door slams open and Robin slides in, looking angrier than I've ever seen, well, just about anyone. Pandy and I look up in surprise from our card game in time to see Michael follow him in, looking tired and bored.

"Chill dude," Michael instructs. He takes off his coat, then goes to the fridge and pulls out a bottle of water.

"What's going on?" asks Pandy, calmly setting down her cards in a way I could never manage. I'm already in panic mode already, terrified at the idea of what might happen if this fight between Robin and Michael escalates. Things with them have only started to ease. Robin spent weeks not even looking at Michael. Michael took it with grace, but I don't know how he'll react to another display of aggression.

"You can't send her down there." Robin shakes his head but Michael shrugs lazily. I see Robin's fingers tense and relax, but his hand stays by his side. I exhale.

"I'm not sending anyone anywhere." Michael's expression is deliberately casual. He looks dramatically bored as he looks through the pages of a folder. I see Pandy's eyes flick to him and suspicion flickers across her features.

"What's going on?" I parrot. Robin looks at me as though just realizing that I'm there. I try again. "Who are you sending where?"

"Michael's set up a protest. We were supposed to wait. This is all way too soon." His phone pleads for attention and he looks down at the screen. "She's there. I'm heading down."

"So soon?"

I blink. There's something in Michael's tone that's almost mocking. I turn my head to look at him but he's moved. He's now sitting on the couch, ankle-over-knee, with his arms spread wide over the back and his face impassive.

"I'm coming too." I stand and grab my camera, lying conveniently right next to me in its bag on the floor. Everyone in the room looks at me in surprise. "I need to finish my damn essay."

"It's Vin, right?" Even though we're in the car now, Robin hasn't filled me in on any of what's going on.

"It's Vin," he finally confirms, pulling onto the highway.

I tug on my seatbelt, mulling over what I heard. Robin was so angry. Angry at Michael for sending Vin ahead into this situation. But why? Seems like a bit more than brotherly concern to me. "Before I charge headfirst into a scenario that I know next-to-nothing about, can you at least tell me what really happened with you and Vin? You said she was pushed the other way. What do you mean?" A reasonable request, I think, and I settle in to wait for his answer.

Robin exhales. "It was a few years ago, when we first met through the EA. We started doing a lot of projects together since we were both new."

"And she liked you." I state this, instead of ask it. I can tell. I can tell by the careful way he treats her. I can tell by his look of guilt.

Robin pauses, then nods. "That wasn't the problem, but it didn't help anything."

"But you didn't like her?" I need to hear it again.

"I was too angry to like anything. Dating wasn't something I wanted to bother with." *He never does anything but casually dates*, I remember Michael saying. Interesting.

"What happened?"

"There was this protest. A pretty harmless one, at least for back then. Vin and a few others were at a construction site, blocking the guys from doing their work. The construction site called the cops to break up the protest. When they got there, most of the group scattered, except for Vin. The cops had to forcibly remove her."

"Ouch," I offer with an eyebrow raise. That doesn't sound like a push over the edge to me. It sounds like a kid throwing a temper tantrum.

"They were rougher than they should have been."

My comeback dies in my throat.

"They said it was necessary. We couldn't prove otherwise, so we didn't have a case. That was when I backed off. I don't want cops to be my enemy because, frankly, they're going to win. Vin, though..." he trails off.

"She was probably angry," I offer.

Robin nods. "We all were. But I saw it as a reason to hold back, and she saw it as a reason to keep fighting."

"What did she do?"

Robin closes his eyes for a second. "Anything she could think of. It made us all look bad. The worst one was when she broke into the mayor's office. She was caught before she could do anything, but she was looking for his safe." He shakes his head in disbelief at the memory.

"Jesus." I pick at the edge of my fingernail. "Was she high?"

"Probably not. It's just what she did. She wanted to use the money for our own projects." Robin knocks his fist against the steering wheel and curses under his breath as a car in front of us slows down and puts on its blinker.

"Was she convicted?" I try to imagine Vin and her lazy smile in a jail cell. The image sickens me.

"No, luckily. Security kicked her out, but the cops didn't get involved. Oh, come on!" Robin hits the steering wheel again as the car in front of us changes its mind.

"How did she swing that? Breaking and entering and attempted burglary are some pretty serious offenses."

Robin hesitates for a fraction of a second, then says shortly, "Michael handled it."

I almost say, "He's good at that," but, seeing the look on Robin's face, I decide to stay quiet. Another situation handled by Michael, and another shield up against him. Why is there so much darkness suspected in his methods?

"She calmed down after that. But then things like today happen." The car in front of us finally exits and Robin zooms ahead.

"You're worried about her," I remark, looking out the window to try and ascertain where we're heading. Despite my cool exterior, I'm starting to feel nervous. I take a deep breath as we whiz around a corner. "She was why you were at the hospital the day I found your hoodie, wasn't she?" In the back of my mind, a fragment of dialogue from my first EA meeting plays. *He's taking Vin to get her cast off.*

Robin nods and swears at his GPS, which has just led us down a dead-end. Throwing the car into reverse, he answers, "She broke her arm after trying to climb onto a bulldozer."

We pull into a parking lot and Robin turns off the car. I take my camera out of its bag and follow Robin out of the car and around the side of the building. A sign we pass reads "Atlantic Paper Mill".

"What are you guys protesting here?" I wonder aloud. The cutting down of trees?

"They don't just make paper," Robin murmurs. "Oh, Jesus Christ…"

There are people everyone, shouting and holding signs. I squint at them, trying to figure out what all this is about. "Keep the water clean—no more tourmaline!" Tourmaline isn't toxic. I take out my camera and start photographing like mad, trying to get as many pictures of this insane scene as possible.

"Vin!" Robin yells plunging into the crowd. I see him grab a wrist and then Vin, hair and all, is pulled toward him. She stumbles and drops a rock that she had been holding. I snap a shot just before the rock hits the ground.

"Hey Robin." Her sleepy expression is gone. She's grinning like a maniac and her eyes are wild. "Come to join the party?"

"Jesus Christ. Vin, we have to go."

"But the fun's just started!" She laughs and takes a few steps back toward the crowd, winking at Robin.

"You compromised our standing. This probably just ruined the whole project. The project is probably ruined now." Robin is rubbing his temples and staring at Vin in angry disbelief.

"We can't let these bastards get away with this!" Vin stamps her foot and picks her rock up again. Robin leaps over and wrenches the stone from her grasp.

"We won't," he promises, taking her free hand with his. "But right now we have to go."

"Fine." Vin softens and lets Robin lead her away from the crowd. I follow them, still snapping away. They reach the car a few seconds before I do, and Vin climbs into the front seat. Annoyed, I let myself into the back.

"Hi," Vin says, turning around to look at me. She gives me a pointedly confused look, but before I can introduce myself recognition snaps across her face. "You're the photographer! How cool that you were here today. I hope you got a lot of good shots." She turns back around and settles into her seat clicking the seat belt firmly in. Robin starts the car and puts it into reverse, not looking at me even as he leans around his seat to see what's behind him.

"We'll see if I'm allowed to use them," I mutter.

Robin, clearly fighting back impatience, inhales deeply and says, "Anything is fine if just Geri sees it."

"You're not mad at me, are you?" Vin asks, reaching over and touching his hand with hers. Robin doesn't answer. "Come on, Rob. We had to do something."

"We had a plan," Robin answers tightly.

"And Jessica and Mark changed it," replies Vin with a shrug. "We couldn't afford a lawsuit. You know that."

"I was working on it."

Vin turns around to face me again. "Rob doesn't like the way we do things. He's all into paperwork and ideas. I like action. Did you hear about what we did on Halloween?"

"Some of it." I glance uncertainly at Robin. He keeps quiet so I let Vin continue.

"We stole some fireworks from this show at Travis U. We made it look like we were just some troublemakers creating a diversion but *really* we used the fireworks in the quarry where Atlantic Paper Mills is doing a bunch of their mining. We blew up so much of their work."

Despite the images of a mining site getting blasted with fireworks, I only think to ask: "Atlantic Paper Mills mines?"

"Well," Vin begins massaging the ends of her hair. "It's not APM, it's their parent company Gollard Inc. APM is their headquarters though; that's why we were protesting there."

Michael's tale of Boston comes back to me. "And they're leaving toxic residue?"

"They're leaking mercury into the water." Robin's voice is quiet but intense and I can see the tension of everything reflected in his face. My breath catches.

"Our water?"

"Maybe. We haven't tracked it, yet. We took some water samples back in the fall, and just got the results. Valentine's Day was trying to trace the runoff. The EA doesn't have the money to open up court proceedings yet, but I've been looking up other options, maybe a class-action suit." He exhales and hits the steering wheel with his knuckles. "Today really puts a wrench in things."

"Got things moving you mean." Vin throws her hair over her shoulders and looks out the front of the car. "Today raised awareness. The press was even there." She gestures back to me.

"You could have gotten arrested."

"We were peaceably assembled! I know my rights." She has the glove compartment open now, and is rifling through, examining the manuals and tissues that Robin keeps stored there.

"Actually," I chime, "you guys were trespassing, which the constitution doesn't cover. And throwing rocks isn't peaceable."

Vin shoots me a look of contempt. "I wasn't throwing rocks."

"We need to shut it down," Robin mutters. "We need everyone out of there."

"By what?" Vin asks, whipping round to face him. "Calling the cops again?"

Thankfully, Robin doesn't react to the mention of the police. "I don't need to call the cops. I'm sure somebody already has."

"Is that why you came to get me? Because little Virginia needs protecting?" Her voice is rising and I dig my fingernails into my palm. I shouldn't be here for this. "How revolutionary."

"I came to get you so you wouldn't get arrested. You're not going to be any good for us behind bars."

"I'm never any good to you," Vin mutters, and returns her gaze out the window. I hold my breath as I wait for Robin's reply, his reassurance, but he doesn't say anything. The car pulls up in front of Shane's house and Vin slides out the door. As she walks toward the house Robin rolls down his window and says, "Tell Shane to get everyone back here."

Vin responds with her middle finger. "Tell him yourself." With that she turns and stalks into the house. Robin sits for a moment without moving and I hear him take a deep breath.

"I'm sorry."

"For what?" I ask, climbing forward into the front seat.

"This. Vin. Everything." He rakes his hands through his hair and I lean over and kiss his cheek.

"It's okay."

"Want me to take you back?" He turns his key and the car grunts to life. Yes. Yes, I do want him to take me back to my apartment. I want to close my door and not talk to anyone. Or maybe watch a movie. One with Pandy. I want to pull away from this whole crazy scene and make Robin handle all of his drama on his own. But I've done that before. So I shake my head.

"I want to stay with you."

Robin and I sit on his bed looking through pictures on my computer. Neither of us has mentioned the picture of Vin and I'm careful not to open it. Instead, we look through an album of winter pictures I've been working on all season. The air outside is starting to tease us with spring, and I want to make sure I can immortalize as much of the fading season as possible.

"I like this one." Robin points to a picture of a little girl in a red parka and bright yellow boots who is frowning in confusion at the long string connecting her mittens.

"She was cute." I chuckle, remembering her battle to separate her hands. The force of her endeavors nearly knocked her backwards but her mother, standing nearby, kept her on her feet.

The next one is the first one I took of Robin, where he's looking over the EA papers on the couch of my apartment. "I look dumb," he groans.

I gasp in mock offense. "Are you saying I'm a bad photographer?"

"The worst," he says, pulling me toward him and kissing me. "None of your pictures are any good." I laugh and pull away only to close the computer before lying down next to him. He pulls me close and I nestle against his shoulder, breathing deeply. Things will work out this time. This is easy. This is natural. This is right.

Robin shifts slightly and I find myself digging my fingers into his hair and clinging as tightly as I can get away with. *He won't leave*, I tell myself.

"Hey," I whisper into him.

"Hey," he whispers back.

I close my eyes and all of the images from the past week come flooding back to me in an overwhelming stream. I need to talk to Robin. I need to see what he knows, I need to find out if I can glean any reassurance from him that the world is as it should be.

"Pandy thinks Michael is cheating on her," I blurt.

"Why?" Robin asks. His hand moves reassuringly up and down my back and I keep my eyes closed.

"Intuition, I guess." As I speak this answer, I feel a chill. Stupid, *stupid* intuition. "But she's probably wrong, right? I mean, you're around Michael a lot. Have you... noticed anything?"

"No, but I haven't been paying attention. Does he do that kind of thing?"

Oh no. Oh no. This isn't how I wanted it to come up. There was never going to be a way to make me seem like a good guy, but does it really have to sound so awful? "Um." I take a colossal breath and say finally, "He did. Once. That I know of."

"What a scumbag," Robin says, shaking his head. Contempt etches over his features, twisting the mouth that I love so much. Oh God. Guilt hammers at my insides and I know it's finally time for the truth to come out.

"Robin?" I pull away and sit up. My secret, my selfishness, my betrayal is all about to come out. He has to know, but I don't want to tell. I don't want to have done that. Not to my best friend.

"Yeah?"

I pull my legs up to my chest and start massaging my feet. Even though they're encased in a pair of Robin's socks the ends of my toes still feel like ice cubes. I squeeze my feet vigorously and say, "He cheated on Pandora with me." Robin sits bolt upright. "I'm sorry!" I say before he can say anything. I try to look earnestly at Robin but he's staring straight ahead.

"Michael?" he asks finally, his face twisted in dismay. "Really?"

"It wasn't like that!"

"Pandora's your best friend," he says flatly. "I didn't know you would do that."

"I know." My voice is unsteady. "I didn't either."

"Did you sleep with him?" he asks, now turning to look at me. His eyes are dark with solemnity.

"It was a kiss. That's it. I swear." I grab his hand and squeeze it, desperate that he knows I'm telling the truth. "And it was only for like two seconds and I've never done it again and I've never even wanted to."

Robin doesn't say anything. He tips his head back so it's resting against the wall, and I can't look him in the eye anymore. I snatch up the corner of his blanket and begin kneading it furiously between my fingers. It's okay, I tell myself, it's good that this is coming out now. It had to sometime.

"You never did it again?" he finally asks. He doesn't sound angry; his tone is closed off. I can't tell what he's thinking.

"Never," I say emphatically.

"I didn't know you guys had that kind of past." Neutrality has taken over. I'm starting to panic. This isn't a neutral subject.

"We don't! I didn't even really want to kiss him in the first place," I say, relaxing my grip on my comforter. The material slackens but the wrinkles I made stay pronounced. "It was at a party my senior year in high school, and I thought I was drunk even though I wasn't…"

"You don't drink."

"I know."

"I like that you don't drink."

"I know." I pause before resuming my story. "I thought I was drinking but it was only soda. But everything was noisy, and fun, and I was scared about leaving for college. And the thing is, I had spent so long with Michael in the role of Pandora's boyfriend I kind of… I wondered what he would be like to be mine. And we were talking and he actually was drunk and we kissed."

"Did you tell Pandora?"

I flush with shame. "He did. I didn't until recently." Robin nods. "Are you mad?" I ask timidly. He shakes his head and exhales loudly, then reaches over and pulls me toward him

"Not mad," he says. "Surprised."

"Have you ever cheated on anyone?" I ask, looking up at him.

"No. Just been on the other end of it."

"I'm sorry."

"Not your fault." A few breaths later he says, "I wondered about the history between you guys. But since he'd always been with Pandora…"

I run my hands over my cheeks. "It's not history. It's nothing. Pandy even knows about it. Nothing else has ever happened."

"Now she thinks he's got something going on with someone else."

I try to shrug, but my position makes it difficult. "I guess."

"Stand-up guy."

We sit quietly for a bit and I try to absorb reassurance from his embrace. His breath is even and he's still running his hand over my back but still, there's distance. *This should bring us closer together,* I think, nestling as close to him as I can go. *No more secrets.* But somehow, this revelation has left me feeling like he's already packing his bags and buying a ticket out of here.

Chapter Nineteen

My EA essay is finally done and it isn't half-bad, if I do say so myself. The pictures from the protest fill the pages with dynamism and conflict, and my angle practically wrote itself. I explored their passion, their deep-rooted desire to do good, mixed with their frayed edges and internal conflicts. I stayed up nearly all night finishing it, catching one of those rare waves of inspiration that keeps me at work for hours. I'm exhausted, but wired. Robin will have to read this before I turn it in, just to make sure that I've revealed nothing incriminating, but after that I'll be ready to hand it to Geri.

I look at the clock and see that it's 5:30. It's not light out yet, but I feel like if I crash now then I'll never wake up. Maybe I should get some breakfast. I leave my room and find Michael standing in the kitchen frying an egg.

"I seem to find you out here a lot lately," he says. I nod, then tip my head toward the frying pan.

"Not tired."

"Same."

We sit in silence for a bit and I find my hands working unconsciously toward my sternum. My fingers massage the spot, rubbing, rubbing, rubbing at the ache. I need to fill the silence.

"How did the protest go yesterday?" Michael shrugs. I make a second attempt. "It seemed intense. Robin said the project is ruined now?" I make sure that he can hear the question in my voice.

"Robin says a lot of things." Michael's tone isn't sharp. It's dismissive. He flips his eggs and the matter is closed.

"How's Pandy doing?" I'm asking this not because I need to know, but because I want to hear Michael's take on it. I'm feeling shaken from my conversation with Robin last night. I want to hear Michael assure me that everything is normal.

"Didn't you see her yesterday?" He's not giving me anything. "How are things going with Robin?" Quick to change the subject, I notice. His blond hair is flattened, either by sweat or moisture from the stove. He reaches up to try and shape it, but it wilts again.

"Didn't you see him yesterday?"

I watch as Michael moves his spatula over his egg. I'm transported back to high school, to the days when Michael used to make us eggs after a night spent on Pandy's floor. The three of us would set up sleeping bags, and spend the night eating popcorn and watching movies until Michael fell asleep. Pandy and I would use the remaining hours of darkness for all of the talking that we somehow didn't get to during the week. We'd wind up awakening three hours after

Michael to the smell of breakfast being made. Suddenly, I want nothing more than for him to hug me.

The truth is that I've never been in love with Michael. For the most part, the only romantic associations I've had with him have been in the context of Pandora. He was Pandy's sweet, attractive boyfriend and my sweet, attractive friend. I've never longed to climb between the sheets with him or even have him hold my hand during a movie; I've only ever wanted him to listen to me when I'm sad and be around to hang out with while I'm bored. He's the ending to The Little Mermaid: not right to fill my gaps, but enough to hold me over. Sometimes only there to remind me of what I was missing.

Robin looked so concerned when he found out that I kissed Michael. He probably imagined quite a torrid scene. I'll bet he pictured lust-filled glances thrown at each other over Pandy's head that culminated in a can't-keep-our-hands-off-each-other kiss.

I don't know what happened the night at that party. I think all three of us were all terrified. Huge changes loomed in our futures and we knew that soon we'd have to take responsibility. So, while we still had the chance to write it off, we each did something that we'd want to erase, because at that point we still could.

High school was almost like those moments before sleep. The time when you your thoughts swirl around into a pattern that's pleasing in a way you would never allow in real life. The free-for-all before the order of the next morning sets in. I kissed him just to try it, but never went for it outside the dim lighting of the party. It wasn't love. It wasn't lust. It was curiosity. I look at him now, swearing at his eggs as they rapidly turn brown, and can't imagine any of it. I want Robin's lips, Robin's smile, Robin's drastic overreaction to small tasks gone awry.

"You know I never had feelings for you, right?" I blurt.

I know that this is a strange thing to say right now, but I feel like if I keep another thing inside of me I'll explode. I watch Michael for some sign of surprise, or indignation, but instead he just nods and says, "I never had any for you either."

I put my hand to my face, and rub my cheek. This is the right answer—I wouldn't want any answer but this one—but it doesn't feel great to hear. "That's good," I say. I wait for a beat but he stays silent. "I don't know why we kissed," I sigh, speaking mostly to myself. This whole conversation is starting to feel very wrong. I can't. I can't be talking to Michael like this. Especially now that I have Robin.

"I'm going for walk," I say, hoisting myself off the stool. I want to text Robin and ask if he wants to get dinner tonight, but he already mentioned having too much EA work. Tomorrow, he said.

The outside air calms me down a few notches and I walk a couple steps with my eyes closed. The cold stings the inside of my nose and I rub it gently, hoping it won't start running. I look toward the end of the parking lot and feel self-conscious when I see someone standing a few yards off. I look again and realize it's Robin.

"I wasn't expecting to see you." I walk over and kiss his bristly cheek. My lips sting.

"I forgot to give you this." He hands me a plastic bag, and I open it to find a new memory card, still in its packaging.

"You didn't have to do this," I remark, pulling it out and checking to make sure it's the kind I need.

"Yes, I did."

He definitely did. I smile and give him another kiss, before starting in on the plastic packaging.

"I'm sorry for breaking it." He watches me as I struggle with the pack. "It's just this EA thing. It's been stressful."

Of course. Of course it's his group. We're back on that now, naturally. I make myself indulge. "What's been going on?"

"Any chance at a lawsuit is gone. They'd probably pose a countersuit. We can't afford that."

"That sucks."

"Yup."

"Have you ever…" I take his hand and swing it back and forth lightly. "Considered leaving?"

Robin shakes his head right away. No pause, no hesitation, no thought. "I can't leave these guys."

"I'm cold." I say. He wraps his arms around me again.

"Want to get something to drink?"

We head together to his car and before we get in I hug him tightly. "We're really okay?" I ask, looking back up into his face.

"Better than okay," he says, smiling and brushing my hair back from my face. And for a moment I believe it.

Chapter Nineteen

With my EA essay finally finished I dive full force into my contest entry. My best picture by far is still the one of Vin, but I'm desperate to come up with a different option. I begin taking pictures of everything and everyone: Michael, Pandora, Robin, our apartments, and the signs of spring that are poking up from beneath the snow. All of it is captured and edited, but none of it yields the passion and intensity that the image of Vin with the firework does. I feel trapped.

Two days before the deadline, I'm desperate. My pictures are flat and lifeless. My entire ability as a photographer seems to be slipping away and replaced by a panicked assessment of other career choices. I suck. My phone chirps at me and I pick it up in a grateful dash, thanking whoever was calling for the distraction.

"Hey, kid."

"Oh. Hi, Jude."

We haven't talked since that time I was walking with Robin. Robin still doesn't know anything about Jude past the fact that I have a brother. I think he's starting to wonder. I hold my breath and wait for my brother to speak. "How is everything?" His usual question. Of course he's just checking in on me, like a good and normal big brother. Just making it seem like he's doing his familial duty. He's good at that.

"Everything is fine. I'm entering a photography contest." I click through to another picture, this one of a dog leaping at a crack on the sidewalk. Trite. Next.

"Oh yeah? That's good. You'll do good." God, he sounds so awkward lately. Why can't we ever hold a normal conversation? Why is he always either drunk or sounding like a kicked puppy?

"Yeah, well, let's hope." My annoyance with men manifests in my voice. Jude, Robin, Michael… all of them seem to be putting restrictions on my life lately. I've all but begged Robin to let me use the picture of Vin, but he can't seem to drop the idea that if I do, she'll get arrested. "There can't be anything linking us to that night," he said again and again, so I eventually gave up. If I'm any good, then I should have more than one contest-worthy photograph, right?

"I've seen your stuff. You've got an eye for this kind of thing."

"Thanks. I don't know, though." A rare moment of showing Jude vulnerability has leaked through. I can't focus on talking to him and going through my work.

"You know what's good. Go with that."

"We'll see." A picture of our front door in the afternoon light. It's static and clichéd. Next.

"Am I going to see you at home ever?" He's teasing, I can tell, but it's true that I haven't seen my brother since the altercation with Pandora all those months ago.

"Maybe. If I win this contest I'll be in Portland for a few days. You guys could come see it, or I could come down and see you or something."

"Yeah."

It's strange, scheduling family time as if they're strangers or distant friends. *Let's see if we're in the same area sometime soon. Maybe we can meet up.* "I'll probably be home for at least a little bit this summer," I offer. In previous years I'd spent the whole summer at home, catching up with my high school friends, going to the pool with Pandy and Michael, and relaxing with my family in the evenings, but this year I'm not sure. I don't want to spend a whole summer in the same house as Jude, and I'm also not sure of Robin's plans yet. Maybe we can take a trip…

"I'll see you around, kid."

"Yup, see you." We disconnect and I stare again at my computer screen in dismay. There's nothing. Nothing. Robin's restrictions weigh on my back and I'm not sure I can break through this barrier. Jude's advice finally registers in my brain. *You know what's good. Go with that.*

Strange that my brother would lead me here. I take a deep breath and close my eyes, making a final decision. Then I open up my email, attach the picture of Vin, and send it off to Geri with the brief but firm note, "This one."

"You seem distracted," Robin comments. We met up in the dining hall for dinner and I realize that I've hardly said a word all meal. I force a smile onto my face and shake my head, trying my best to act normal. "Do you want to talk about it?" Robin asks, not buying my innocent act.

"Just family stuff," I say, moving my mashed potatoes around with my fork. I'm almost tempted to mention Jude just to get Robin off the scent, but this doesn't seem like the right time to bring up my assaulting older brother.

"I have a family," Robin presses, his eyebrows raised. I laugh a little.

"Nah, it's nothing, my brother just called. It's nothing." Robin shrugs and returns to his plate. worry flickers through me as I watch him. Is he mad? "How was your day?" I ask, trying for a new subject. Robin shrugs again.

"Fine."

Oh great, he is mad. He's mad because I'm not telling him about Jude; how would he react then if he knew the real reason for my silence? "Hey," I say gently, desperate to smooth things over. "What's up?"

"Nothing," Robin says, his hand staying limp, "Lots of work."

"Fine," I say pulling my hand away. If he's going to act like this, then fine. We finish the meal in silence. "See you," I say standing up to leave.

"Wait," Robin says, standing too. He pulls me toward him and gives me a kiss. "I'll see you tomorrow?"

"Tomorrow," I agree, and then head outside to walk to the apartment alone.

"I think Robin's mad at me," I say, flopping on the couch when I get home. Michael, who's sitting at the kitchen table, looks up.

"Why?"

"Cuz I wouldn't tell him about Jude." Half-truths are easier than lies.

"Huh." Michael goes back to reading the paper in his hand. I frown.

"Aren't you going to offer any advice?"

"Tell him about Jude."

"I can't!"

"Why not?"

I let out a frustrated sigh, mulling the issue over carefully. "Because I don't want him to see that side of me. My brother is so messed up. How would he react if he knew that the guy who broke your project was his girlfriend's brother?"

"You know about that?"

"Robin told me. Jude is such a freaking nutcase."

"I know."

"I know you know. That's why I can talk to you about this."

"Alright." Michael takes a sip of tea. This is infuriating.

"So you don't think I should tell Robin?"

He shrugs. "It's up to you."

"You're helpful," I mutter. I reach up behind me and grab Santa, who was lounging on the windowsill behind me. "What do you think, sweetie?" I ask her, turning her gray face to me. She meows. I sigh and let her go. "You're no help."

"Why is this an issue?" Michael asks, finally putting down his paper.

"Because," I explain patiently, "Robin's mad at me."

"So tell him what's going on."

"I can't!" This conversation is going nowhere. "Okay," I say, trying to phrase things in a way that he'll understand. "If you had a really messed up family member, would you tell Pandora?"

"Sure." I groan. I'm about to give up on the conversation entirely when Michael asks, "What's going on with Jude?"

"Things have been weird," I say flicking my finger over Santa's ear, "I mean, weirder than usual—ever since… you know, that thing with Pandy… I think he might be getting sober or some help or something. I think he's reaching out, but I don't want to deal with him, so I keep pushing him away."

Michael nods. "Is that why you haven't told Robin about him?"

"Sorry?"

"You feel guilty for not helping him."

"I hadn't thought of that," I say slowly. Santa begins to purr. Michael's theory makes a lot of sense: Jude brings out the worst in pretty much everyone, including me. Nothing I do with Jude ever feels like the right choice. As a result, I always end up feeling twisty and terrible. "You know, Robin should let me not talk about things if I don't want to," I declare. "I don't need to talk about everything."

Michael snorts. "Yes, you do."

"I do not!" I protest, but I can't keep from giggling. Just then my phone dings and I see that I have a text from Robin. I open it.

"What's up?"

"Not much," I reply. "Just talking to Michael."

I expect a reply, but none comes. I frown. "It's okay to not tell him everything, right?" I ask Michael uncertainly. "Maybe even better?"

Michael shrugs again. "Up to you. You might want to tell him about Jude, though, since he's not gonna go away."

"No," I sigh, "he isn't, is he?"

"We need to talk." Robin's reply beeps through on my phone that evening, three hours after I told him I was talking to Michael. I glare down at the words on my phone, angry with Robin for having chosen such an ominous phrase. He must know how that comes across.

"Fine," I reply curtly. "When?"

He's probably mad at me for talking to Michael, or not talking to him, or something stupid like that. There's been plenty wrong with us today, a plethora of potential things for us to discuss. He's probably scaring me on purpose.

But, nags a voice in the pit of my stomach, *what if this is important and he's in the first stages of letting you know this is a breakup?* But we have no reason to break up! Maybe… Oh no, maybe he found out that I sent that picture to Geri. That's probably it; he's probably going to yell at me for that.

Annoyance mixes with relief and by the time his text bings into my phone ("Now?") I've shredded nearly every piece of scrap paper on my desk.

Sure. Now.

My god, it's cold. I pull on a pair of socks but it might be too late. Socks seem better for prevention than repair. My toes squiggle back and forth rapidly but no blood moves down to my feet. I pile up with a sweater and a coat and go outside to wait for Robin.

He's right on time. His car pulls slickly up in front of me, courteously free of slush spray. I climb into the passenger seat and he kisses me—a good sign in my opinion.

"So, what do we need to talk about?" I hate waiting; I won't wait for this. Whatever it is, let's get it over with.

"We can talk about it over dinner." Robin seems relaxed but there's something in his demeanor that's different. He isn't cold or unloving or even nervous or tense, but there's something…

We pull up in front of a Chinese restaurant and Robin gets the door for me. I haul myself out onto the sidewalk and together we walk inside. We're seated right away and as soon as we're handed the menus I look intently at Robin.

"What?"

"The EA's offered me an awesome opportunity."

"Oh, that's great!" I set my water goblet down on the table, almost spilling it in relief. Poor Robin. He probably thought I wouldn't be happy for him. I lean forward and take his hands. He needs to know that I'm in this with him and that I support him no matter what. "What's the opportunity?'

"Remember hearing about the project with Velke Corp? Well, they're a company that's been working on developing a cleaner way to mine."

"Wow, that's awesome!" I'm surprised at my own relief. Hearing about the chemicals being leached into our water must have affected me more that I knew. "And you guys are working with them?"

Robin nods, his smile still tense. I put my hand on his to try to relax him. Everything is okay. He squeezes my hand, and then takes his away. "Yeah. It's liquid mining, really. They pump a solution into the ground that extracts minerals. It mixes with the strata, and after it's pumped out again the solution is discarded and the minerals remain." He's looking intently at me, as if the specifics are important for me to understand. I commit the facts to memory, trying to imagine how a project like this would work. "It also can be used to clean up toxic residue left by other mining projects."

"That's so special that you get to work with them," I beam. I'm running short on ways to show my support. He's still looking at me as if I'm missing something. My head begins to bob up and down as if I'm listening to a song I like. I probably look like an idiot, but I need him to know how on-board I am with his success. Why is he looking at me like that?

"There's one thing about it, though."

I pause mid-nod and carefully ask, "What is it?"

"It's in Vancouver."

The colors in the room are suddenly over-saturated and everything is moving a bit more slowly than before. "For how long?"

"A year."

"And you're going." This isn't a question. I can see in his face that he's already made up his mind. The description of the project, his serious expression, all of it was to let me know that "no" isn't an option. The nod that follows doesn't tell me anything new. He's going.

"I can't do anything if I stay here. The tourmaline project is dead. If I go to Vancouver, I can get some real work done. This is big, Katie. I could help." He's not apologizing. I can see it in his eyes. He's explaining.

"When do you go?" I don't care to know the answer, but I need something to say.

"I leave in September."

"Alright. Have fun." I lean back and straighten, dropping my napkin onto the table. Robin looks at me, waiting for more, but I don't have anything else to say.

"Thanks," says Robin finally and I give him a tight smile.

"I guess it's time to order." I signal the waiter and tell him clearly what it is I want to eat. I have no idea what I'm saying. Robin mumbles something to the waiter too. Then the man disappears, leaving us alone together.

"The study program they're offering me is for a year. I was thinking I could go and do that and you can finish school and afterwards…"

"No," I cut him off, shaking my head like a maniac. The group that got him arrested, the group that dove headfirst into a protest that shouldn't have happened, the group that has no idea of the right way to go about things is sending him away to Canada. And he's going. "After all of this…" I thought he knew. I thought after he left me waiting there under that bridge that he'd... No. I didn't. I always knew that it was going to end like this, right from the start. I deserve this. "No. I can't."

I can't believe you went.

Robin knew this was coming just as well as I knew that he was going. I see him swallow, then nod. "Yeah. Yeah, I know."

Chapter Twenty

The next two weeks pass in disconnected images, the pieces of my jigsaw life being flipped over one at a time with no relation to anything else. I tell Pandy what's happening with Robin after I get home. She seems so sad but I can't understand why. I can't understand anything, actually. Robin calls, and calls, and calls. Why? There's no point, no reason…

The contest entry. That's done. I should probably tell Robin, but why? There's no point in that anymore. It's over. Robin calls some more. I haven't seen him since he told me. It's a long time to go without seeing Robin, but what would be the point in seeing him now? In a few months, I'm never going to see him again.

The spring air taunts. Warmth kisses and flirts with me, whispering of picnics and classes skipped in favor of cloud watching. People are boisterous and energized, putting radios in windows and sending music streaming over campus. Everyone's spirits are lifting, it seems, except for mine. And, strangely, Pandora's. I can't remember the last time I've seen a smile on her and her words are few, only offered when prompted. I look for Michael to try and cheer Pandy, but he's almost always off with the EA or busy with its work. That goddamn group.

My friend's melancholy is the only thing that pulls me out of my angry haze. I wake up early even though it's a Saturday and busy myself brewing Pandy a cup of tea for when she's up. I pull out a box of coconut chamomile— her favorite—flip the switch on our electric kettle, and settle down to listen to the water gurgle and hiss. Just as the switch flips up there's stirring in Pandy's bedroom. I walk over to her door and smile as she emerges, looking tired and tousled.

"For you," I say, carefully handing her the mug.

"Thanks," she says, taking it and yawning. She pads over to the counter and places herself heavily on one of the stools. It's as if standing is too much work. I wait patiently until she's taken a few sips and wakes up a little before I sit down next to her and look her right in the face.

"I was thinking we could talk."

Pandy nods sleepily. "How have you been doing?"

"Actually, I was thinking we could talk about you."

Pandy, her face carefully neutral, asks, "What about me?"

"You've seemed so down lately. I want to know what's up."

Pandy rips a paper towel off the roll and wipes her mouth with it, leaving tiny white fibers on her lips. "Nothing you don't already know."

Her pajama bottoms are ridiculously worn. The ends are in threads and the seam around the crotch is threatening to tear apart with one false move. For all of the shopping Pandy does, it's odd she hasn't gotten a replacement. These pants have got to be six or seven years old.

"I don't, though. I mean, I know you were worried about Michael, but you didn't have any reason to be. I was wondering if anything's changed." I reach over and tear a loose thread from her shirt.

"Nothing's changed," she answers stonily. A flash of anger passes through her eyes. All at once I realize how selfish I've been, not only the past couple weeks, but since Robin and I began.

"I just want to know what's been going on," I say as gently as I can. Pandy softens.

"He's never around anymore, and neither are you. My classes suck, and everything's just been really crappy."

"I'm so sorry," I say, giving her a hug.

She nods and looks down into her mug. "It's not your fault. I can't even imagine what you're going through. I'd do the same thing if it was me and Michael. It's just..." She trails off and her blue eyes fix sadly on the wall.

"I know," I say, letting go and taking my seat again. God, the counter is dirty. When was the last time either of us cleaned this place?

"How are things with Robin?" she asks, taking a steadying breath and pushing her hair back over her shoulders. It's gotten a lot longer, I notice. She usually keeps it around her shoulders but now it's nearly halfway down her front. The weight of the hair has elongated her curls, giving her a less girly and more sophisticated look. I like it, but I don't know it. Why have I just seen this now? She's lost some weight around her face too. Is it on purpose or from neglect? Has she been eating?

"I haven't talked to him," I answer, tugging on the ends of my own hair. It's grown out too, but I tend to only cut it in the summer, so that's not unusual. Pandora's religious about her hair.

"You should."

"I should. I know. I'm just still so angry."

"I know the feeling," Pandy says, taking a dignified sip of tea. She looks older and almost regal, sitting at the counter with such deliberate composure. Where's the feisty little girl I've always known and loved?

"So," I say, deciding to get down to some of the real issues before I lose Pandora entirely, "you have to have a guess of who Michael's new girl is, even if she doesn't exist. Has he been mentioning anyone more than usual? Or not mentioning someone that he used to mention a lot?"

"I have an idea of who it is," she says evenly, setting her mug down on the table with a tap.

"Who?" I ask, my eyes growing wide and my pulse quickening. *She's probably wrong,* I think again and again, but I'm nervous. What if Michael does have feelings for someone else? Our whole group would split up. My world will fall apart. And poor, *poor* Pandy...

"I think it's you."

"Me?" I gasp, once I've regained my vocal capabilities. Pandy nods, her jaw set. "No, it's not me. I haven't... I don't... There's nothing going on between us!" I'm babbling, not entirely sure what words are coming out of my mouth. But she has to know. She *has* to.

"I know there's nothing going on between you," she answers calmly, "but I do think Michael has romantic feelings for you. Have you noticed that when he stopped hanging around here was when you and Robin started dating? He's been a mess ever since. I think he wants you."

I can't speak. This doesn't make sense. Michael was never supposed to like me. Ever. Not even when we kissed. That was just... that was idiotic. There are no excuses for it, but what I am certain of the fact that it didn't mean anything. In fact... my brain kicks back into gear and I shake my head. "No. We actually talked about this recently."

"You what?" A fire ignites in Pandora's eyes and I balk.

"Not like that! I don't even remember how it came up; I think we were talking about you... But anyway, I told him that I never had any feelings for him and he told me the same thing! It wasn't anything, I swear," I plead, looking into her eyes, but Pandora looks murderous.

"Of course he said that," she snarls. "Katie, what *right* do you have to start talking to my boyfriend about that?"

"I... I don't know... I thought it was okay..."

"How is that okay?" she demands, jumping to her feet. Her seat clatters backwards on the floor and even though her full height doesn't amount to much I know she could take me. "How is it okay to talk to my boyfriend like that?" She punches each word with emphasis and I raise my hands to my head, trying to think straight.

"It wasn't like anything!" I respond. I look at her face, so full of anger and accusation, and begin to feel defensive. "We have never *ever* revisited that subject any other time, ever. We just talked about it that once. Once." I hold up one finger to underline my point.

"Just like you kissed once?"

I open my mouth but can't answer.

"Go away," she hisses, before sweeping off her stool and stalking back into her room. I stare after her, shaking with rage, then grab my coat and head out the front door.

Well. Well that's the last time I'm going to try to be nice to her. Of all the nerve! What right does she have to talk to me like that? I have only ever been a good friend to her and she just responds and treats me like this. Well, fine. I'm done. She can work her fake Michael problems out herself. Insecure bitch.

This thought startles me and I stop in my tracks, raising my hand up to my forehead. What on earth is going on? I never think like this. Not about Pandora. If she's feeling insecure about Michael, it has to be for a reason. Even if that reason isn't me.

My head is so foggy on the walk home that I don't register that someone is calling my name until I feel a hand on my arm. I snap out of my reverie and turn to see Michael, windswept and panting, standing in front of me.

"Hi," I say robotically. There he is, standing right in front of me like a normal person. He looks cold and a little tired, but all-in-all pretty normal. How strange that this person, the one right here in front of me, can be the cause of all the venom that passed between Pandora and myself. He has no idea.

"I was calling you for like ten minutes," he says, running his hands through his hair.

"I didn't hear," I answer. He is so tall. Was he always this tall?

"Are you okay?" he asks, looking at me closely. I could fall apart to Michael right now. Collapse into his arms and sob out my problems like I have so many times before. Except it's different now.

"Fine," I answer, tugging my arm out of his grasp and continuing my walk. I quicken my pace but Michael's long strides easily keep him next to me.

"Something's up, I can tell," he presses.

I stop. "Robin's leaving." It's the easiest answer. And the hardest. Michael, having been gone for much of the last two weeks, doesn't know about this. I stop dead in my tracks and shudder.

"Vancouver?" Michael asks. I nod and run my hands over my arms.

"You knew?"

"I actually helped him get into the program,"

I nod. Of course. They love the EA, both of them. And Michael... Images of Robin's fist colliding with Michael's face fill my mind. Robin was so, so angry. And Michael accepted that. Now he's helped Robin fulfill... I guess I have to call it his dream, and hasn't asked for anything in return. I rest my forehead on Michael's arm. "I don't think I can make it work," I whisper, wiping my eyes.

"I don't think you can either."

"What?" I snap my head up and look at Michael in surprise. That wasn't what I was expecting to hear.

"Long-distance is practically impossible. You guys haven't been together that long, and you've never seemed compatible to me."

I my shoulder slump and wait for the onset of tears. "I always thought we had such a connection..." Michael lets out a brief chuckle and puts an arm around me. He's warm.

"It's always hardest for the people involved to see what's going on."

"I thought they were the only ones who know what's really going on," I answer, leaning against him. "Well, I guess that's not always true. Pandora's been thinking that you like someone else. I guess emotion can blur the truth sometimes..." I don't know if I said this because I'm still angry with Pandora or because I want to shock Michael, but the words are out of my mouth before I can think about what this means. I hold my breath as I wait for Michael to respond.

"She's right."

A car whizzes past and I feel like it's hit me. For the second time today, my whole world cracks. I stare at Michael with an open mouth. He must mean something else... he can't... he must mean... "Who?" I ask, feeling a deep and desolate sense of betrayal.

Michael shoves his hands into his pockets and looks down at the ground. "Come on, Katie, who do you think?"

I try frantically to come up with someone. Any of the EA girls? But I don't really know any of them, except for Vin. He's always kind of flirted with Jemmy... "I don't know," I say, shrugging helplessly. God, is today really happening? I close my eyes and breathe, hoping that this is all some crazy dream.

"Katie, come on," he says again. I open my eyes and look him in the face and my nausea punches my stomach. No. No. *No.*

"Michael, I don't know who it is," I snap, pulling my coat around me and taking off at a brisk speed. Still, he's right here next to me. Curse his long legs!

"Katie, stop."

I whirl around. "What?" I demand, glaring at him. "What do you want?"

Michael shoves his hands back into his pocket and sighs in agitation. "Look, I don't know what's going on, but things haven't felt right lately."

"So?" *Don't say it, don't say it,* I silently urge.

"We never gave us a try."

"That was for a reason!" I explode. God, Pandora was right. She was right, and I'm a horrible person, and a bad friend.

"Robin's no good for you," says Michael as he steps closer to me. We're both standing on the freezing sidewalk. I bet he thinks it's romantic.

"Pandy's too good for you," I spit. Dizziness floods my head and I'm having trouble breathing. This is all so surreal. I don't know whether to laugh or hit Michael right in the face a la Robin.

"You're right." He's stopped moving and now has his hand on his forehead.

"Mike…" I walk to him and close the distance between us. He looks at me, not angry, not hurt, but scared. I reach out and touch his arm. "You have to figure this out. Maybe… maybe take some time away from Pandy to think."

"Yeah." Michael nods, looking down at the snow. "Do you think we…?"

"Mike, sweetie, no. I can't. I just can't. Not now. Maybe…" I swallow and then shake my head. I don't know what I'm saying. "I can't."

"Yeah." He says again. Then I turn and leave him on the sidewalk, listening to my sneakers squeaking on the sidewalk. I didn't realize it was raining.

Chapter Twenty-one

Everything is clear now. My mind has crystallized into a frozen calm, and everything in front of me finally makes sense. There was some sort of apology with Pandora—I don't remember what happened, but I know we hugged at the end. I checked the mail and saw that I had a letter. After that I went into my room and thought (and cried) for about three hours, and I now finally see everything as it should be. Robin is coming over. I need to tell him what's going on.

The letter in the mail was like a mallet to the head. When I opened it up, there was both cheering and conciliatory hugs. Pandy grinned at me in the way that she's recently adopted. She seems to think that if she stops smiling, I might break. I don't think I will, though. Or maybe I wouldn't be able to tell.

The door to my bedroom creaks. I close my eyes and listen as Robin walks in.

"Come here," I say quietly and he obliges, sitting gently down next to me on the bed. I pull him in and kiss him, allowing for one more moment for everything to be okay. He puts his hand behind my head like he did the first time we kissed, and for a moment I just am, letting our lips touch and feeling his breath tickle my face. Then I pull away.

"I want you to know that I didn't use the picture of Vin for the contest." I push my hair back over my shoulders. Robin pauses, then nods. He doesn't know how close I came. How that picture would have gone straight through if it weren't for Geri's simple answer: "You sure?"

I wasn't sure. I wasn't sure of anything. The picture of Vin had lost its mysterious luster, and I couldn't tell any longer if it was better than the others, or if none of them were special. Mostly, though, I didn't want to send an entry out of anger. So I left the emotional bombshell sitting on my hard drive, and chose the picture I took the day I hid Jude's phone call from Robin. Something about that green bug's struggle with the leaf pulled me in; I don't know if it was the improbability that it could stay attached while crawling along upside down, or the fact that a leaf seemed so big to the tiny creature. Whatever it was, I saw some potential, and it seems like someone else did, too.

"Did you win?" I see his gaze land on an envelope lying on my bedside table bearing the trademark lettering of the contest. Even though I only just received it, I've practically memorized the words.

"No."

"Sorry." Robin's shoulders slump.

"I probably wouldn't have won anyway." I look down at the letter on the desk and wonder if this is true. Even with the picture of the bug... "I got a job offer."

"Hey, good for you!" I can tell he isn't sure how to speak. He isn't sure why I asked him here, and he isn't sure where we are. I can tell he's hoping I've changed my mind.

"It's in Chicago." I didn't trust the letter at first. Why on earth would I get a job offer from a contest I lost? But I've read it and read it again and there's no questioning it. The panel of judges, the ones that Geri was so determined I impress, came through for me. "One of the judges liked my work, and says that he wants me to come and intern for his company."

The letter was handwritten and tucked in with the typed response of the competition. The contest letter thanked me for entering but explained in gentle terms that they had chosen someone else to be featured in the Portland gallery. I hadn't been surprised, but I was disappointed. I then pulled out the smaller note, read it and almost dropped it.

Martin Fitzgerald, an alumnus of Travis University, pleasantly told me that he had been impressed by my work and that there was an opening for an intern at his company, should I be interested in furthering my career in photography. Doubtful at first, I had gone straight over to Geri who confirmed that she knew Martin and that the offer was legitimate. Something in her gaze made me wonder if she was really that surprised, but all she said on the matter was a simple, "He knows Professor Davies."

"Is it a photography studio?"

I shake my head. "No, it's actually an advertising firm. But, you know, I could make some good connections." I never saw myself in advertising. I don't know where I saw myself, but it was exciting, outdoors, and with my camera, not in an office, looking over commercial prints. But this, this letter right here in front of me, is offering me a chance to put my foot into the professional world of photographs. It could lead anywhere.

"So you're moving there."

"Yeah." My hands are dry and cracked. I notice a fissure in my skin running from my pinky halfway down my palm. It reminds me of the lacerations from the bridge. "Robin… Even if I did want to wait, it wouldn't make sense. You're going to be in Canada. I'm going to be in Chicago. It would be hard enough to wait a whole year as it is, but we don't even know where we're going to end up."

Robin turns his face away, but not before I see the crushed look that arrests his features. "I get it," he says with a brisk nod.

"I'm so sorry," I say, my voice cracking. "I wanted it to be right, I really did, but us… all this… I don't think I'm supposed to wait for you, baby. I'm so sorry." He nods again, and I hear him sniff. No, please no. Don't let him be crying.

I thought about it. I thought about it and thought about it, and I know that it's right. But right now, when I'm here on my bed seeing Robin's slumped shoulders and realizing that I may never be able to kiss him again, I don't know how it possibly is.

"I want you to know that this isn't a punishment," I say, gently touching his shoulder. I feel the soft material of his sweater beneath my hand, the very material that I found on the chair in the hospital that day. "I'm not going to punish you for the good you want to do. If I thought this could work, I'd try so hard. You know I would. But we're not compatible anymore. Maybe we were back then, but now..." Our difference in priorities, the lack of trust I've felt from the start, and the deep feeling of betrayal that his leaving reopened puddle together like warm ice cream. All I want is for us to be okay. I don't want to do this.

But then my toes grow cold, and suddenly I'm back to being the girl under the bridge. "I broke. Back then. I broke so badly that even now I couldn't accept it. I wanted this to work. I wanted it to work so badly, but it's not going to. I think we were put together this time so that..." I've never believed in closure. What can anyone ever do to seal an ending up nicely? But here we are, put back together just for a few months so we can get as close to that as possible. So we can understand.

"I know." Robin's voice is cracking, and he sniffs again. He's crying. This pushes me over the edge and I burst into tears, falling down on my pillow and sobbing into it like a heartbroken teenager. His arms wrap around me, and I cry harder. This is the last time.

"I'm so sorry," I weep. I repeat this again and again as he strokes my hair and whispers, "It's okay, it's okay."

And I lie on the bed feeling his warmth next to me for one last time until I wake up and find he's gone.

Robin leaves early for Vancouver. There's no point in a summer together—it would only be prolonging the inevitable. School ends and rooms are packed up, leaving only the bare bones of the life we built there over the past year. I cast one last glance around our place and then step aside to let Jude in to take the heavier boxes out to the car, my diploma resting precariously on top.

I finally told Robin. Just before he left he asked what my plans were before Chicago. There was no point in trying to protect him or his image of me so I answered honestly, "Taking care of my alcoholic brother and seeing if I can get him back on track." I told him about Jude, and about that day when Jude broke their display.

Robin just smiled a little—not that wide, beautiful smile that I'm used to, but a smaller, sad one—and said, "You're a good person Kate."

Then he left. I keep half-expecting him to walk into my room. No, I don't. I'm wildly and desperately hoping for it but I know he won't. Especially now that I'm leaving. I cast one more gaze around the apartment. It seems so small without our things. Pandy will be home all summer too, but I know that mostly I'll be focusing on Jude. Ahead of me lies a summer of weight and responsibility. Robin was my break, my sweet vacation from the heaviness of real life but in the end he turned out to be another lesson. I guess I'm stronger now, but it doesn't feel that way. I feel shattered.

"Are you ready?" Jude asks, hoisting the last box into his arms. He looks better. Maybe things won't be so awful with him. Maybe this summer could even be about him helping me, like he used to.

I nod. "Ready."

I don't unpack when I get home. I haven't fully unpacked in four years, always keeping certain items in boxes or suitcases to tote back and forth just to make everything a little easier. Tonight I leave everything where it is, except one box that I packed up myself. Once everyone else in the house has gone to bed, I slip over to the box and open it up. Inside, I encounter lengths of heavy blue fabric. I pull the blanket out and wrap it tightly around me, allowing myself this one reminder of Robin. Just for tonight.

Chapter Twenty-two

"Have you talked to Michael?" I dump a handful of clothes onto my bed and shake my head, thinking for the millionth time that I need a haircut.

"No," Pandora answers, catching a sweater that I throw her and folding it neatly before sliding it into one of the big cardboard boxes. It's still four weeks until I have to leave for Chicago, but I'm already packing, keeping what I want and tossing what I don't.

Michael and Pandora decided to take a break at the beginning of the summer. Pandy didn't tell me the details but I have a horrible suspicion it might have to do with me. I wonder what he told her.

"He'll come back," Pandy says calmly, coming and standing next to me by my bed. "He's probably going to play around, but he'll come back. I'm the only person who can see through him."

How can you be so certain? I want to ask. *How do you know he's not gone for good?* But instead I stay quiet, and fold my blue penguin t-shirt. She seems so positive that the relationship will work out, but how can you ever be sure that anyone is meant to be together? I tap my fingers together and start humming—a habit I've gotten into whenever I start thinking about Robin—and shove together the top of an overflowing box. The cardboard wrinkles and complains, but I force the whole the top closed, and sit down on it.

"Anything else?" Pandy asks, looking around the room. I shake my head.

"That's it for now. Thanks for the help," I say, giving her a hug.

"No problem. But Katie?"

"Yeah?" God, my hair is long. I tug on the ends; they feel brittle and cracked. I wonder how short I should go.

"You don't want to do this."

"Do what?" I sit down on my bed and begin rifling through the contents of my bedside drawers, mentally labeling things "keep" and "toss". Pandy stops me, taking my hands in hers.

"You don't want to move to Chicago."

I glance up at her. "Yes, I do."

"No, Katie, you don't. It's the Midwest. You hate the Midwest. You love mountains, and lakes, and trees…"

Taking my hands from hers, I shrug and continue to sort. "So? I love a lot of things, but you can't have everything all at once. I'll make connections, and maybe they'll lead me back here."

"They won't! They'll be Midwestern connections. And Katie…" She takes a deep breath and sits down next to me. "You have too much talent to take a job you don't want."

I stop for a second and look at her. Her eyes are so earnest that it nearly makes me want to cry. "Pandy, I don't. I'm a twenty-two year old fresh out of college with a degree in photography. This is the next step. This is what we do."

"But Chicago?" Her face is crumpled in dismay. "It's freezing in the winter and roasting in the summer."

I crack a smile. "Kind of like here."

She doesn't look convinced. I look down at her bright green sneakers and notice the rubber on the front is starting to come off. I should go shopping with her before I go. We can get her some new shoes, and maybe see a movie after. We should do it soon. She reaches down and tugs at the loose elastic.

"What else would I do?" I ask softly.

The quickness of her response shows me that she was anticipating this question. "We could start a company together. Right here in Hartford. It could be... communications, or digital media, or... I don't know, something! But we have words, and pictures, and that's what people want..." She trails off as I reopen the top drawer. "It's a good idea for later."

"Yeah," I say, tossing a stack of books to the floor. "Later. Hey, listen, I have to get ready for tonight. I'll call you tomorrow."

Pandy nods and gets up from her bed. "Sure."

She leaves the room and I slump down on my bed, feeling totally exhausted. The walls are bare; my fairy posters are packed up and ready to go into the attic. I don't need them now. The only remnant of my love of the mystic is my Grimm's Fairytales book, something I can't seem to leave behind. I tucked it in the back of my shelf so I can't see it anymore, but even when my eyes are closed, I can feel its presence. It's terrible and reassuring all at once.

I have a date tonight. An old classmate from high school, a goofy boy named Kent, got in touch with me over Facebook and asked if I'd like to get a drink with him. I always thought Kent was pretty cute, and since I'm leaving so soon I didn't see the harm in agreeing. Now I wish I turned him down.

I've talked to Robin a little since he left. We never said it, but there's a mutual understanding between us that it's dangerous to depend on regular communication. The destructive power of waiting for him is the reason I knew that we couldn't stay together. He doesn't have regular internet access anyway; a few Facebook conversations and one Skype call is as far as it's gotten. I don't know if he has a new girl. I haven't asked.

His work is going well. The company he's doing a partnership with is taking steps that the EA never got around to, researching cleaner ways to manufacture their products and cut back on their carbon footprints. Robin seems to be a key part of that. It sounds like he's being fulfilled. Now it's my turn.

I have an image of the beautiful girl he's bound to fall in love with, pale skin and dark eyes an adorable French-Canadian accent, but who knows? Maybe it'll be Vin.

I'm free now. I think I realize what's happened. Robin and I came together for a reason, and the reason was so that we could part peacefully. We did that, and it's time to move on. I'll be in Chicago soon with a new job and new people to meet, and hopefully Robin will fade away.

Starting a company with Pandora. I grin at the idea. I can picture it, she and I sitting in some tiny office while she types furiously and I design pictures. The thought makes my heart ache, and I quickly drop it in favor of images of the crowded streets of a big city.

Michael stayed in Maine with the EA, continuing the fight against mining from the home front. I haven't spoken with him either, but it seems best to keep away until he's figured everything out with Pandy. Whenever I think about it, I get this sickening sense that I might be losing him. I'm terrified imagining a life where he'll never walk through the door again, never bring food, never call me Katie-cat. But there's nothing to be done. I have to let it all play out.

I need to get ready to go. I convince myself that making an effort is the polite thing to do, so I pull on a sundress and rope my hair back into a ponytail. I look alright, I guess, but that's as far as it goes. I'm not excited, not happy, not dreaming about a kiss or even the drink we're going to have. I just want this to be done.

Six o'clock rolls around and I set off toward the bar where we agreed to meet; I didn't want to depend Kent for a ride home. I get there at six-fifteen, a quarter hour before the time we agreed upon, so I order a shirley temple and sip it slowly while I wait.

How did I get here? How did I end up back home sitting in a bar waiting for a date with Kent McKernan a few weeks before I move to Chicago? I look at my reflection in the mirror behind the bar. I look the same, except for some new makeup, but I can't find myself in the image.

Kent ambles in at six twenty-five. He sees me right away and grins. "Started already?" He gestures to my half-empty drink. I try to smile back.

"I got here early."

"That excited to see me." He winks and orders a beer. He leads me to a table in a quiet corner where we settle in. "What have you been up to?"

I stifle a yawn as I give the spiel I've been using all summer. "I just finished school and I have a photography internship in Chicago that I'm going to be starting."

"Cool, cool." Kent nods and takes a slug of his beer. "I love Chicago. I lived there for a few months right after high school."

"Neat," I reply flatly, watching him have another go at his drink.

"Very. It's a great city. Lots of culture."

"So I've heard. Anyway, what about you?"

Kent says something that I don't hear. Is this what dating is going to be from now on? It was so much easier in college when there were parties and events and classes and plenty of ways to meet and get to know men. But now here I am, sitting in a bar with a guy I care next-to-nothing about just because he finds me attractive. Am I going to be sucked into a *Sex and the City* style of dating until I finally find the guy I'm meant to settle down with? Is that what grown up life is?

"So yeah, it's all been pretty good," Kent finishes, grinning at me over his quarter-empty mug.

"Awesome." I have my polite voice on. There's nothing I can do to get rid of it. I sneak a peek at my cell phone and see that we've only been here for ten minutes. Great. I promised myself I'd stay for at least an hour but at this rate…

"Do you want another one?" He nods at my glass.

"Oh. Sure. I think I'll have a Coke this time though."

"Got it." He gets up and walks to the bar and I slump down in my seat. I can't wait to get out of here. For lack of anything else to do, I look over to the bar to watch Kent get the drinks. He's talking to someone. Ugh, this is going to take ages. I'm so not extending my hour; if he wants to use up his time talking to some guy at the bar, so be it. A couple minutes later he heads back to our table and I see the person he was talking to is following him. He invited someone on our date. Excellent.

The room is so crowded I can't make out who it is, so I boredly look down at my phone, determined to send them each a message of how rude it is to interrupt a date. The chair next to me slides out.

"What's a girl like you doing in a place like this?"

My head snaps up and I stare in shock. There he is, sitting in his chair like he owns it, grinning at me like nothing ever happened. "Mike!" I squeak, and proceed to launch myself at him. It's as if hugging him tightly enough will make up for his absence over the past few months, or prevent him from going again. He's laughing, and I am too. After I disentangle I ask, "What are you doing back?"

"The EA's on break. I decided to come home."

I squeeze his hand, my cheeks almost cramping from grinning. "I'm so glad. How long are you here for?"

"We'll have to see, won't we?" He winks and I feel like a helium balloon.

It's hard to keep Kent in the conversation. I try to be polite and keep him involved but my attention is entirely wrapped up in Michael. He's *here*. After a bit, I relax and let Michael and Kent talk. They discuss school, jobs, high school friends, and plans for the future while I lean back against my chair and beam like an idiot. I don't know how much time passes but finally there are two empty mugs on the table. Kent takes one last swig out of his almost-empty glass, stands, and says, "I think I'm going to call it a night."

"Bye!" I say, waving enthusiastic. He smiles, waves back, then lopes out.

"Sorry." Michael says after Kent leaves.

"For what?" I feel a little dizzy. Michael nods toward the door.

"Interrupting your date."

I let out a short laugh and glance at Kent's disappearing back. "No, it's really fine. I'd rather hang out with you anyway. So, tell me everything. What's been going on?"

Michael takes a thoughtful sip of his scotch (when did he start drinking scotch?) and stares moodily at the candle in the middle of our table. The flame, despite having been burning for at least a few hours, is still leaping like an excited puppy. Michael licks his thumb and forefinger then quickly extinguishes it. It hisses into darkness.

"I've been thinking a lot about everything."

"About Pandy?" My drink is about three-quarters empty, but I leave the last bit of cola in the bottom of the glass. I'm giddy with anticipation, but sick with fear. *Come back*, I beg silently.

"Yeah. Pandy." Michael drains his drink. "I've liked you forever."

"What?" The back of my foot collides with the leg of the chair and I fall forward with a gasp of pain. "Me?"

"You."

"But…" Blood is seeping into my sock now and I screw up my face against the sting. "But this is only a recent thing. Only since Robin." His name seems out of place here. My feelings toward Robin belong in a box.

"I've always wanted you." His eyes lock with mine, and my breath catches. Always…

Specialness sparkles inside me as I mull over what this means. He wanted me at that party. He wanted me all of those times that I've walked around in PJ shorts, and tank tops with no bra. He wanted me on Halloween, and Valentine's Day, and was jealous of Robin…

He wanted me every goddamn time Pandy was in the room.

"No." I flail my head back and forth as if enough of the movement will repel Michael's words. "No. You didn't. Michael, you didn't. Maybe you've stopped loving Pandy, but you spent a long time only wanting her."

"I always wanted you," he repeats.

The images are different now. Pandy and Michael dressed up as the King and Queen of Hearts, Pandy's face every time Michael walked into the room, the conversation she and I had where I promised her nothing was going on between Michael and me. "You suck." I say, getting to my feet. I flinch as my foot shouts in protest.

"Katie, do you know how much I've wanted this?" His gaze is strong. "I called the cops on Robin, for chrissake. I sent him to *Canada*."

I still, my head pounding. "He was right," I finally whisper.

Michael is sitting in his chair, staring at me with a look of calculated hurt, but I don't see Michael anymore. Layer after layer seems to be peeling away. His handsome face, intelligent blue eyes, upright posture... all of it so familiar, but right now I don't know him at all. He called the police to get his friend arrested, an action malevolently intended to keep Robin away on Valentine's Day. He's a man who will do anything to get what he wants, and right now that happens to be me.

"How could you do that? How could you do that to your friend?" I demand, slamming my hands down on the table.

"I want you Katie," he repeats, his voice and eyes intense. I feel like the air around me is draining away.

"Go to hell," I snarl, throwing money down on the table. "I'm done." And I leave him there, a king without subjects, to find a new batch of pawns. Let him plan, scheme, manipulate, and find girl after girl to chase.

I'm done.

I'm done with the lies and with trying to make things fit the way I want them to. I'm done getting played, getting hurt, and going for the things I think I should have, instead of the things I want. As soon as I'm out the door and the cool evening air wraps around me, I pull out my phone, hit my speed dial, and wait for the call to connect. As soon as it does I say, "Pandy? I'm in. Let's do it."

Chapter Twenty-three

"There's so much room!" Pandy dances around the new space and I grin as I set the boxes I'm carrying down. Santa, startled by Pandy's erratic movement, darts under the sofa that we got Jude to bring in for us yesterday.

"I don't think we need this much room, but it is pretty awesome," I concede, walking over to one of the windows to look out at the street.

I was nervous about choosing this space but Pandy convinced me that it was the right thing to do. The overpass that rushes above us reduced the price enough to make me not want to pass out every time I thought about it. I don't mind the noise, and Pandy was willing to do anything to get us into our own place. So we wrote a check, signed a lease, and packed up all our things. It's hard to believe that we're here.

Turning down the job in Chicago felt good. The anxiety and regret I was expecting was surprisingly absent and instead I felt light, cheerful, and excited. My mother thinks I'm being stupid. Geri too, despite all of her emphasis on looking for something better, was horrified when I told her. I did it through email, sending her a note thanking her for all of her help this past year and letting her know what my plans were for the future. I casually mentioned that Chicago wasn't going to work out and that my friend and I decided to start a company (Grant and Winters Communications). All I got back was a resigned message wishing me the best. A week later, though, she sent another email with a request for us to design a poster for her engagement party. It seems that some forgiveness must have taken place.

She will soon be Mrs. Geraldine Davies.

"I never pictured those two together," I mused, turning to Facebook and finding increasing numbers of pictures of them together. How did I miss that?

"I did," Pandy replied with a spark in her eye. Pandy knows everything.

Pandy's parents, thank God, were much more supportive than my own. They loaned us enough money to buy the LLC certificate and the first month's rent for the apartment-cum-office we're renting in Hartford. Now we're officially setting up shop, decorating with everything from pictures that I took, articles that Pandy wrote, and a framed list of our first three clients: Geri, Pandy's dad (who needed a press release), and a local grocery store chain that wanted new fliers. So far, I think, we're not doing too badly.

After sending Geri the engagement party flier we received two more orders from her: invitations, and a wedding photographer. Pandy shrieked and danced around as soon as we got the request, and I sat and stared dumbly at the order. The wedding is going to take place at the house by the stream where Geri took me the very first day of my photography intensive. She and Davies are buying it.

I keep trying to imagine what it will be like to go back there, this time as a paid professional. I imagine walking down the incline, into the trees, and over to the river. I'll sit on the stump where I first sat and told Geri that I missed someone. A year has passed since then, and in some ways, I'm in exactly the same place. I still miss him more than anything. But I can think of his face now.

In other ways, everything is different. My pictures, *my pictures*, are going to be the ones that Geri and Davies (or should I call him "Owen" now?) will keep for life. I'm going to capture one of the biggest moments that they'll share, and give it its own kind of immortality. This is what I want to do. My work will be preserving every moment of joy that I can. I'm done exploring yearning, loneliness, longing, and all of the other emotions that, in the end, knock you flat. I want to take the joy of right now, and turn them into little forevers, kept on a mantelpiece.

I never told Pandy what happened that night at the bar. I haven't spoken to Michael since. He's still in Maine, throwing himself into the EA for all he's worth. His Facebook posts are eerily detached from the life that Pandy and I have now. They're full of pictures with people we don't know and projects that we're not involved in, but every day it's hurting a little less. I think Pandy might be feeling it too.

At the bottom of the box I'm unloading lies a framed print of my favorite picture of Robin. I forgot it was in here. I pull it out and look at it, feeling my breath catch. The ache he left behind isn't going away. I pull my legs up under me and run my hand over the frame. There he is: laughing at me with his arm stretched out invitingly. I can't remember what he was laughing about. I asked him once what he was thinking when the picture was taken and all he said was, "That I wanted you to sit down next to me." I place the frame on the floor.

Pandy crouches down and looks at what I have. "You must really miss him," she says, smoothing my hair with her hands. I nod, afraid to speak. "Have you talked to him at all?"

I shake my head. In the four months since Robin left our communication went from sporadic to non-existent. The last exchange we had was about three weeks ago when I got a cheery and impersonal text from a number I didn't recognize saying, "New number. I can get calls and texts now. Robin V :)". It was clearly the kind of thing sent out to his entire contact list, so I didn't bother replying and he hasn't reached out since.

"Katie, did you ever think…" Pandy sighs and picks the picture up off the floor before replacing it in the box. "Did you ever think that maybe you don't have to do this?"

"I'm t-trying," I hiccup as the tears start, "but I don't know how to do it. You're so b-brave, but I'm not. I miss him, I miss him so much." My head falls to my knees and tears seep into my pants. I don't want to cry; I'm so tired of crying.

Pandy hugs me. "That's not what I meant. What I mean is, do you really have to not be together?"

"We're not s-supposed to be." I take a shuddery breath and try to pull myself together, coughing and rubbing my hand over my wet face.

She shakes her head impatiently. "I know you have this whole past-life theory, and maybe it's true, but even if it is, are you sure this is the answer that you're supposed to get out of it?"

I look at her through blurry eyes. "We met again in this life to sort everything out. It hurts a lot, but I know that we're both meant to move on. I just wish that knowing this made it hurt less."

Pandy gives me a hard look. "How do you know?"

I look down into the box and at the picture of Robin, "We're falling into the same pattern."

"So what? Last time he left and you didn't wait. This time he left again, and you still didn't wait. What's the lesson there?"

"To not be angry." I put my chin back on my knees look miserably at my feet.

"Are you angry?"

"No." The picture laughs up at me. "I'm sad."

"Good, then you've learned your lesson. Now call the darn boy, and tell him you miss him." She shoves my phone into my hand.

"But…!" I protest, but before I can do anything Pandy selects his number and presses send. "No!" I squeak, but it's too late. The phone is ringing.

"What do you have to lose?" Pandy murmurs. "You're already not together."

She's right. I'm in the middle of taking a deep breath when I hear a click on the other end of the line and I start talking before he can. "Hi!" I squeak, and begin to cough. Once I catch my breath I gasp, "It's me."

"Kate!" he says at the same time I do. "Hi!" There's something unsettling about his voice. It's overeager, nervous, and a tiny bit… guilty? I'm imagining it. I forge on.

"Robin," I say firmly, getting to my feet and beginning to pace. "I miss you. A lot. I haven't stopped missing you. And… And I think I made the wrong call, saying I won't wait, or I don't know, maybe it was the right one at first but I'm not happy. Not being with you makes me unhappy, and, if the offer is still open, then I want us to do this." Saying all of this feels crazy, absolutely crazy, but there's no turning back now. I close my mouth and dance from foot to foot. I hear him exhale on the end of the line. He starts to say something but I hurry on, unnerved by his reaction. I need to postpone his answer for as long as I can.

"I mean," my pace quickens and soon I'm nearly sprinting around the room. "I get if it's too late. It's been such a long time. And I screwed up. You wanted us to be together, but I was too stubborn. But now… Things are different. And even if you don't want to be together now, maybe when you come back to the states we can try it. I mean, it's fine to do whatever you want in Vancouver, I guess, I just really, really want to… be with you." I'm out of breath. There's no way to keep going.

He's quiet. My heart plunges. Pandy is staring at me in curiosity and I turn away. If Robin is going to break my heart, I want to be alone. I stagger quickly toward our door. "That's…" he says finally, "That's really…" My hand closes around the door handle. "That's…" I tug the door firmly open and stare ahead of me in shock.

"A relief." Robin lowers his phone and grins at me. He's standing here, right here in front of me. Under the overpass. Under the bridge. I hurl myself forward and land in his arms.

"What are you doing here?" I shriek into his neck.

"Pandy told me where you guys were living. I wanted to come and see you."

"I can't believe it," I sob, my voice muffled by his coat. His smell, his body, the material of his jacket… "I can't believe you're here."

"I can't believe I ever wasn't." His arms wrap tightly around my waist and his face is in my hair. I grip him tighter and tighter, determined never to let go.

"I missed you so much. How were you here? How were you right outside when I called?"

Cars whiz overhead and Robin laughs nervously. "I've been out here a while."

I look up at him. "Why didn't you come in?"

He brushes back my hair, still fragrant and soft from my trip to the salon yesterday, and looks down into my face. "I didn't know what you wanted."

"You said Pandy told you to come…"

"She did. She did. But… I haven't heard from you in a long time. I didn't know if you had met someone else."

I shake my head. "There is nobody else. I looked."

He laughs and we stand together out on the street, wrapped tightly together while the September sun shines down on us. Finally I ask, "How long do I get you for?"

"I'm not going back."

"But…" Guilt contaminates my joy, and I look into Robin's face. "But you love the EA. And Vancouver…"

"Didn't make me happy," Robin finishes, shaking his head.

"Why?"

He kisses me. I close my eyes and put every ounce of my being into experiencing the kiss. Once he pulls away he runs a finger along the bottom of my lip and says, "Because I should have stayed."

After Robin helps set up my bed we sit on it, talking and cuddling until the place grows dark.

"There's so much environmental work to be done, I don't see why I had to be there," Robin says, tracing a pattern lightly into the palm of my hand. "There's plenty to do here. We ended up sorting out some projects for me to work on from afar."

"For me?" I ask, resting my head on his shoulder.

"For you," he answers, kissing my hair. "At some point I might end up going abroad again, but for now I'm right here."

"I'll go with you," I whisper.

"I'll stay," he murmurs back.

We hear Pandy walking around outside my bedroom door and Robin asks, "How are she and Michael doing?"

"Who knows?" I'm not sure I'll ever be able to figure them out. Part of me thinks that they're meant to be together but I also know the damage Michael is capable of doing. "Pandy will figure it out. Hey Robin?"

"Yeah?" He has his fingers in my hair and is twirling my curls gently.

"How did you know that it was Michael who called the cops on Valentine's Day?" I look up at Robin and he looks back down at me.

"Because I remembered."

I let this sink it, allowing Robin's words seep into me and confirm what I already knew. "Even before the story," I finally say. "But I thought you trusted him."

"With everything but you."

"I had no idea," I say, shaking my head.

"I know." Robin laughs and untangles his fingers from my hair and we lie together quietly, free for now, or maybe forever.

"I love you," says Robin for the seventh time, squeezing me tight.

"I love you," I say for the eighth, and close my eyes. I'm beginning to drift, but this time I smile. I've finally left the bridge. I slide my feet down into the warmth of my blanket, and surrender to the rhythm of Robin's breath.

Sisters Fawn and Penny Anderson each have their own reason for loving More Please Bakery. It's the place that helped Fawn heal after an earth-shattering betrayal, and an escape from Penny's stalling relationship. But Fawn can't forget her bittersweet history with the bakery's handsome owner, Penny has a growing interest in the delivery boy, and the shop's bank account is getting low.

When Penny lands them a celebrity client, reality TV star Delaney Roosevelt, Fawn dives in headfirst trying to come up with the perfect design. However, pleasing the starlet isn't easy and soon heartbreak and scandal descend on the shop.

As the sisters face their romantic and professional demons they are forced to decide what is worth holding onto, and what they need to let go.

Chapter One

Bubbles erupted furiously all over the granite countertop. Moisture wrinkled Fawn's hands, but she continued her assault on her kitchen, half-convinced she could scrub it into oblivion. It was funny, really, how the angrier she got at the house, the more brightly it shone. The stupid, stupid house.

She shoved a handful of hair away from her face and wiped her forehead with her arm. Her breath was coming short now, in bursts of protest at her frenzied activity. *Why,* her lungs seemed to pant, *is this the kitchen's fault?* On a normal day the house was her best friend, and her kitchen was the special thing that kept them close. She lived, cooked, explored, and created in the house in North Quincy that she'd never have been able to afford alone. But then there were days like today. Days when the walls felt like they were going to crash in on her shoulders, and her only defense against it was to try to wash the melancholy away.

Today. Fawn stilled her sponge. There had actually never been a day like today.

She resumed her bubbly siege. The counter was glinting violently, threatening her with what she didn't want to see. One wrong angle, one stray fragment of light, and her face would appear in its surface. Right now, she must look like an evil queen, all pale skin, dark hair, and angry eyes. Stupid eyes. If only she could scrub those clean.

She had been looking, of course. You don't find that kind of thing without looking for it. But all the same, she hated to have found it. She had been on her way home from work, smelling like bread and sugar. She'd stopped by the newsstand to buy a paper, almost convinced, at this point, that she really did just want to read the day's news. But she had flipped past the news, right to the section she feared the most. An offensive approach seemed to her like it could help minimize the shock.

It didn't.

The newspaper ink had pounced on her, staining her fingertips black with words designed to hurt her. And so the washing had begun.

These were the days that made Fawn miss the aftermath of the divorce. Back when there were pictures to burn, mugs to break, clothes to throw into the street, and love letters to shred. Jamie had liked turning to the ancient art of letter writing. Maybe it was the novelty of seeing words that hadn't been produced by a computer, or maybe it was plain old narcissism. Whatever it was, he couldn't resist seeing his own words scrawled across sheets of paper. This was why, in a horrible display of masochism, Fawn had been buying the paper every single day since their divorce was finalized.

She knew there was that one heartbreak left. Jamie wasn't one for the internet, and neither was Fawn, for that matter, so their divorce had stayed mercifully out of the digital realms. But now here she was, down two years' worth of newspaper money, reeling from the final blow. She could have bought a subscription. It would have been cheaper. In retrospect, she should have. But who knew it would take this long?

She turned up the volume on her radio, hoping the pop song she'd grown to recognize, but not quite know, would help drown her agitation. *It doesn't matter*, she told herself again and again. *It was always going to happen. Now it has.* That was why she had been looking. As much as this hurt, not knowing would have been so much worse.

The song hit the one part of the chorus that she knew. Fawn paused in her cleaning and joined in on the electronically-enhanced "ooh"s so recklessly that she almost didn't hear the phone. Sighing, she switched off the radio and made her way over to the wall, one of the only people left in the world who had a landline.

"Hello?"

"Fawnie?"

Fawn's stomach lurched at the sound of her sister's voice. *Please*, she prayed, *please don't let Penny have seen.*

By herself, Fawn could believe the wound was an old one. She could believe that the two years--three months and six days--that had passed were enough. That it didn't matter anymore. But Penny knew better.

"What's up?" Fawn asked, trying to sound cheerful. That was difficult. She was still out of breath from her kitchen cardio and had never been good at softening what was sharp.

She heard Penny exhale, pause, and then giggle. "I have a question for you."

Fawn's eyes narrowed, her panicked plea momentarily forgotten. "Oh?"

"Okay, well, remember how I bought a car at the beginning of the semester?"

Fawn ran her fingertips across her forehead. Beads of sweat leapt onto her hand. Better than ink. "I do."

"Well, it turns out that, on top of school stuff, it's coming to a lot more than I can afford."

"College is expensive," said Fawn dryly. "Imagine that."

Penny paused, and when Fawn didn't say anything more, continued. "I really need the car. I wouldn't be able to get anywhere otherwise."

"Because driving in Boston makes so much sense." Fawn picked up a stack of magazines from her coffee table and began flipping through them. She was certain a couple had articles she hadn't yet read but couldn't remember which.

"I'm fine in the city, but if I don't have a car, how am I going to get anywhere else? Like to see you?"

An unwilling smile crept onto Fawn's face. Penny's sweetness was so political. "So, you need money?"

"No!" Penny sounded aghast. "Well, yes. But I don't need you to give me any. Well, I do. But not for free."

"What are you talking about?" Fawn dumped the pile of magazines into the trash can, enjoying the thud. Andrea Roosevelt—an actress more famous for her myriad of divorces than her work onscreen—smiled wryly up at Fawn from the trash can. *You and me both, sister,* Fawn thought.

"I was wondering if I could have a job at the bakery?" Penny's tone rose steadily in pitch until she was nearly squeaking. Fawn looked at the phone in surprise.

"My bakery?" Silence.

Fawn took a deep breath, trying to imagine Penny in her workspace. Would she be behind the counter? In the kitchen covered with flour? In the office with the paperwork? The paperwork. Was there room in those numbers for another employee? "I'll have to ask Lenz."

That certainly wasn't a conversation she wanted to have. Things were strange enough with her boss as they were; she didn't need to add...

"I already did," Penny said hurriedly. "He said it's fine, but I have to check with you."

Of course Penny had gone over Fawn's head. She had learned long ago to never leave anything important up to the whims of a sister. Again, Fawn found herself smiling. Poor Lenz. He never had a chance.

"I guess it's decided then."

Oddly, Fawn felt a surge of hope. Lenz was willing to take Penny on. Maybe that meant he had seen something in those unforgiving numbers that Fawn hadn't. For all of the ferocity Fawn had for her job, and for all the love and dedication she had for gathering the frayed edges and weaving them back together, there was something about an owner no employee could surpass. More Please Bakery might be Fawn's passion, but it was Lenz's blood.

"Thank you!" Fawn could almost hear Penny bouncing in excitement, her curls bobbing around her shoulders. "I'll be awesome, I promise. I'll be the most awesome employee there. Besides you, of course."

Fawn let laughter fill the space between them. Once it quieted, she ventured, "Penny, you know, you could move off campus. Save some money. It's not too long a commute from here."

She kept her tone deliberately casual, trying not to reveal how much she wanted her sister's fireball energy in her big and drafty house. How she simultaneously felt too young and too old to be living alone. Especially after today.

"Dad's already paying for all that," Penny breezed. "I just want enough to be able to go out sometimes. Maybe have a vacation."

Fawn sometimes forgot how much younger her sister was. For Fawn, money was almost like a family member, something she kept close tabs on that alternately made her feel proud and anxious. For Penny, it was an elusive friend, hard to keep in touch with, but always so much fun. A bank balance that sent a worried streak through Fawn's heart would make Penny's eyes widen in wonder. Fawn remembered that age. Her view on money hadn't changed until Jamie.

She stared through the kitchen and out the window behind the sink. She had always wondered why so many kitchens had windows behind the sink. She wondered that even back when she and Jamie were looking to buy. God, that had been ridiculous. It seemed it then, with their shiny new bachelor's degrees and a giant wedding present check from his uncle; and it seemed it now, five years and one unraveled fantasy later. Was the window placed there to try to make the task of washing dishes more enjoyable, or to rub in the fact that one was stuck over a sink of hot soapy water when he or she could be outside enjoying the day? Fawn herself never had a problem with doing dishes, but Penny did. Fawn would be crazy not to put Penny out front with the people, anyway.

"Fine," she sighed. She grabbed a nearby sticky note and scrawled "*cashier*". "But Penny? Don't be late."

Devour this sweet tale now!

Fall in love with Amy's Amber and Jeremy (and three other couples!) in this romance anthology!

books2read.com/passion

Acknowledgements

First and foremost, I'd like to thank my husband, Ravi Both, for his pivotal role in getting this published. Without his help and support (and extensive Facebook friends list) this book never would have seen the light of day, and would still be sitting on my computer as a "good idea to revisit later".

Second, I would like to thank my mother, Linda R. Spitzfaden, for her endless feedback, edits, and patience as I forced this from a draft into a real-life book. I am so grateful, and so much better a writer than I would be without her.

Third, I want to thank Sara Voorhis and Marissa Frosch for enabling me to bring this back in its new and improved form. I'm so excited to see where this goes, and so thankful for your help and support. It's an adventure I love being on with you guys.

Finally, I want to thank each and every one of you who voted for me and Untold in the Writers Voices contest in 2013. Without you, this literally wouldn't have happened, and being able to achieve a lifelong dream solely because of the support and encouragement of those around me means more than I can ever say. Thank you.

-Amy

AMY SPITZFADEN

Amy is a chick-lit and women's fiction author from Temple, New Hampshire where she lives with her husband, Ravi. She won first prize in the 2013 Writers' Voices Chelson Award for *Untold*.

She graduated with a literature and writing degree from Maharishi University of Management in 2012 and works as editor and social media manager at PSCS Consulting when not writing.